"Someone's watching us."

"Do you think it's him?" Wade asked.

She nodded. "I do. I know it's foolish, but I do."

He shrugged. "If you think he's watching, play along." And as he said it, he leaned closer, brushed his mouth across hers. Softly, barely touching. Then again. "Might flush him out to see you kissing another man," he said. His lips brushed hers again. "Shake him up." He spoke with his mouth close to hers. E̶̶ breath, every movement of h̶̶ ̶̶le of heat right dow̶̶

"I unders̶̶

"Good. Th̶̶ ̶̶ it, Edie."

He didn't h̶̶ her twice.

Dear Reader,

Happy (almost) New Year! The year is indeed ending, but here at Intimate Moments it's going out with just the kind of bang you'd expect from a line where excitement is the order of the day. Maggie Shayne continues her newest miniseries, THE OKLAHOMA ALL-GIRL BRANDS, with *Brand-New Heartache*. This is prodigal daughter Edie's story. She's home from L.A. with a stalker on her trail, and only local one-time bad boy Wade Armstrong can keep her safe. Except for her heart, which is definitely at risk in his presence.

Our wonderful FIRSTBORN SONS continuity concludes with *Born Royal*. This is a sheik story from Alexandra Sellers, who's made quite a name for herself writing about desert heroes, and this book will show you why. It's a terrific marriage-of-convenience story, and it's also a springboard for our twelve-book ROMANCING THE CROWN continuity, which starts next month. Kylie Brant's *Hard To Resist* is the next in her CHARMED AND DANGEROUS miniseries, and this steamy writer never disappoints with her tales of irresistible attraction. *Honky-Tonk Cinderella* is the second in Karen Templeton's HOW TO MARRY A MONARCH miniseries, and it's enough to make any woman want to run away and be a waitress, seeing as this waitress gets to serve a real live prince. Finish the month with Mary McBride's newest, *Baby, Baby, Baby,* a "No way am I letting my ex-wife go to a sperm bank" book, and reader favorite Lorna Michaels's first Intimate Moments novel, *The Truth About Elyssa.*

See you again next year!

Leslie J. Wainger
Executive Senior Editor

Please address questions and book requests to:
Silhouette Reader Service
U.S.: 3010 Walden Ave., P.O. Box 1325, Buffalo, NY 14269
Canadian: P.O. Box 609, Fort Erie, Ont. L2A 5X3

MAGGIE SHAYNE
Brand-New Heartache

Silhouette

I N T I M A T E   M O M E N T S™

Published by Silhouette Books

America's Publisher of Contemporary Romance

SILHOUETTE BOOKS

ISBN 0-373-27187-5

BRAND-NEW HEARTACHE

Copyright © 2001 by Margaret Benson

All rights reserved. Except for use in any review, the reproduction or utilization of this work in whole or in part in any form by any electronic, mechanical or other means, now known or hereafter invented, including xerography, photocopying and recording, or in any information storage or retrieval system, is forbidden without the written permission of the editorial office, Silhouette Books, 300 East 42nd Street, New York, NY 10017 U.S.A.

All characters in this book have no existence outside the imagination of the author and have no relation whatsoever to anyone bearing the same name or names. They are not even distantly inspired by any individual known or unknown to the author, and all incidents are pure invention.

This edition published by arrangement with Harlequin Books S.A.

® and TM are trademarks of Harlequin Books S.A., used under license. Trademarks indicated with ® are registered in the United States Patent and Trademark Office, the Canadian Trade Marks Office and in other countries.

Visit Silhouette at www.eHarlequin.com

Printed in U.S.A.

MAGGIE SHAYNE,

a *USA Today* bestselling author whom *Romantic Times Magazine* calls "brilliantly inventive," has written more than twenty-five novels for Silhouette. She has won numerous awards, including the *Romantic Times Magazine* Career Achievement Award. A four-time finalist for the Romance Writers of America's prestigious RITA Award, Maggie also writes mainstream contemporary fantasy, as well as story lines for network daytime soap operas.

In her spare time, Maggie enjoys collecting gemstones, reading tarot cards, hanging out on the Genie computer network and spending time outdoors. She lives in a rural town in central New York with her husband, Rick, five beautiful daughters and two English bulldogs. She is also the proud grandmother of two.

Prologue

It made him sick that he liked her so much. In Wade's mind, she represented everything he hated about this town, this high school. When he passed her in the hall, she looked right through him, just like most everyone did.

Wade Armstrong lived in a rusty, lopsided trailer with three junk cars, none of which ran very often, in the driveway. His old man was the town drunk and got tossed into jail at least once a month for being disorderly at one of the local bars. Even, every now and then, the one her mother owned. He didn't remember his own mother. They said she hanged herself when he was three.

He didn't think Edie Brand was so much better than him. Sure, she had a mother, but her old man wasn't in the picture. Folks said he'd had another family on the side. Wade heard he'd been shot down in a gangland execution. That might be way more romantic than hanging yourself, but the old man was just as dead.

Of course, there was more standing between him and

Edie Brand than that. Edie's mother owned a saloon, kept
her daughters in decent clothes and shoes. Wade's father
spent most of his time in saloons and most of his money
on whiskey. Wade's own clothes never looked like much
and were rarely a perfect fit. He couldn't afford to be fussy.
His part-time job at the garage in town barely paid enough
for him to keep the power and heat turned on in the trailer
and buy a few groceries now and then.

Edie lived in a house. No mansion, but it was worlds
above his place. Still, her family was almost as scandalous
as his own. She just had a way of outshining her background. A way that almost made him jealous, though he
would die before he would admit it out loud. Why the hell
couldn't *he* breeze through life as if he were just a hair
short of royalty, despite the truth?

Hell, he knew why. Because guys were different. The
jocks in this school detested him, and they never let him
forget how far above him they saw themselves. It wasn't
overt. Just the looks they'd send. The way they would
huddle in a group and watch him pass, talking softly, then
laughing aloud. Matt McConnell was the worst offender.
In various little ways over the years, he'd managed to
make Wade feel about as important as a piece of gum on
the quarterback's shoe.

Wade turned, leaned against his locker, and watched
Edie Brand as she walked away from him, hangers-on
milling around her like gnats around a bug light. Everyone
wanted to be near her—as if she gave off some kind of
magnetic energy that drew them. He didn't know what the
hell it was. True, she was beautiful. More than just your
normal, garden-variety prettiness—Edie Brand was *beautiful.* Movie star beautiful. Her smile made people act like
idiots, tripping over themselves to get closer.

That could easily include him, unfortunately. It was a

constant effort to appear as if he didn't give a damn whether she was on the planet. God, he was pathetic.

She didn't even know he existed. He was sure of that much. When he met her in the halls at school, she never looked him in the eye, always kept hers averted. Never said hello, and he would be damned if he would speak first. He was invisible to her. Her whole crowd—the jocks, the cheerleaders, the popular kids—ignored him. They didn't mess with him, but they didn't speak to him, either. He didn't exist in their world. They were content to keep it that way.

He would show them someday. He would show them all.

For now, though, he just watched, and willed her to look his way as she stopped at her locker, faced it and began spinning the dial on the lock while smiling and talking to her admirers. His fantasy spun out in his brain the way it always did. This was his senior year. The prom was coming up. She was only a sophomore. Not that it mattered—he wouldn't go anyway. But in his fantasy, he did. He rolled up to her farmhouse in a long black limo, and he got out wearing a tux. She came to the door in a white dress that reached the floor, looking just like an angel. Smiling with those baby-blue eyes, right up at him.

Hell. It was a dumb dream. He couldn't afford a tux or a limo. He would be lucky to get one of the junk heaps on the lawn running long enough to drive to the school gym and back, and a tux would be out of the question. He'd been idiotic enough to check the prices for rentals. Then there would be tickets, a corsage, dinner out somewhere beforehand, like all the socially acceptable couples had. Maybe if he didn't eat for a week...

A squeal of girlish laughter shook him out of his thoughts, and he looked again at Edie Brand, as her friends nudged her and giggled. Matt McConnell was standing near Edie, holding her hand, smiling at her, waiting.

She parted her lips to speak, and Wade found himself straining to hear, moving closer without even realizing it.

"Sure, Matt," she said. "I'd love to go to the prom with you."

Something burned like acid in Wade's chest as he watched the confident high-school quarterback lean close and plant a kiss on Edie's cheek. And he vowed he would hate that girl forever.

Chapter 1

Thirteen Years Later...

"Hey, boss, you hear the latest?" Jimmy rolled out from under a red Taurus headfirst, faceup, wiping his hands on a grease rag.

Wade stopped halfway between the tiny office attached to the garage and the communal coffee urn, a cup in his hand. "What news?"

"Your favorite pinup girl is back in town."

He managed not to spill the coffee. In fact, he was pretty sure he managed not to show any reaction at all. It shouldn't be difficult. Hell, he barely thought about Edain Brand anymore—or Edie B., as she was known in the media. He only had her sexy catalogue photos pinned up all over the shop because she represented everything he hated, everyone who had ever brushed him off as unworthy. Looking at her reminded him of all the things he had to prove to the upper-crust folks in this town. That he was as good as they were. That he wasn't anything like his old man. That they had been wrong to judge him as if he were. That he could be successful. He wouldn't be happy until he was the most successful person in Big Falls. And he had a damn good start on it, too. Armstrong Auto Repair & Body Shop had four full-time employees. Wade didn't even have to work on the cars anymore. He still did once in a while, just to keep from going soft, but he didn't *have to*. He was even thinking of opening a second garage over in Tucker Lake. And by week's end, he planned to buy the nicest house in Big Falls, just to drive his point home.

"Boss? You hear me? I said Edie B. is back. Shelly saw her in town today."

"I heard you. What makes you think I care?"

Jimmy frowned at him, glanced at the catalogue pages lining the walls, the calendar that had gone out of date five months ago but still hung there. Then he looked at his boss again. "I don't know. I just thought you'd want to know."

"Already knew," he said. "She's been back in town since her sister got married, last Christmas. Just been keeping to herself." It wasn't as if he had been paying attention or anything. Nor had her brother-in-law Caleb, Wade's only real friend, breathed a word. He'd just happened to see her name in one of the celebrity gossip rags at the checkout counter of the local grocery store when he'd been picking up snacks and beer for the Super Bowl, and he'd picked it up to read the article. The piece said Edie B. had left L.A. when her contract with the sexiest lingerie catalogue in the world, *Vanessa's Whisper,* had expired in December, then dropped out of sight. There had been all sorts of speculation as to where she'd gone and why, from plastic surgery to a secret marriage to a dread disease. Even more questions were posed about her plans for the future.

Would she renew her contract with *VW?* She was their top model, but it was common knowledge her price had been dropping over the past year, as hot new faces and lean new bodies arrived on the scene. Would she continue modeling, the paper asked, or maybe move on to acting?

That theory had made him smile. Those tabloid writers sure had short memories. Five years back or so, Edie B. had landed a bit part in an action flick that had gone straight to video. It hadn't been easy to find a copy. Wade had to hunt it down on the Internet to get his hands on one. Just out of curiosity, of course.

He'd almost winced for her when he'd watched her acting debut. She was terrible. *Terrible.*

"She's been holed up at her mother's place this whole time," he went on as Jimmy watched him with arched brows. He knew that because he'd been kind of keeping an eye out for her ever since he'd read that article, back in January. And he'd glimpsed her once or twice. Checking the mail, shoveling the walk. He'd seen her out mowing the lawn one day last week. "She's been hiding out like a whipped pup."

"What do you suppose happened to make her want to do that?"

Wade shrugged. "Don't know, don't care." He wondered about it, too, though. She'd always been in the spotlight, right in the center of attention and loving every minute of it. For her to retreat so well that none of the locals even knew she'd been in town for five months was damned out of character. But what the hell did he know? "Apparently, whatever it is, it's over now."

"Then why isn't she back in L.A.?" Jimmy asked.

"Jimmy, how about we stop gossiping about the local underwear model and get on with fixing this car, huh?"

Jimmy shrugged, grinned and slid his creeper back underneath the car.

Wade headed for his office again. But he paused on the way to glance up at Edie Brand on her hands and knees, back arched, hand making a claw like a cat scratching at the camera. She wore a push-up bra and thong panties made of fake leopard fur. Her blond hair was teased and perfectly tousled, and her teeth were bared between shiny pink lips.

Damn, she looked good.

Edie B. looked into the camera as if it were her secret lover. Her face was flawless, her hair piled and curled and gleaming like gold. Her practiced smile was unwavering as she answered a TV entertainment reporter's questions regarding her daring outfit for the Couture Network Fashion Awards, where she was presenting that night. Who designed it? Were there sequins involved? What color would it be? And what was really going on between her and the drummer from that hardcore band?

She answered every question without giving away a thing. And she looked good doing it. She'd been at the top of her game that day.

Her mother came into the living room, looked from Edain, slouched on the sofa, watching herself on TV, to the television, where the year-old taped interview rolled on. Then she looked back at Edie again. "I thought I told you the pity-party was over, daughter?"

Edie thumbed the stop button and dropped the remote control onto the sofa beside her. "I went out today," she said, a little defensively. "I even did my hair and makeup first. Ask Mel, if you don't believe me."

"It's true, Ma," Mel called from the kitchen. "She

bought cute little outfits for the twins and some fresh flowers for the dining-room table.''

Vidalia Brand nodded slowly, eyeing Edain as she did. "Well, that's a start, I suppose. Too bad you came home and resumed wallowing in ancient history so darn fast."

"I know how little it means to you, Mom, but I was at my best in that piece I was just watching."

"Oh you were, were you?"

"Yes. I was."

"That piece aired the day after a schoolroom shooting. A six-year-old girl died, Edain. And you were on the TV talking about your clothes. It was far from your finest moment.''

Edie looked up slowly. She honest to God had a love-hate relationship with her mother. She loved the woman, respected her for having managed to raise five daughters on her own. And she owed her own good looks to her mom's genetics, if not her coloring. God, even now, Vidalia Brand didn't look half her age. She had a killer figure, and thick, raven hair with a few strands of silver just starting to line it, and the cheekbones of a royal.

Unfortunately, though her love for her mom was requited, the respect was not. Vidalia had never gotten over Edie's career choices. And she probably never would.

"The shooting hadn't happened yet when we taped the interview," Edie said slowly, trying to hold her temper.

"It had happened when they ran it, which ought to tell you a lot about the values in that make-believe world where you've been living for the past ten years."

Edie looked down at her hands in her lap, unable to answer that. It was true. She knew that.

"I like to think there was a reason you left that life, Edain. Like maybe that you finally realized you didn't belong there. And if you think *that*—" she snatched the remote up and hit play, then paused it on Edie's perfectly made-up face and false smile "—was your finest moment, then you are sadly misinformed."

"I was at the height of my career."

"You were pretty. It didn't matter what you thought or how you felt, just so you looked good, and you did. To you, that's some kind of peak?" Sighing, Vidalia shook her head. She shut the TV off, tossed the remote down. "Are you going back to modeling underwear for a living or not, daughter? It's time you made a decision."

"Don't you think I've been wrestling with that question for the past five months? Don't you think it's killing me, not knowing?"

"No, I don't. You've got too much money, that's what your trouble is. You can afford to mope around the house, licking your wounds and pouting, for just as long as you want. No pressure to get off your backside and earn a living."

Edie bristled. "I'm pitching in more than my fair share around here! I even work at the bar after hours."

"Uh-huh. And that's what you're gonna do for the rest of your life? Mop floors after hours and spend your days watching old tapes of yourself on TV? Hmm?"

"No! Of course not!"

"Then what *are* you gonna do?"

"I don't—"

"Don't you tell me you don't know. I didn't raise any airheads, Edain Brand, contrary to public opinion and TV spots like that giggling, vacant-eyed one you call the peak of your career. So don't you tell me you haven't given this some thought. You always knew your good looks wouldn't sustain you forever."

Edie crossed her arms over her chest, refusing to meet

her mother's eyes. "I always thought retirement would be another ten years off."

Her mother made a noise.

Edie said, "Well, at least five."

"And?"

She shrugged. "I don't know."

"You don't know." Vidalia said the words as if they made her stomach hurt. Then she stomped away, up the stairs.

Edie sighed in relief, thinking the conversation was over, but that was a mistake. Because seconds later Vidalia came down again with Edie's big black camera case in one hand. She placed it carefully on Edie's lap. "Lie to your mother, will you?"

Edie shook her head, confused. "This doesn't mean anything. It's just a hobby."

"The hell it is, girl. I saw the photos you've taken since you've been home. Maya's twins. Your sister's wedding, such as it was. The Falls. The snow on the trees after that freak storm. You're good, Edie. And you know about a camera. Goodness knows you've spent enough time in front of one."

Edain licked her lips, hesitant to admit to something she knew her mother would leap on. "I...*have* toyed with the idea of opening a photography studio of my own."

Vidalia Brand smiled, nodded once, firmly, and said, "Then do it."

"I don't know, Mom. I'm not sure I—"

"Moping time's over, daughter. Get out of this slump you're in and start making a life for yourself, or I will personally kick your backside all the way back to La-La-Land. If you think I'm not serious, you just try me."

"I know you're serious."

Vidalia nodded again. "You'd better." She drew a

breath, blew it out again, then sat on the edge of the sofa. She glanced just once toward the kitchen, but Mel had the good sense to keep out of the line of fire, though she'd peeked in a few times during the discussion. "What are you running from, Edain? Something sure chased you home in a hurry. You haven't been yourself at all since you came back. You barely see anyone besides family. You keep to the house as much as possible. What is it?"

After a long pause, Edie said, "Maybe I'm not myself because I'm not sure who that is anymore."

"Bullcookies."

Edie sniffed, lowered her head a little. "No. It's true. You always used to tell me there was more to me than a pretty face, Mom, but I didn't bother to find out what. That pretty face was all I needed to get where I wanted to go. Where I...thought I wanted to go. Now, I...I don't know. I'm close to thirty. Models fifteen years younger are taking the slots that used to be mine. It's getting harder and harder to keep up with them." She shook her head. "Something scared me, you're right about that. I thought that was the only reason I left, but I just can't drum up any enthusiasm for going back. I don't want to work out until I drop or live on carrot sticks anymore. You know I've put on ten pounds since I've been home?"

"Ten? You could use another twenty. You're nothing but bones. A grown woman is not supposed to have the body of a prepubescent girl and the breasts of a nursing mother, you know. It's unnatural."

A snort came from the kitchen.

"Shut up, Mel."

"Sorry. Frog in my throat," Mel called.

Her mother sighed, because the body image that Edain's work perpetuated was another sore subject with her. Along with morality and dignity and about a hundred other issues.

Still, she softened and searched Edie's face. "What scared you, honey? You tell me, and I'll see it gets removed from creation, whatever it is."

That made Edie smile. Her mother meant every word of it, she knew that. The woman would fight a pack of rabid wolves bare-handed for her daughters. Even the one she so disapproved of. "It doesn't matter, Mom. It's been months. I think it's over."

Vidalia looked doubtful, but nodded all the same. "So, you gonna get on with your life or what?"

She smiled gently. "I suppose I could go see Betty Lou at the real estate office. At least see what's available that might make a nice photography studio someday. In case that's the decision I make."

"That's a start," Vidalia said. Then she turned to look through the dining room into the kitchen. "It's safe to come in now, Melusine. You can stop pretending to check on my pot roast. We all know you can't cook anyway." She glanced at Edain with a smile. "Bring the cordless phone along, will you, Mel? Your sister wants to call Betty Lou Jennings, over at the real estate office."

Mel came in, telephone in one hand, phone book in the other. She was the toughest pixie ever to live in Big Falls, tiny and dark as an elf, strong and hot-tempered as a Brahma bull. She sent Edie a sympathetic look as she handed her the phone. Edie took it with a sigh.

"I suppose now is as good a time as any."

Two hours later she was driving her SUV into a curving driveway, where another vehicle was already parked. She came to a stop and stared at the tall, darkly stained house. It had a modified A-frame center, with two wings angling back on either side. There were huge skylights on both sides of the steeply pitched center roof, and floor-to-ceiling windows in the front. It was huge. And it sat on a hilltop, with the falls providing a stunning view from a short distance away.

When she'd spoken to Betty Lou, describing what she wanted—something large, airy, open, with plenty of natural light—she hadn't expected the woman to tell her she had the perfect place, much less that she was showing it to a client that very afternoon. Edie had to wonder if her mother had cooked this up ahead of time with the real estate agent, who was an old friend.

Still, the place was spectacular. God, if she knew for sure she were going to stay in Big Falls, she would buy it this minute, without even having seen the inside.

This was it, Wade thought, walking slowly through the house he'd been all but drooling over for the past ten years. A Tulsa architect had built it here, planning to retire in it, but the isolation had proven too much for him to handle in his old age. He'd longed for tropical climates, so now the place was vacant and up for sale.

It was a dream. And the way it sat slightly above the rest of the town appealed to him for its symbolism. No one could look down on him up here.

He heard a car pull in, figured Betty Lou had arrived. She'd left a key in the mailbox for him, told him to come on up and look around, that she would meet him here. He couldn't help but show up a little on the early side. He'd been waiting a long time for this. He already had a buyer for his little place in town. He planned to close on that deal by week's end. That would bring enough for the down payment, and he had a good enough credit rating to finance the rest. Everything was in place. He was ready.

Footsteps came up the stairs from the lower-level foyer. He turned, expecting to see Betty Lou Jennings, whose shape and demeanor reminded him of a bumblebee. Instead, he saw *her.*

She met his gaze, seemed a little startled, but hid it quickly enough. "I'm looking for Betty Lou—"

"She's running a little late," he managed without stammering, because, damn, she looked better than in her photos. The fact that she had clothes on didn't take a thing away from the sex appeal that wafted from her like musk. It had only been hinted at before she'd left high school and Big Falls all those years ago. Now it was full grown, and so was she. Eyes so big they could swallow him whole. Skin like satin. Her hair was pulled back, pinned up, nothing like the bedroom styles she wore for those sexy photos. But her lips were just as plump, and he knew that wasn't collagen. They'd always been that way.

"I'm sorry," she said. "I don't think I—"

So she didn't remember him. No wonder. She'd barely noticed him. "Name's Armstrong," he said quickly, cutting her off.

Her brows drew together briefly, but then she was busy glancing around the room, and he didn't think she was checking the place out with the eye of an interested buyer. She looked more like a woman alone with a snake, searching for something to whack it with.

"Betty Lou will be along any minute," he said.

"I'm sure she will." She shuffled her feet, looked nervous.

"So are you looking to buy this place?"

Her eyes shot back to his. "I was thinking about it. Of course, I haven't even seen it yet, so it's hard to say."

"Well, we can remedy that right now." He moved closer to her, almost against his will, curved a hand around her elbow, felt a shot of pleasure at touching the woman whose naked flesh had fueled so many of his nighttime fantasies. He had to forcibly remind himself of his goal here. Eliminate any competition he might have for this place. Quickly. "This is the living room. The fireplace is my favorite part." He led her toward it, trying to resist the catalogue page that flashed into his mind. Her, sprawled suggestively on a bearskin rug in front of a fireplace a lot like this one.

When she looked at him, he wondered if he'd groaned out loud or just mentally. He tried to cover by getting back to his goal. "Of course, it's a huge risk, having a natural fireplace. Easy as hell to burn the place to the ground if you don't know what you're doing."

"Good thing I grew up with wood heat, then, huh?" she asked. She made it sound completely innocent, but he could tell she had guessed what he was up to. "You looking to buy this house for yourself, Mr. Armstrong?"

He shrugged, turning away from the fireplace. "Then, of course, there are the windows. Floor to ceiling," he said in his best tour guide voice.

"I can see that," she said. Almost as if she were talking down to him.

He bristled but tried to hide it. "They'll make it damned uncomfortable in here. Roast you right out in the summer, I imagine."

"Unless you turn on the AC," she returned.

He pursed his lips. It was going to take more than questioning the house's merits to get rid of her, wasn't it? Fine. He had more. He had plenty more. "It'll take a creative mind to figure out how to cover them. For privacy, I mean. Then again, I don't suppose you worry about that too much."

She narrowed her eyes on him. "And why do you suppose that, Mr. Armstrong?"

He shrugged. "You don't seem like the shy, retiring type."

"Because I was a model?" She faced him now, hands on her hips, and he could see she was angry.

"Because there's not much of you that hasn't already been seen by everyone who cared to look."

"That was my job, caveman. It doesn't mean I'm going to parade around in my underwear in front of open windows."

He lifted his brows and his hands. "Hey, don't get defensive on me. I didn't mean anything. Hell, I'd be the *last* one to complain about your work. Ask anyone in town." He turned away again. "Now, as you can see, this main area could double as a dining room. The kitchen is right through—"

She stopped him, a hand closing tight around his upper arm as he started toward the kitchen. He winced in pleasure. God, he liked her touching him. "What do you mean, you'd be the last one to complain?"

He turned an innocent look on her. "Only that your photos provide a valuable service to a great many men on cold, lonely nights, Edie B. Myself included."

"When you can't get a real woman, you mean?" she snapped back.

"Exactly. Sometimes there's just no one to keep a fellow company besides you, and good old Rosy Palm."

She frowned. "Rosy Pa—" She went silent, her mouth gaping. She was only speechless for an instant, though. A second later she clamped her jaw, smacked him across the face and turned on her heel. She was out of the house so fast it must have been some kind of record.

Her tires spat gravel in their wake when she left.

Wade smiled broadly, rubbing his cheek. "For a second

there, I was afraid I'd never get her out of here," he said
to the empty room.

He probably shouldn't have been quite so mean. But it
served her right for not recognizing him. She should at
least have found him vaguely familiar. But no. She was
the same arrogant little brat she'd always been. Still
thought she was better than him. Just like so many others
in this town.

Screw it. He would show them all. The minute Betty
Lou Jennings arrived, he was going to tell her to mark this
place sold. To him.

Chapter 2

She spun her tires as she tore out of the driveway onto the curving dirt road that twisted away from the gorgeous house and got about a hundred feet before she realized what that manipulative SOB had done. He had driven her away on purpose—because he wanted the place for himself.

She was so furious she damn near had steam coming out her ears. Wade Armstrong. He had *always* been trouble. Everyone knew it. And he had *always* managed to intimidate the hell out of her. Dark, brooding, moody—she had been as turned on by him as every other girl in high school. But she had been equally afraid of him. Rumors about Big Falls' own bad boy had abounded back then. They said he could make a girl do anything he wanted her to. And that he always did just that, on the very first date. They said he only went out with older women, because girls her age couldn't keep up with his appetites, and there was a ton of speculation about him and the young English teacher who had only kept her job for one school year. She had taken a special interest in Wade Armstrong, and the next thing everyone knew, she was gone.

Edie had been completely intrigued by him. And convinced that if she so much as looked him in the eye, he would see that in her eyes and approach her. And if he asked her out, she didn't think she had it in her to say no. And then she would be in big trouble, her reputation ruined, her popularity in the toilet, and her virginity another trophy in Wade's collection. Her mother would have *killed* her.

So she only looked at Wade Armstrong when he wasn't looking. She avoided him as if he were poison. And she remained afraid of him.

"Well, not anymore," she muttered, jamming the brakes. "I'll be damned if I'll let some sexually depraved grease monkey chase me away from something I want."

She was going to turn around and drive right back there. She was going to stomp up to the arrogant bastard and tell him exactly what she thought of him. She was going to...

A car came around the bend, slowing as it drew nearer. Edie saw the magnetic "Betty Lou Jennings Real Estate" placard on the side, cranked her window down and waved. Betty Lou stopped so the two cars were side by side, facing in opposite directions. It wasn't a problem on a winding dirt road like this one. No traffic to worry about. Edie bit her lip, hoping Wade Armstrong would stay right where he was for a few more minutes. That was all she needed.

Wade was standing in the living room, choosing a spot for the big-screen TV that was so sorely out of place at his little house in town, when he heard a vehicle's tires rolling over the gravel driveway. He tensed a little, and his belly went tight. He shook the reaction off—it wasn't Edie Brand. She wouldn't be back after the way he'd sent her packing. Pacing to the window, he glanced outside, just to make sure. And it puzzled him that he found himself half-hoping it *would* be her in her little powder-blue Jeep out there. He liked sparring with her. Liked to watch her face heat with color and her eyes spark with anger. Liked it when her lips parted and no words came out. Loved it when she touched him.

But then, so would any red-blooded American male between the ages of ten and dead.

By the looks of things, she was planning to stay in Big Falls for a while. Maybe a long while, or she wouldn't be looking to buy a house. That knowledge kept digging at him for some reason. He would brush it aside, but five seconds later he would be thinking about it again, as if it meant something to him, when in fact he couldn't care less.

Betty Lou Jennings got out of her station wagon and came up the steps, and Wade opened the front door before she reached it. She looked up fast, startled, and then a troubled V formed between her eyebrows.

Well, his news ought to put a smile on her face. "I'm taking the house," he announced. "I made up my mind yesterday. Got my little place in town sold already, and it's more than you need for a down payment. Rob at the bank says my loan is going straight through, no problems. It'll take about a week to get the official papers signed, and then we can close the deal."

"Oh." She wasn't smiling. She wasn't looking him in the eye, either. "You sold your place, you say?"

"Signed the contract yesterday," he said. She did not look happy. Her short, round little frame was perfectly still, her eyes staring straight ahead. "Sorry about not us-

ing your agency, Betty Lou—it was just one of my employees who bought it. He's getting married. I made him
a decent deal.''

''It's...not that.''

''Well, then, what's wrong?'' He watched her force herself to meet his eyes, and he got a bad feeling in his belly.

''I'm so sorry, Wade. I...the place is sold.''

He blinked, repeating the word in his mind, and then
aloud, because he didn't think he could possibly have
heard her right. ''Sold? It's *sold?*''

Betty Lou nodded, her short brown hair bouncing with
the jerky motion of her head. ''I've been waiting for you
to make up your mind for a month, Wade, and I had no
reason to believe you wouldn't keep dragging your feet for
another one. I have kids to feed, you know.''

''Yeah, but—'' He turned slowly, pushing a hand
through his hair, totally blown away.

''She wrote me a check, right there on the spot, for the
full amount. No haggling, no banks, no questions. She just
took it. Just like that.''

Wade stopped with his back to Betty Lou, one hand on
the back of his head. He froze there for an instant, then
slowly lifted his head, eyes narrow. ''It was Edain Brand,
wasn't it?''

''I...well, I...yes. It was.''

''That bossy, arrogant, egotistical little—''

''Wade, really. There are other houses in town. I have
at least three I can show you this very afternoon.''

''I don't want any other houses,'' he said, enunciating
each word and keeping his tone completely level. ''I want
this house. She doesn't. She only bought it to stick it to
me.''

Betty Lou lifted her brows. ''Don't be ridiculous, Wade.

No one drops two hundred thousand dollars just to get revenge.''

"That's pocket change to her.''

"Well, what on earth did you do to make her angry enough that you think she would do such a thing?''

He looked up then, having nearly forgotten Betty Lou was there. He had been talking mainly to himself. So what *had* he done to make the great Edie B. angry? Not much. Just called her a slut and told her that men around the world enjoyed manual stimulation while looking at her pictures—himself included. Not in so many words, of course, but he supposed he'd been less than tactful.

"Guess I insulted her.''

"Guess you must have.'' Betty Lou glanced at her watch. "Look, I have to run. Don't worry about this, okay? We'll find you a great place in no time, I promise. Okay?''

"Yeah,'' he muttered. "Whatever.''

She turned and hurried back down the flagstone path to her car. Wade followed her outside, pulling the door closed behind him. Betty Lou had forgotten to ask for the key back. Not that it mattered. Not now. Damn. *Damn* that woman for showing up and screwing up his plans.

He was furious, fuming as he drove back toward town. And then he saw her little Jeep parked on the shoulder of the road. He told himself to keep right on going. That it was a foolish, stupid thing to do, stopping when he was this angry. But he stopped anyway. He got out of his pickup and walked up to her car, glanced inside. She wasn't there. He hadn't expected her to be. There was a footpath here that led out to the falls. You could drive right up to them from the other side, but from this end you had to walk. And it looked as if that was what she had done.

Wade squared his shoulders and marched onto the meandering path, fully ready to tell the woman just what he thought of her high-handed tactics and the way she threw her money around. He followed the narrow trail through the woods. It wound downward, ending at the riverbank, near the base of the falls. And that was where he found her.

She was sitting on the rocky bank with her knees drawn to her chest, head lowered on her crossed arms. Crying. Not a soft, quiet, delicate kind of crying, with a sniffle and a few tears. No, she was really bawling. Hiccuping, with sobs in between, her shoulders shaking with the force of it.

He didn't know what the hell to do. He sure as hell couldn't confront her now, tell her off the way he'd intended, not when she was like this. His throat felt oddly tight—he couldn't seem to swallow for a while.

He froze, just watching her there for a long moment. Then, silently, he withdrew. He made his way back to his pickup and drove back the way he'd come until he found a place where he could park reasonably out of sight. Then he sat there, and he waited. An hour went by before she finally came dragging back up the path, got into her car and headed for home. Only then did Wade return to the garage.

"Well, I hope you're happy," Edie said as she stomped through the door of the farmhouse. She heeled off her suede walking shoes and sank into a kitchen chair. "I bought the place."

Her mother looked up from the coffee she'd been sipping, a stack of open mail beside her, peered over the tops of the glasses she refused to wear in public and said, "Maybe you should go outside and try coming in again with a better attitude."

Edie sighed, lowering her head. "Sorry. It's not your fault. Not really."

Her mother laid the letter she'd been reading aside and got to her feet. She leaned through the doorway into the dining room, and called, "Selene, you still around, sweetie?"

"Yeah, Mom?"

"Go on up to your room and get us some of that calming tea you brew. I think your sister could use a batch."

Selene's footsteps pounded away, up the stairs. At that moment the kitchen door burst open again, and Maya stepped through it, carrying a baby on each hip.

"My land, you'll be crippled before they start school!" Vidalia scolded. But she smiled as she hefted little Dahlia away. Turning, she handed the five-month-old to Edain, then relieved Maya of the other one. "CC, boy, you get any bigger, you'll have to start carrying me instead," she said, laughing. "Yes, you will. Yes, you will," she chirped as she carried the baby to a chair and sat down with him.

Edie held Dahlia on her lap and tried to be cheered by the huge blue eyes and spit bubbles, but it wasn't helping much. Maya hung her jacket on a peg near the door and came in, poured herself coffee. "So what's new around here?"

"Well, your morose sister finally got herself out and about today," Vidalia said, her attention fully on her grandson.

"I thought I saw you driving out this afternoon. What did you do, Edie?"

"Not much. Bought a house I hadn't even fully seen, is all."

Maya blinked, looking from Edie to her mother and back again. "You...you bought a house?"

"Yeah. The big A-frame on the hill overlooking the falls."

"Oh, gosh, that place is *fabulous!* But...so...does that mean you're staying?"

Sighing, Edie shrugged. "To tell you the truth, I hadn't even really made up my mind what I wanted to do. I only went out there to look at the place, just in case I decided to stay."

"She's thinking of opening a photography studio," Vidalia filled in.

"That's a wonderful idea!" Maya exclaimed, clapping her hands together.

The baby in Edie's lap smiled and clapped her hands together, too.

"It was just a thought. I really don't know if that's what I want to do."

"Well, then...I don't get it," Maya said. "Why'd you buy the place if you still haven't decided?"

She drew a deep nasal breath, lifted her head, met her sister's eyes. "I ran into Wade Armstrong out there. He wanted to buy the house himself, and he insulted me and pissed me off and—"

"Language, Edain," Vidalia cut in.

Edie bit her lip. "He *ticked* me off so badly that I left. And then I realized that was what he intended, to chase me off before Betty Lou got there so he wouldn't have any competition for the house. So when I met her on the road, I stopped her, and I...I bought the house."

Maya just sat there staring at her. She finally glanced at her mother. "Is she kidding?"

"I don't think so. And we always thought Mel was the hot-tempered one."

Selene came trotting into the kitchen then, her silvery-blue eyes curious, a mason jar half full of finely ground herbs in her hands. "Hi, Maya. Hey, Edie," she said, waltzing through the kitchen. She paused to lean over each of the babies, cooed and tickled them hello, then turned to put water on to heat. She found her metal tea balls in a drawer and began measuring herbs into them. "How many for my calming brew?"

"Just Edie," Vidalia said.

Looking over her shoulder, Selene lifted her brows. "What's got you all out of sorts, sis?"

Edie sighed, saying nothing. Vidalia answered for her. "Edie just dropped four years' income on a house because some man made her mad." At Edain's glare, she amended. "Sorry. Four months' income for her. Four years to anyone else—more than that to most folks."

Selene lifted her brows, glancing at Edain. "Wade Armstrong, I'll bet."

Maya closed her eyes, shaking her head slowly. "Knock it off, would you? That really creeps me out."

Selene shrugged. "So what happened, Edie? Did you go into his garage and see all the—"

"Selene, your water's boiling," Vidalia said quickly, a sharp edge to her voice.

Edie heard it. She frowned and looked at her mother, who looked away.

"He insulted her," Maya said, hurrying to fill in the tense silence. "And he wanted the house himself, so she bought it right out from under him, to get him back."

Selene lowered her head quickly, but not before Edain saw the smile. "Bet he didn't expect that. Heck, he has most people around here believing his big bad scary routine. They're too intimidated by it to mess with him."

"He hasn't changed a bit then, has he?"

"Since high school?" Selene asked. "Nope, not a bit. He's still a loner. Still carries a big chip on his shoulder and walks around as if daring anyone to try and knock it off.'' She carried a steaming cup of fragrant tea to Edain and set it down in front of her. ''And he's still nuts about the most popular girl in town.''

''I pity her, whoever she is,'' Edie muttered as she lifted the cup to her nose to sniff the contents.

Selene smiled crookedly. ''So, now that you have a house, you gonna move out and leave us, sis?''

''Not right away. I mean, I need to think about furniture—the whole place needs to be decorated. And besides, I like being close to the babies.'' As she said it, she bounced Dahlia on her knee and tickled her underneath her chin.

''Well, there's no hurry,'' Vidalia said.

''Nooo,'' Maya said, drawing the word out. ''But it will sure burn Wade Armstrong's buns to see the place sitting empty. I mean, he must know you bought it just to spite him.''

''He's an arrogant jerk who thinks the only thing I'm capable of doing is posing in my underwear. He had it coming.'' Her sisters and her mother were looking at her. She pursed her lips. ''He *did*.''

''Okay. He did. The question remains, what the heck are you going to do with a house you're not even sure you want?'' Maya asked.

''Oh, she wants it.'' Selene spoke slowly and with an authority that seemed out of place coming from the youngest of the sisters. ''Deep down, some part of her knows that. Ticking Wade Armstrong off was just an excuse.''

Vidalia tipped her head to one side. ''I never can figure out if you're more witch doctor or headshrinker, girl. But you do make a good point. Don't you think so, Edain?''

''No, I don't think so.''

"Neither did I, when she said I was going to have twins," Maya muttered, half under her breath.

Edie pursed her lips and sipped her tea. It was good. It was delicious, but she wasn't going to give her know-it-all kid sister the satisfaction of saying so.

"No need to make a decision now, anyway, Edain," Vidalia said, patting her daughter's hand. "You can stay right here just as long as you want to. Just so long as you don't try to hole up in the house like a hermit. You're a beacon, girl. You need to shine, or you'll just flicker out." Then she glanced at the clock on the wall. "I have to go. Kara's all alone over at the Corral, and it'll start getting busy soon." Getting to her feet, Vidalia set her grandson back in his mother's lap.

"I'll ride over with you, Ma," Selene said, snagging a light jacket from one of the pegs beside the door. The two headed out without another word, and Edie was certain they would be discussing her all the way to the family business—the OK Corral.

"I have to get home," Maya said. "I left bread in the oven."

"You're gonna make that man of yours fat," Edie said. She got up, though. "Come on, I'll help you carry the rug rats up the hill."

"Thanks."

Together they put the babies' sweaters and hats back in place. It was May, but it was also evening, and there was a breeze. As they walked along what was now a well-worn path that led up the hill a hundred yards from the farmhouse to the dream house Maya and her husband, Caleb, had built, Edie couldn't help but admire the place. It was large and homey. A log cabin fit for *Home Beautiful,* big enough for a big shot like Caleb—whose father was one of the richest men in the country—yet cozy enough for

Maya, the original homebody. There was still some work
under way. The driveway hadn't been paved yet, and the
two-car garage was still unfinished. But the wide front
porch was just what Maya had always talked about, and
there was already a swing set in back, though the kids were
way too young to enjoy it yet.

As they neared the house, Caleb's car pulled into the
long gravel driveway that wound from the far side of the
house down to the road. He got out, spotted them coming,
and started toward them, a warm smile on his face. Edie
still couldn't get over the way that man's eyes lit up when-
ever they fell upon Maya or the babies. He was hopelessly
in love with his little family. God, Maya was so lucky.

He met them halfway, wrapped his wife in his arms,
baby and all, and kissed her deeply. Then he took little
CC from her, smooching the baby's cheek until the kid
laughed aloud. He relieved Edie of her niece in the same
manner, then grinned. "Hello, Edie. Heard you bought a
house today."

She blinked at him. "My goodness, news travels fast
around here."

"Oh, not really. I just had some inquiries as to whether
there were any legal actions that could be taken to block
the purchase."

"What?" She blinked at him, then understood. "Wade
Armstrong?"

"I really can't say. But it doesn't matter, anyway.
There's nothing in the law to stop you from going ahead
with it. If you...you know, want to."

"You sound as if you think I shouldn't!"

He shook his head quickly. "I didn't say that."

"He and Wade are friends," Maya said. "But this is
family. Right, Caleb?"

"Well, yeah. Sure. I mean, I..."

"And Wade Armstrong can just find himself another house. Right, Caleb?"

He hesitated. "Technically," he said at length, "either one of them could probably find another house."

"Caleb…"

"Come on, Maya, I don't want to disagree with you on this. But…it was kind of mean, what your sister did. Wade's been getting things lined up to buy that place for a month now."

"Well, he didn't move fast enough."

"Because someone richer came along and used her money like a weapon," he said. And it hurt. Edie winced.

"*Caleb!*" Maya sent him a scowl.

"No, Maya. Caleb's right," Edie said slowly. "That's exactly what I did. Wade made me angry, and I struck back. With my money. Just exactly like a weapon. And it wasn't very nice." She sighed, lowered her head.

"I only know because I've been there," Caleb said, his voice gentle. "It doesn't make you a bad person. You just had a brief flash of temper, is all."

She nodded. "So he's really been planning to buy the place for a whole month?"

Caleb nodded as his daughter pulled his hair and his son stared at him as if transfixed. "He sold his own place, too. I don't know what he'll do about that."

Edie swallowed, lowering her head. "God, why do I let my temper get away from me like that?"

"Nobody's perfect."

She sighed. "I suppose I could undo this thing before it goes any further," she said with a sigh. "It would probably be the fair thing to do. He did see the place first."

"He's not a bad fellow, Edie. But he does have a bad attitude about people lording it over him. Thinks he has something to prove. This really hurt."

She nodded. "Thanks, Caleb. I suppose if I'm staying in Big Falls, I shouldn't start out being known around town as that bitch who throws her money around to get her way." She drew a breath, stiffened her spine, told herself it was no big deal. She could afford to have a dream house built to her own specifications if she wanted to. But it wasn't the idea of letting the house go that was bothering her. It was the idea of admitting her mistake.

Caleb read her face. "I can call him for you if you want."

"No. I'll, uh, I'll do it myself. I'm an adult."

He nodded, turned and started toward his own dream house with a baby on each hip. Maya leaned closer, hugged Edie hard. "I'm sorry he's so darned…" She seemed to search for the right word.

"Ethical? Moral? Fair-minded? Decent?" Edie asked. "You're right, he's all those things. He's also right. The rat."

"Just don't do anything unless you're sure."

"It was a temper tantrum, Maya. I'll think about it some more, but I suppose if I don't have that house, I'll get over it. See you tomorrow, okay?"

Maya nodded, then turned and hurried after her husband. Edie sighed, squared her shoulders and began marching back down the hill to the farmhouse, the phone and the meal of crow she was about to devour.

She knew, deep down, that she had reacted to far more than just Wade Armstrong's petty little insults and slams. It wasn't him at all, she reminded herself. She had become hypersensitive to men who saw her as a sex object. And that had nothing to do with Wade Armstrong. He was just your garden-variety lech. Just one more who saw her as nothing more than an airbrushed, glossy bit of flesh in sexy clothes.

No, her reactions were because of one particular man, one who'd taken it too far. Crossed the line. Frightened her so badly she'd left L.A., left the business, left everything behind. But that man, she reminded herself, was a part of her past. History. He was a sick, disturbed nobody who had only been able to get to her because she was so much in the public eye. Now she was home. Her life was her own again. *He* wouldn't even know where to begin to find her now.

She walked the rest of the way down the hill to the friendly back door, hauled it open and stepped inside. Then she paused. A small brown cardboard box sat on the kitchen table. Exactly in the center. For a minute a chill whispered down her nape, and she shivered. But then she told herself that was ridiculous. It was a simple delivery. This was Big Falls, Oklahoma. If you weren't home and your door wasn't locked, delivery guys routinely set their packages just inside the door. Especially if they knew you. And *everyone* here knew everyone else. This was not a big deal.

She walked up to the table, her steps slow, her eyes darting through the doorway into the dining room, her ears straining to hear any sign of anyone else inside the house. She looked at the box. It had her name on it.

"No postmark," she whispered. "No address."

It hadn't been left by any delivery guy. She swallowed the dryness in her throat, edging along the counter until she reached the knife drawer. She slid it open, closed her hand around the largest handle in it, pulled a cleaver out.

Still looking, still listening, she moved silently closer to the table, and with her free hand she reached out and flipped open the lid of the box. Leaning closer, she peered inside, her gaze darting downward only briefly, in case someone came at her from elsewhere in the house. She thought of just running back up the hill, shouting for help. But not for the world would she put Maya or those babies at risk.

Inside the box, unwrapped, lying loosely, were a pair of handcuffs.

Then, very clearly, she heard two solid footsteps coming through the back door, stopping right behind her.

Chapter 3

Wade strode up the path to the wide-open back door of the Brand house. He'd seen Edain Brand go in that way only a minute ago, and she had left the door swinging, so he assumed she was still lingering nearby.

When he paused at the entrance, she was standing with her back to him, looking at something in a box on the kitchen table. When he took a step toward her and opened his mouth to announce his presence, she spun around before he got a word out, brandishing a meat cleaver.

He ducked reflexively, bringing up one arm in self-defense—even though she didn't follow through on the swing once she saw his face.

"You!" she accused. At least it sounded like an accusation to him. Just what she was accusing him of, he couldn't begin to guess. "You did this, didn't you? You sick, vile—"

"That's about enough, Edie." He reached out and clasped her wrist, rendering her cleaver-bearing hand harmless. Then he took the cleaver away. "Now, just what is it you think I've done? Let me guess. Maybe I did something really horrible—like swooping in to buy a house I didn't even want just so you couldn't get it." He frowned. "No, wait. That was you."

"You're not one bit funny. And if you think this twisted little *gift* is, then you're more warped than I realized."

"Gift?" For the first time, he took a good look at her face. She was pale, not her usual flawless color, and her eyes had an expression in them he hadn't seen before. "I didn't send you any…" He looked past her, at the box on the table; then he moved toward it.

She stepped into his path, but he put a hand on her shoulder and moved her aside without a hell of a lot of effort. He looked into the box, saw a pair of handcuffs in the bottom. He turned, lifted his brows. "Secret admirer?"

She averted her face so quickly that he found himself frowning again.

"You didn't send it?" she asked. "This isn't some kinky little insult to get revenge on me for buying your house?"

"No."

She closed her eyes quickly, whispered "damn" on a soft breath.

"Disappointed?" he asked. "You were actually hoping I harbored some sexy little bondage fantasies about you?"

"Shut up."

"'Cause I do. I mean—of course I do. But I didn't send the handcuffs." He glanced at them again. "Nope. In my version we use silk scarves. Red ones. And—"

"*Shut up,* Wade."

He shut up. Not because she said so, but because she'd called him by his first name, and he felt it all the way to his toes.

"You haven't changed a bit, have you?" she asked him. "Still trying to intimidate people, just like in high school. Well, I may have been scared to death of you then, Wade, but I'm not anymore. So just knock it off already."

He couldn't speak for a minute. He had been so certain she didn't remember him at all—that she hadn't even noticed him in high school. "You...were scared of me?"

"Everyone was scared of you."

"So what are you scared of now?" he asked.

She shook her head. "Look, what did you come here for?"

"Doesn't matter. What are you scared of, Edie?" He glanced at the box. "The guy who sent you those?"

"How can I be, when I don't even know who it was?"

He frowned. Then he had a thought and reached for the lid, intending to flip it down and check out the label, the address, postmark, that sort of crap. Edie closed her hand on his wrist, moved it away from the box, and placed herself between him and the table that held it.

"It's none of your business, Wade."

He studied her face, blinked slowly as he tried to figure her out.

"You came here to try to talk me out of buying that house," she said slowly. "You wasted your time. Not only am I going ahead with the deal, but I'm moving in tomorrow."

"And rubbing my nose in it tonight, apparently."

"Get out, will you? I want to be alone."

"You're a lousy liar."

She walked to the door, stood beside it, waiting for him to leave.

"What was with the meat cleaver, Edie? Tell me that and I'll go."

"You startled me. That's all."

"That's all? And you were standing there looking at a pair of handcuffs with a meat cleaver in your hand because…?"

"Because I freaking felt like it."

He studied her, wondering if he could be mistaken. But no, he was certain she'd been scared witless when he had stepped in here. And Edie Brand had never been anyone's fool, despite her public image. If she were scared, there was a reason.

"I'll tell you what," he said. "I'll leave. But first I'm gonna have to go on up the hill and tell Caleb about your anonymous gift."

She stabbed his eyes with hers. "Don't do that."

"Why not?"

She licked her lips, looked away, seeking a plausible lie, he was certain. "Look, I don't want anyone to know about this. I need you to keep it to yourself, Wade. I mean it."

"All right. I will. On one condition."

Her head snapped toward him. "If you think for one minute you can blackmail me into giving back the house…"

"Uh, no, that's not the condition I was thinking of."

She went silent for a moment. Then she looked at him, and her eyes widened and her cheeks heated.

"Neither was that," he said, before she could accuse him. Damn, she thought awfully little of him. Then again, so did most of the locals. "I was going to say, I'll keep quiet if you'll let me take you somewhere."

"Where?" she asked, her eyes suspicious.

"Anywhere," he said. "Your sister's place, the saloon, I don't care. I just don't feel right leaving you here alone when you're scared half to death of some anonymous pervert, okay? Maybe I'm an idiot, but that's the way it is."

She blinked and kept looking at him as if she'd never

seen anything like him before. Finally she nodded, her head moving in short, jerky motions. "Okay. Fine, you can take me to the saloon. I, um—" She glanced at the box.

"You want me to throw it away?"

"No. I should keep it."

He frowned at her, tilting his head. "Come again?"

"They teach you these things when you start getting a following. Any oddball gifts like that should be tucked away, in case a problem surfaces later on. I'll just...take it up to my room." She turned away, grabbed the box and started for the dining room with it, but her steps slowed, and he read her fear again.

For God's sake, did she think there might be someone in the house?

He didn't ask. He just fell into step behind her, even putting a hand on her elbow. And he figured he must have guessed right, because she didn't jerk away or snap at him. He walked with her through the dining room, into the living room and up the stairs. She went into her bedroom, knelt down and shoved the little box under the bed.

He knelt down, too, peeking under there. He saw a larger box but couldn't see what was inside it. Sighing, he got up and moved through the bedroom, checking the closet, the bathroom; then he strode out of the room and down the hall, and checked every other room, as well. She didn't yell at him or tell him to stop. He checked every room upstairs; then they went down, and he did the same again, even to the basement. When he finished, he took her arm and led her out to his truck. She locked the house when they left. No one locked their doors out here. No one.

She swallowed hard. "That wasn't actually necessary."

"No, I didn't really think it was."

They were both lying. And he was more curious than ever as to what kind of trouble Edie Brand had dragged home from L.A. with her.

She sat quietly in Wade Armstrong's tow truck as he drove. It was nice, for a glorified pickup truck. Leather seats and lots of room. It was black, bigger than normal pickups, with a boxy nose and a chrome grille that looked like a leering grin. To her, anyway. He had a pair of those headlights that looked like the eyeballs of a giant bug mounted on the hood. As if his normal headlights weren't bright enough all by themselves. In the back, where the box should have been, there was a towing contraption instead. She sat there, feeling awkward, unable to come up with anything to say. She hadn't played fair. She had bought his house out from under him, and he had returned the slam by coming over just when she was more scared than she had been in months and making everything all right.

Not that she would ever admit that. But maybe it wouldn't hurt to be halfway civil to him. Considering. She slid a sideways glance at him.

He sat there behind the wheel, looking straight ahead. He was as good-looking as he'd always been. Better, maybe. But not in a handsome way. More in a dark, brooding kind of way. He had a hard face. Skin that was dark and shadowed with stubble. Eyes that tended to be too narrow and squinty. Brows that were too thick and usually bent in a scowl. His jaw was square. She wondered for a moment just what it was that made the whole package seem attractive to her. Then she decided it had to be his mouth. He had a great mouth. Lips on the full side for a man, and coral colored and moist, the dip above the upper one a little deeper than usual. His mouth was wider than the average, too, and he had nice teeth. Big and even and strong-looking.

His neck wasn't bad, either. Corded and thick. She liked that. And she liked that he didn't cut his black hair off severely but let it curl over his neck just a little. Kept that wild image of his alive. The nonconformist. The rebel. It curled over the tops of his ears, too. But it was definitely his mouth that drew her eyes back again. Yeah, his mouth was his winning feature. If she photographed him, she would have him biting into a juicy peach, a little trickle on his chin, those lips on the fruit as his teeth sank in.

"Damn, woman, you keep staring at me like that, I'm gonna think you mean it."

She blinked and jerked her gaze away from his lips, fixing it on his eyes. Only she couldn't, really, because he had put on a pair of dark sunglasses the second they got into the truck.

"Think I mean what?" she asked.

He shook his head slightly, licked his lips, and she wanted to tell him to do it again. But she resisted, as he focused on the road. The sun was going down now, aiming at them right through the windshield. Edie reached up automatically and folded the sun visor down to protect her eyes.

He did the same. And that was when she saw the tiny, dashboard-size calendar there. One of those peel-and-stick numbers, with pages smaller than business cards, and a single photo on the top.

In this case, it was a photo of her. She was wearing a black push-up bra and a pair of thong underpants to match. She had a black furry cat in her arms and cleavage to spare.

"Come on, Wade, don't do this."

"Do what?" He glanced at her, then followed her gaze

to the calendar. "Oh. I kind of forgot it was there. Does it embarrass you, Edie?"

"No. Well, yes, but—" She sighed, shook her head. "It was a catalogue shoot. I didn't even know it was going on a calendar until six months later."

"They put it on the big wall calendar for '99. April. Then they recycled the same shot for this little dashboard model for 2000." He shrugged.

"Yet here it is, almost 2002, and the thing remains on your visor."

"What, you think I put it up there so I'd know the date?"

She looked away, felt her face heat.

"If it really bothers you, I'll take it down. Right now."

Stiffening her shoulders, she lifted her chin. "It doesn't bother me. Why should it? I looked great." She licked her lips. "At least, I did for a while. By the time that cat got through with me, it wasn't so pretty."

"Didn't take to being photographed, hmm?"

"He didn't mind that so much as he did the poodle that some twit brought onto the set. It let out one yap, and all of the sudden I felt as if I'd fallen into a paper shredder."

He laughed softly. She liked the sound, in spite of herself. And when he glanced sideways at her, she realized she was smiling at him.

"Don't think this means I'm over the whole house thing, Edie. I'm not."

"I didn't expect you to be. For what it's worth, I know it was a lousy thing to do."

"Yeah? So why don't you undo it, then?"

She licked her lips. "I can't."

"What do you want? A profit? I can probably—"

"No. It's not…look, I can't go into the reasons, but maybe I can find some way to make it up to you."

He lifted his black eyebrows. "Baby, I like the sound of that."

Her good humor fled instantly. "That is not what I meant. Pig."

He pulled into the parking lot of the bar and came to a stop. "Can't hate a guy for trying."

"Yeah, actually, I can. You know, there's a lot more to me than the way I look, Wade Armstrong."

"Oh, I'm sure there is. Like any red-blooded male, I just don't happen to care."

She pursed her lips tight, shoved her door open and slid out of the truck. "Thanks for the ride. Slug." She slammed his door closed.

Wade looked at her, shrugged as if he were completely innocent of any wrongdoing, and then backed out of the parking lot with a wink and a wave.

He was in his little house, which was located around the corner from the garage, and was just big enough for a guy to be cozy. Two bedrooms, but he only used one. The other had become a weight room for him and the guys who worked for him. He had a Nautilus machine in there, weight bench, dumbbells, a treadmill and a punching bag. His mountain bike hung on the wall, boxing gloves underneath it. And there was a mini-basketball hoop fastened to the inside of the door.

The living room was just a place to watch sports on TV, although his roommate, Long Tall Sally, thought of it more as a place to nap. She was stretched out on the floor now, snoring happily, and he figured it was easily five feet from her hind legs to her forepaws when she lay like that. Maybe more. The kitchen was basically the place where the beer and junk food were stored. Sally pretty much agreed on that, he thought, only for her it was Great Dane chow and water. It was nothing special, his little saltbox in town. But now he was wishing he didn't have to let it go.

He leaned over, idly scratching Sally's head. She sighed contentedly in her sleep, twitched a long ear. Maybe he didn't have to let the place go, he thought. Hell, Tommy Hall was a friend as well as an employee. Wade could probably explain things to him. Yeah. That was what he would do. He would call Tommy and tell him what had happened, that he couldn't go through with the sale. Tommy would tear the contracts up. Sure he would, he was a friend.

Wade reached for the phone.

Someone knocked at the front door, bringing Sally's head up fast. She scrambled to her feet, tripped, got her footing and loped to the door, tail wagging. Frowning, Wade set the phone down again and went to answer the door. The young man he'd been about to call stood there grinning at him. Sally barked hello, and he petted her automatically.

"Hey, Tommy! I was just gonna call you, buddy. How you doin'? C'mon in. You want a beer?"

"Yeah." Tommy came inside as the dog danced beside him. He was a tow-headed, crew-cut fellow, too big for his own body. He wasn't from Big Falls, but Wade knew he'd been an outcast as a kid, just like himself. Wade could tell. He could spot another social reject from across a crowded room. There was a scent they gave off, though you couldn't exactly smell it. Maybe it was an energy. Or just something in their eyes. But it was real.

Tommy scuffed his feet over the doormat, then headed straight to the sofa while Wade ducked around the corner into the kitchen to pull two beers from the fridge. He popped the top on one, handed it to Tommy, then opened his own. He didn't sit down. He was too nervous to sit.

And feeling a little guilty too for what he was about to do. Sally came and sat so close to his side that her body was pressed to his leg from ankle to calf. She did that when people came by. Her way of showing her loyalty, he supposed.

"You, uh...you aren't packed," Tommy observed, looking around the place.

"Uh, no. Not yet."

"The closing's the end of the week, though," Tommy said, looking around. "Right?"

"That's what we said, yeah." Wade took a sip of his beer, paced away from the kid. Sally moved with him.

"That's good." Tommy said it with a sigh that sounded relieved. "I promised Sue we could move in over the weekend. She would have my hide if I had to go home and tell her I got the date wrong." He shook his head, grinning. "You don't know how stir-crazy she's getting in the apartment, Wade. She's just about climbing the walls."

Tommy's wife-to-be, Sue, was usually a pretty easygoing sort. At least, Wade had always thought so. Laidback, never snappy or mean, didn't care for gossip. Wade liked her. "Since when is she so miserable in the apartment?" he asked. "I thought she liked it?"

"She did, but..." Tommy licked his lips, took another swig of beer, then looked Wade in the eyes and got all serious. "That was before we knew we were having a baby."

Wade blinked and felt his heart drop to waist level. "Baby?"

Tommy nodded, his face splitting in a smile. "You look as shocked as I did when she first told me. I thought I was gonna pass out cold." He turned his head, glancing down the hall to the two doors that stood opposite one another. "The weight room's gonna be a nursery. And she's just about dying to get in there and measure it up for wallpaper and curtains and carpet." He licked his lips, a shadow flitting across his eyes.

Wade picked up on the reason for that shadow immediately. Wallpaper, curtains and carpet could be summed up in one word. Money. "Sounds to me like you're gonna need a raise to go with this baby, Tom."

Tommy's eyes snapped to Wade's instantly. "I wasn't trying—"

"I know. Trust me, you've earned it." Wade lowered his head, found the dog's deep-gray speckled face staring right back up at him. It almost seemed she knew there was a problem. "I don't suppose that apartment of yours is gonna be available once you leave?"

"Nah, the owner's got a waiting list." Then he frowned. "Why, Wade? I thought you were gonna buy that big place up by the falls."

"Someone beat me to it," he said. Then he plastered a smile on his face quickly. "Nothing to worry about. I'll just find a bigger, better place to buy."

"Not in this town, you won't." Tommy leaned forward, elbows balanced on his knees. "If you don't have anywhere to stay, Wade—"

"Look, this is not your problem. I'll be fine. I can room at the boardinghouse until I find what I want."

"But what about Sally?"

At the sound of her name, the dog spoke. "Ree-rah-roo," it sounded like. She was always doing that, and Wade always thought she knew exactly what she was saying, even if no one else did.

"I'll take care of Sally, don't you worry. It's not a problem, Tommy."

"Are you sure, Wade?"

Wade nodded, keeping his smile firmly in place, petting his dog reassuringly. Then he took a large bracing drink of beer and followed it up with an exaggerated belch that had Tommy laughing and shaking his head, and made Sally look at him with her head cocked to one side.

"If you're sure," Tommy said finally.

"Sure I'm sure. A deal's a deal."

Tommy drained his beer, got to his feet. "Then I guess I'll see you Saturday. Let me know if you need help moving any of your stuff out."

"I will. Same goes for you, moving stuff in. And I imagine putting a crib together is gonna be a bit different from rebuilding a carburetor, so I'll help with that, too, when the time comes."

Tommy got a funny look in his eye. "I can hardly imagine it. Me, a father."

"Think how the poor kid's gonna feel." Wade chucked him on the arm as he said it.

"Thanks a lot, Wade. I mean it. Thanks."

"Go home and tell your wife no duckies in my weight room. I never liked duckies. I want something rugged on that wallpaper or the deal's off. Teddy bears, something like that."

"Roo-roo!" Sally chimed in.

Wade nodded at her. "Right, girl." Then to Tommy, "Puppies would be acceptable, too, she says."

Tommy grinned. "I'll tell Sue." He crushed his beer can in his fist, handed it to Wade and headed for the door.

After he was gone, Wade wandered down the hall with Sally walking so close he almost tripped over her big feet. He looked at his weight room and shook his head. "I'm gonna have to strangle that Edain Brand."

His phone rang, and he turned and walked back to the living room, plunked down in his favorite recliner, yanked the cordless off the end table beside it and said, "Yeah?"

"Wade, it's Caleb. Just wanted to let you know who to thank, pal."

Wade lifted his brows. Caleb was a good friend, a tal-

ented lawyer and an all around nice guy. It had taken Wade
a while to see that, because he tended to dislike rich bas-
tards like Caleb on sight. But although Caleb was rich—
filthy freaking rich—he was not a bastard. However, none
of that applied to this situation. Caleb was married to the
enemy camp here. "Who to thank for what?" Wade asked.

Sally seemed to be getting tired of following him. She
returned to her spot in the middle of floor, in case he
needed something to trip over, and stretched out again.

"For Edie changing her mind about the house," Caleb
said. "I'm the one who made her see logic. Not that I
want any gratitude or anything, but, uh—"

"She changed her mind?" Wade came to his feet. "She
changed her mind? When?"

"Earlier tonight. Hell, I thought she'd have told you by
now. It was before you showed up at the house, and then
took off with her. Where did you take her, anyway?
Date?"

He released a sharp burst of air that could have been a
laugh but wasn't quite. "I took her to the saloon and
dropped her off. And she didn't say a word about having
changed her mind about the house."

Caleb was silent for a moment. "She told me she was
thinking seriously about canceling the purchase. Even said
she was going to call you herself to tell you."

"She told *me* she'd be moving in tomorrow."

"Well now, Wade, that just doesn't make any sense.
What could have changed her mind from the time she
walked back down the hill from our place to the time you
pulled in the driveway? Hell, it couldn't have been more
than five minutes."

Wade pursed his lips and thought about the box on the
Brands' kitchen table, the handcuffs inside it, and the way
Edie had acted scared half out of her mind when he'd come
up behind her. Beyond that, he'd been ninety-nine percent

sure she had been afraid there might be someone in the house. She sure as hell wouldn't have left with *him,* of all people, if she had felt safe there. "I think something's going on with your sister-in-law, Caleb."

"Something like what?"

"I don't know, exactly." Wade had given his word he wouldn't tell anyone about the gift. Now he wished he hadn't. But he had, and he couldn't break it. "Has she said anything about why she left L.A.?"

"Nope."

"You think it could have been a guy? You know, an overbearing boyfriend, bad breakup, anything like that?"

"I don't think so. At least, she hasn't mentioned it to Maya, and they're not the kind of sisters who keep secrets from each other. Why, Wade, do you think someone's giving her trouble?"

"Maybe."

"And what would that have to do with her changing her mind about the house?"

"Couldn't say." He could speculate, though. Whoever she thought had been around was someone she didn't want around her family. The Brands were a tight bunch. Notoriously tight. Maybe she wanted to keep the sender of that odd gift away from her homestead. Hell, she'd damn near panicked when he had threatened to tell Caleb about it. Maya and Caleb had twin babies, just a hundred yards from the farmhouse. And the sender must have the mailing address....

Unless the package had been hand delivered.

Which would explain her reaction to him coming up behind her even better.

He nodded to himself. "I'm gonna look into this, Caleb."

"Yeah? Why is that, Wade?"

He tipped his head to one side. "Well, hell, I want my house back."

"Uh-huh. And?"

"And nothing." But he knew there were other reasons—the main one being that he was the only one who knew about the gift. And since he had promised not to tell, he couldn't hand the information off to anyone else. So until he could wriggle out of that promise, no one else would know as much as he did about what was going on. Even though what he knew was damn little.

"You sure about that?" Caleb asked.

"Get over it, Caleb. Just get over it. And listen, keep an extra eye on things around the place for a while, okay?"

"I have kids, Wade." The reminder came in a low, serious tone of voice.

"I know you do. I'm on this, okay? No reason to be worried. When there is, I'll let you know. All right?"

"All right."

"Talk to you later." Wade hung up the phone. Sighing, he got to his feet, picked up his empty can and Tommy's crushed one, and carried them into the kitchen to drop them in the recycling bin. Sally followed him with her eyes but didn't get up. Then he opened the fridge and stared inside, wondering what he ought to eat for dinner. But as he stared, he wasn't thinking about food. He was thinking about Edain Brand and the handcuffs in that box and the fear in her eyes.

He swung the fridge door closed and said, "Guess I'll get dinner out tonight. Wonder what they've got on the grill over at the OK Corral?"

Chapter 4

The OK Corral was hopping by 9:00 p.m. The place was damn near packed, and Edie found wending her way through crowds of mostly male bodies while carrying mugs of beer was far more difficult than she remembered. Her sisters made it look easy. Except, of course, for Kara, but she stayed mostly in the kitchen in back, grilling up finger foods. They didn't serve full meals at the Corral, but they kept the deep frier churning out mozzarella sticks, chicken fingers and onion rings at a steady rate. And Kara, still laboring under the assumption that she was both a full-fledged klutz and something of a jinx, preferred manning the frier to carrying breakable tumblers and spillable liquids.

She wasn't a klutz, of course. She had a body some of the models Edie had worked with would kill for. Six feet tall, slender as a reed, with a neck like a swan's and legs that didn't seem to end. She just hadn't learned to be comfortable in her own skin yet. But she would; Edie was working on that. If there was one thing she could do besides pose in skimpy lingerie, it was teach a tall gangly young woman how to walk.

She delivered drinks to a table full of men who looked at her as if they were trying to see through her clothes, then took the empty tray back to the bar and set it down.

"Watch yourself out there, Edie," her mother said as she topped off a frosted mug from the tap.

"It's packed." Edie brushed a wisp of hair off her forehead with the back of her hand.

"It's a Friday night, and it's springtime. Those young men are randy as billy goats. We got twice as many males as we do females in here tonight, and adding booze to that mix is like tossing it right onto an open flame. Watch yourself. And don't serve anyone you think has had enough."

Edie nodded slowly. "They're just locals, though. No one dangerous."

"Honey, just 'cause they're local don't mean they're saints. Big Falls has its share of jackasses, just like any other town."

As if to punctuate the warning, Edie felt a body slide up close beside hers, and when she glanced up, she saw a vaguely familiar face grinning at her. "Hey there, Edie B.," he said slowly. "You wanna dance with me?"

"No room for dancing in here tonight," she said. He was the son of the guy who owned the drugstore, she thought, searching her brain for a name to put with the face. "Besides, I'm not much of a dancer."

"Sure you are. You were in high school."

"Yeah, well this isn't high school." Pete, she thought. Peter Dunnegan. That was his name.

"No kidding." He put his hand on her hip. She caught it at the wrist before it could slide around to cup her backside, tugged it away and dropped it like garbage.

"Grow up, okay?" She saw her mother on the other side of the bar, reaching underneath for something, and she knew the baseball bat was going to come out momentarily. She held up a hand. "I've got it covered, Mom. I didn't survive a decade in L.A. without learning a thing or two."

Her mother frowned but straightened again. Edie's admirer said, "You sure did learn a thing or two, I'll vouch for that. Hell, from the looks of you in those catalogue spreads, I'll bet you learned a lot. Why don't you come over to my place and show me, hmm?"

"It's time for you to leave," she said. She gripped his arm, started pushing him toward the door. "Let's go."

"To hell I will!" he yelled. The place went quiet as he jerked his arm away and whirled on her. "No trashy little slut like you is gonna tell me what to do."

Vidalia came around the bar, baseball bat in hand. Mel vaulted over the top of the bar with murder in her eyes. But neither of them had the chance to do what they intended, because someone else grabbed Pete by the collar, spun him around and smashed a fist into his face.

He went down like a sack of feed, a startled expression on his face, his nose spurting blood.

Edie looked up to see Wade Armstrong standing there, rubbing his knuckles. He gave her a wobbly smile. "No need to thank me."

"Thank you? *Thank you?*"

"You're welcome. But really, it was nothing."

"You're right, Wade. It was nothing, and I had it under control." She rolled her eyes and looked down at Pete. "You all right?"

"Screw you," he spat, and scrambled to his feet; then he turned and headed out of the bar.

"Dammit, Wade, that was a paying customer. One of Mom's regulars."

He gaped at her. From behind him, Vidalia said, "Edain, hon, I don't think he'd have come back anyway, once I whaled on him with Babe, here." She slapped the baseball bat into her palm a few times to make her point.

"That was a nice job, Armstrong," Mel was saying. "I'd have used an uppercut to the chin, but that right cross was nicely done."

"Thanks." He wasn't looking at Mel, though. He was looking at Edie, and he seemed confused and maybe a little insulted. "You'll have to watch out for him," he said. "He probably won't try anything again, but his pride's been wounded—and in public, to boot. He may give you some trouble down the line."

"He wouldn't be the first," she said. Sighing, she lowered her head. "Well, come on and sit yourself down. I should at least buy you a drink."

"Don't put yourself out." But he did move through the bodies to the bar, then took the stool the idiot had formerly occupied. The guy next to him immediately got up and moved, and when he patted the vacant stool, Edie took it.

Her mother shoved a glass at her. "Go on, drink it down. You've been as tense as a bowstring, girl, ever since you got in here tonight." She drew a beer and slid that across to Wade. "Your usual."

As Vidalia moved away, Wade leaned close to Edie, speaking so near her ear that his breath sent a shiver through her. A good shiver. But the effect was ruined by his next words. "Did you tell her yet? About the package?"

"No." She looked toward her mother to make sure she was out of earshot, felt like clubbing Wade for bringing it up here. "And I'm not going to, either."

"Okay, okay. Drink your whiskey."

She put the shot glass to her lips and downed the whiskey in one quick swallow. It burned like fire in her chest, but it warmed her, too. She set the glass down.

"How about the fact that you're moving out tomorrow? Did you tell her that yet?"

She averted her eyes, shook her head. "That's not a conversation I want to have in a barroom full of people. I figured we'd talk about it after closing time."

He nodded, sipping his beer thoughtfully. "I had a phone call from your brother-in-law earlier," he said matter-of-factly.

"Did you?" She asked it as if she could not possibly care less.

"Yeah. He somehow got the idea that you'd decided you didn't want the house after all. He called to find out if you'd told me yet. Hell, I was confused. Especially seeing as how I saw you five minutes after he says you made that decision, and you had totally changed your mind by then."

She ran a forefinger around the rim of the shot glass, looking at it rather than at him. "Don't I have the right to change my mind?"

"Sure you do. I'd just like to know why, is all."

"Well, you're not going to. I have my reasons. They're private. And that's all I have to say on the subject."

He nodded slowly, lips pursing. "It had to do with the package," he said. "Or the fellow who sent it."

She shrugged. "Not necessarily."

"I wasn't asking. This much I know, not being blind or a fool. You're moving out to keep whatever you're afraid of from getting too close to your family."

She frowned at him as if she thought him insane. Inside, she was reeling at his accuracy. "You have a really big

imagination, Wade. That's one of the things I don't remember about you from high school.''

He smiled slightly. His lips were even tastier looking
when he smiled. ''I didn't think you remembered anything
about me from high school, to be honest.''

''Oh, I do. I remember a lot.'' She had to force her eyes
not to linger on his mouth. Why it intrigued her so much,
she couldn't even imagine.

''Tell me,'' he asked. His tone had changed. His eyes,
too, in some indescribable way.

''Someday maybe I will. For now, though...'' She slid
off the bar stool and stood up. ''I've got drinks to sling.''

She walked away, but she felt his eyes on her from then
on, and even though she avoided having to talk to him
again, she continued to feel them all night long.

They closed up at midnight, when the last of the patrons
had left. Legally, the Corral could remain open till 2:00
a.m., but they rarely did. Once things wound down, they
tended to push the stragglers along toward home and lock
the place up for the night. They split up into two vehicles,
Vidalia's pickup truck and Mel's Jeep, and headed home.
Then they all trooped in the back door, kicking off shoes
as they entered.

Selene stepped inside, heeled off one shoe and then
stood still, lifting her head and looking around. ''What the
heck is that?'' she asked.

''What?'' Everyone else looked, too, listened. Edie even
sniffed the air, wondering what her baby sister was referring to.

''Don't you feel it?'' Selene asked. Then she rubbed her
arms and gave her head a shake. ''Someone or...
something has been in this house.''

''Someone or some*thing*?'' Mel rolled her eyes.

"You've been watching that vampire slayer show again, haven't you, Selene?"

"Never miss it. But that's beside the point." She heeled off her other shoe and started through the house. "I can't believe you guys can't sense the negative energy."

"Oh, for crying out—"

Vidalia held up a hand. "Be nice to your sister, Melusine. Selene, hon, if you feel something's wrong, you feel it. Nine times outta ten you're right." She nodded to the girls. "Split up, check the house, make sure all the doors and windows are locked up tight while you're at it."

"I'll take this floor," Kara said. She opened a drawer and pulled out a rolling pin, then went creeping toward the living room.

"I'll come with you, hon," Vidalia said. "Mel, Edie, you two take the basement."

"I don't think it's still here," Selene said. "But I'll check upstairs."

"Not by yourself, child," Vidalia said, but before she finished, Selene was off, jogging through the living room, tromping up the stairs.

"Go after her," she told Mel and Edie. "Kara and I will do the basement once we finish here." Vidalia glanced at the cellar door. It was locked, and that seemed to reassure her.

Mel and Edie ran upstairs after Selene, who was already opening doors and closing them one by one. They caught up to her as she checked the third bedroom, but she was already shaking her head slowly. "No. It was never up here."

"That's reassuring," Edie said. She wished she could bite the words back the minute she said them, but too late. Mel just sent her a funny look.

They checked Selene's room last, with Edie wishing the

whole time she could just tell them that Wade Armstrong
had already checked the entire house, and that the vibes
Selene was sensing were from someone who'd come and
gone hours ago. But she couldn't. Telling them that much
would necessitate telling them more, and if they knew she
was being harassed by some perverted, obsessed fan, they
would never let her move into her own place. They would
want to protect her. They would put themselves in danger.

Selene's room, like the others, was undisturbed.

In fact, even if the intruder had gone through every room
in the house, Edie thought idly, he wouldn't have bothered
Selene's room. It was the most peaceful place Edie could
imagine. Little fountains bubbling here and there. Low-
wattage bulbs kept it softly lit, and the ever-present aroma
of incense clung to everything. There was no clutter in
Selene's room. It was like a miniature temple.

Selene opened her closet, fumbled around inside, and
came out again with a tiny bundle of twigs in her hand.
"Sage," she said, when they looked at her with their eyebrows raised. "I'll just smudge the house a little and get
rid of the bad energy."

"Oh, man," Mel said, tipping her head skyward. "That
crap smells like pot. You know what people will think if
they come by and smell that stuff?"

"If I don't do it I'll never sleep. Besides, who's going
to come by at this time of the night? And it does not smell
like pot, it smells like sage."

Mel threw up her hands, shaking her head as she stalked
out of the room. "I'll go check the basement. If I'm lucky
the boogie man will get me before your stinky smoking
weeds do." She headed out of the room in a hurry.

Edie glanced at Selene. She felt bad about letting the
kid take so much ribbing when she was dead-on accurate
in whatever she was sensing. How that could be, she didn't

know, didn't even try to guess. Her sister had something. She always had.

"You all right, Edie?" Selene asked, voice soft, eyes probing.

"Yeah. I, um...I should go help Mel."

"All right." Selene flicked a long-nosed lighter and touched the flame to her tiny bundle of twigs. They flared up for a moment; then the flame lowered, waned and died. Smoke immediately started wafting from the smoldering ends of the twigs. Selene set them into a copper bowl and picked up a fan made of feathers. She was always picking up feathers when she found them lying around outside, from wild turkeys, crows and whatever other large bird happened to drop one for her collection. She followed Edie down the stairs, waving her fan and sending smoke into the shadows and nooks and crannies of the old house.

She was a strange one, all right. Edie picked up the pace and caught up to Mel halfway down the cellar stairs.

Mel had a flashlight in one hand and a tire iron in the other.

"Gee, you're not nervous, are you?" Edie asked.

"Not really. But if Wanda the witch up there is right, I'm thinking a tire iron might have a little more impact than smoking stinkweed."

They reached the bottom of the steps. The stair light was on already, and Edie reached out to flip the switch that would light the rest of the basement. It worked; the lights came on. She'd been half expecting the switch to have no effect, like in some horror film. Then again, sometimes in those kinds of movies the lights went off *after* appearing to work just fine.

Edie walked close to Mel, glad of the tire iron her scrappy sister carried. They both pretended to be unconcerned, but they were both a little scared. Even Mel couldn't deny Selene sometimes nailed things in ways that defied explanation.

They traversed the entire basement, though, and found nothing amiss. Then they headed back up the stairs, much more relaxed than before.

The scent of Selene's sage lingered but wasn't overpowering. Still, Mel made a show of waving the air in front of her face and wrinkling her nose. Selene smirked at her. Her sage and bowl were gone, apparently returned to her bedroom. And no doubt Vidalia had already made some comment about how a recital of the Lord's Prayer would have been just as good and asking why Selene insisted on such heathen practices. Selene had probably already responded that sage had been used by indigenous cultures for centuries to ward off negativity, and that since God put it on the planet in the first place, using it couldn't possibly be in any way sinful.

It was a conversation repeated so often, with various twists, that Edie could have recited it almost verbatim. She was glad she had missed this round.

"Do you suppose we could all go to bed now?" Kara asked, leaning against the door frame between the kitchen and dining room. She yawned.

"I think so," Selene said.

"I know so," Mel put in.

Edie opened her mouth but closed it again without saying a word. She needed, at some point, to sit down with her family and tell them she had decided to move into her own place. The suddenness of it would worry them. They would ask questions. But despite their tendency to hover and be overprotective of each other, they also did their best to respect each other's privacy. At least, that was the stated policy, she thought with a pained smile as she headed up the stairs to her room.

She would break the news at breakfast. That would be soon enough. That would be *plenty* soon enough.

She changed clothes, cleaned and moisturized her face, brushed her hair and teeth, and went to bed. She stopped thinking about how infuriating Wade Armstrong was. About how insulting Peter Dunnegan had been. And about breaking the news to her mother that she was moving. All those musings quieted as she lay there, hovering on the edge of sleep.

But when the other things went still, that left room for the one thing, the big thing, to take center stage in her mind.

She chased it away, but her eyes were heavy. It was late. She slipped into sleep without warning, and she was there again.

Her newly hired bodyguard a half step behind her, Edie walked unsteadily along the wet sidewalk that led from the nightclub where she'd been partying toward the car that waited at the curb. Inside the club there had been a crush of people, shoulder to bare shoulder. Music pounded and sweat scented the air. Outside, it was nice. Quiet in the wee hours, or quiet by L.A. standards, anyway. No one around to speak of, light traffic, just headlights gliding past every now and then, with the sounds of tires hissing over wet pavement. She got halfway to the car and stopped dead.

Mike closed a hand on her elbow. "You okay?"

"I left my purse." She looked up at him sheepishly, and maybe a little drunkenly. Mike was old enough to be her father, a short, stocky man with a face like a bulldog. As bodyguards went, he was one of the best. He came highly recommended.

"Would you...?" she began.

"Not till you're safely locked in the car." He kept hold

of her, kept moving forward. He held out his hand to the valet who waited by the open passenger door. The valet dropped the keys into his hand, and he tucked them into his pocket. "In you go."

Edie sank into the front seat of the plush sedan. It was not her own vehicle. It was Mike's car. He'd insisted. He was bossy for a bodyguard. After all, he was supposed to be working for her, right? So where did he get off being so bossy? She wasn't even sure she honestly needed a bodyguard. Hell, aside from a few kinky anonymous gifts and some really graphic letters, there was nothing. Certainly no physical risk, despite the threats. But her agency had insisted she hire someone once they caught an eyeful of those notes.

Mike locked the car door and closed it, sent her a smile and headed back to the entrance of the club. The valet stood at attention, his back to her door. Mike must have told him to stand guard. Great.

She leaned her head back against the softness of the seat, folded her hands in her lap.

A hand slid around her face from behind, clamping tight over her mouth before she could scream, even as another one gripped her wrists so hard she thought they would break. Her eyes flew wide, but she could see nothing. A face rubbed against her cheek, and a voice whispered near her ear, "Did you get the gifts, Edie? And the letters? Did you?"

She twisted and pulled in his grasp.

"Answer me!" He made a whisper seem like a shout. "Did you get them?"

Edie nodded, her eyes wide, growing wet now.

"Then you know what I'm going to do, don't you, Edie? Yeah. You've been waiting. That's why you sent your goon back inside. Isn't it?"

She shook her head side to side, tried to kick her feet.

"Stop!" he barked in her ear. "Do you want me to have to kill you Edie? Do you?" Something cold encircled her wrists and snapped in place. Handcuffs. Oh God. Then his hand was free again. It vanished and returned with a knife, its blade sharp and deadly. "I'll kill you. Now you sit perfectly still like a good girl. Don't make a sound, Edie baby. I just want to see, that's all. We won't have time for more. Not tonight."

His blade moved, easily snapping the buttons off her silk blouse one by one. He used the knife to push the blouse open, exposing the black lace demi-bra she wore underneath.

She felt him shaking his head slowly, side to side. "You've been a bad girl, Edie. I told you in the last note, I didn't want you wearing bras anymore. Not outside the shoots. When you're not posing, I don't expect any underwear at all, do you understand? Do you?" He dug the point of the blade into the rounded, soft part of her breast.

She nodded fiercely, but the blade pricked her anyway. She felt blood, just a trickle. "I'm going to have to punish you, Edie. You've got to do what I tell you or face the consequences. Do you understand?"

She nodded again, her eyes shifting toward the club and the rigid back of the useless valet. How long would it take Mike to get the purse? How damn long in that crowd of idiots?

His mouth attacked her neck then, wet and sloppy. She felt his tongue, and his teeth bit down cruelly. And all the while that damn knife was pressed to her throat. Her stomach turned. She wanted to vomit. "Get off me," she whispered. "Just get off me and go. I won't tell, all right?"

He stopped lathering her neck and sat up. "Get off you?" He asked the question as if incredulous. "Oh, Edie,

*why did you have to go and ruin it, hmm?'' He dropped
his knife and closed his hands around her throat so fast
and so hard she couldn't breathe, much less cry out. She
thumped the window once, and he jerked her to the middle
of the car so fast that she couldn't hit it again. Her head
was pounding, her eyes straining, her entire body shaking
in need of air. He was going to kill her. She was going to
die.*

*And then he was gone. Just like that, the pressure was
off, the hands were gone, and she collapsed against the
seat, sucking in huge, choked breaths. She lifted her head
to look in the rearview mirror and saw the back door
standing open, the back seat empty.*

*Tears rolled hot and burning down her cheeks. She
clawed for her door handle, found it and shoved it open.
The valet turned as she started to get out of the car. Then
his eyes went wide as Edie fell to her knees on the sidewalk. She glimpsed Mike coming out of the club, running
toward her, and then she passed out cold.*

Edie came awake with a start, her eyes wide, her hands
on her throat. Then she lay there for a full minute, trying
to convince herself that she was home, in Oklahoma, not
in L.A. That her monster was a long way away from her.

But he wasn't. He had been here, in her haven, she could
feel it. She reached for her light, turned it on and sat up
in the bed. She probably wouldn't sleep another wink tonight. Reaching under her pillow, she pulled out the present Mike had given her as a parting gift. It had been tucked
away in her closet since she'd been home. But now she
felt she needed it again. It was snub-nosed, deadly black
and fully loaded. Mike had been the only person in L.A.
who had taken her fear seriously. Her agent had been just
barely sympathetic, his most memorable comment being,

"Hey, you pose half-naked for a living. You telling me you didn't *expect* something like this?"

That had hurt most of all, because it reminded her, painfully, of her mother's warnings, her disapproval, and her constant reminders that you reaped what you sowed. Edie had considered Vidalia Brand a judgmental, prudish pain in the backside at the time. Now she wondered if her mother had been right all along. If maybe, in some way, she had brought it all on herself.

And now, Edie mused, she had brought her problems back home to share with her family. God, the thought of that animal touching one of her sisters the way he had touched her...

She was going to have to make sure word got around town that she had moved out of her mother's place tomorrow. It wouldn't be hard in a small town like this. The rumor mills worked with amazing—even alarming—efficiency.

But in the meantime... She glanced at the clock, calculated the time in L.A. and then reached for the phone beside her bed. She dialed Mike McKenny's home number, and he picked up on the third ring. Just the sound of his voice helped a little. He was a strong, sharp man. A good bodyguard. And he sounded glad to hear from her.

"Hey, Edie, my favorite former client. How are you?"

"I don't know, Mike. That's kind of what I'm calling to find out."

She could almost see his expression changing from light to serious. "What's going on?" he asked.

She drew a breath, sighed. "Look, I know you said he would never trace me back here, but I think maybe he has."

"Why?"

That was Mike, straight to the point. "I got another

package. A pair of handcuffs. No return address. The box was left on the kitchen table.''

"Describe them," he asked.

She sighed, not wanting to think that much about her troubling gift. "Standard, like maybe police issue?"

"Uh-huh. And the note?"

"No note. There was nothing."

He sighed deeply, and she thought she heard his fingers drumming in time with his thoughts. "I don't think it's him, Edie."

She released her breath in a rush. "Really? Oh God, I'm so glad. Why not, Mike? Convince me."

"He always leaves a note, for one thing. For another, his toys usually come from the sex shops. He would be more likely to send you a pair of satin-lined or leopard-fur-covered love cuffs than cold steel handcuffs. It's not his pattern."

"So then, this is what? Another insane fan?"

"Look, you did do that spread with the bondage overtones last year. Weren't there handcuffs in that piece?"

"Hanging from the bedpost. But I wasn't wearing them."

"The implication was there. It may not even be a dangerous fan, Edie. Maybe just a horny one. They could be a gag gift, even. Have you pissed anyone off since you've been home?"

She blinked and thought of Wade Armstrong. "Yes, actually, I have."

"Uh-huh, I thought so. Listen, do you need me to come out there?"

She took a breath, sighed. "How's Richie doing?"

"His T cells are down a little. It's not serious yet."

She nodded at the phone. "You stay where you are,

Mike. You're probably right, it's probably a pissed-off redneck. God, I can't believe how scared I was.''

"Don't get overconfident here. Take precautions, be on your guard. And call me if anything else happens, okay?''

"I will, Mike. And thanks. You're one in a million.''

"Any time,'' he said.

Edie hung up the phone and lay back in the bed, feeling a lot better than she had been. Then she started thinking about Wade Armstrong. He had arrived only seconds after she had found that box on the table. Maybe he'd been there the whole time. Maybe he just put the box there, then went out front and waited for her to have time to find it. He had probably only come back to enjoy seeing her scared witless.

She mulled that over. He hadn't *acted* as if he were enjoying her fear. Then again, he didn't know about the stalker she had picked up in L.A. He probably hadn't expected her to react with more than disgust at the suggestive gift. Maybe he even felt a little guilty after seeing how much it upset her. Yeah, that was it. No wonder he had given her the ride and defended her against Peter Dunnegan. Guilt.

The bastard.

On the other hand, what if he *hadn't* been the one to send the lurid present to the house? What if...?

No. It wasn't her stalker. It wasn't.

She was almost glad now that she had stolen Wade Armstrong's house out from under him, the lowlife. She was going to enjoy rubbing it in his face every chance she got.

Chapter 5

"I don't get it. I just don't get it, Edie."

Edie hadn't planned on Maya and Caleb and the twins being present when she made her big announcement at the breakfast table. She knew their presence would make things a little more complicated the minute they arrived, but she was out of time. And the entire family was going to have to know sooner or later anyway.

"What's to get?" Edie asked, as casually as possible. The others around the table were quiet. Mostly just looking at her as if she'd lost her mind. Her mother wasn't. She was searching, her eyes narrow and knowing. "I bought the house, and I want to be in it. Why should I wait?"

"Because just last night you were on the verge of changing your mind and letting Wade Armstrong take the place," Maya said.

Edie shrugged, sipped her coffee. "That was just guilt talking. Wade Armstrong's a big boy. Why should I give up something I want just so he can have it? We're not children sharing a sandbox here. We're both adults. I was the first one to come up with the money and sign on the dotted line. That's the way business is done in the real world. And Wade Armstrong, of all people, understands that."

"Why do you say that?" Caleb asked, his voice careful, level.

"What?"

"'Wade Armstrong, of all people,'" he repeated. "Why would he understand it better than anyone else?"

"Because he owns his own business. Competition is an everyday event for him. What did you think I meant?"

Caleb shrugged. "Maybe that he would understand more than most because he's been getting jerked around by people with more money than him his entire life. That's all."

"You should talk, having more money than God and all," Edie said, knowing full well she was being unnecessarily snarky to her brother-in-law, and that he really didn't deserve it.

"I try real hard not to club people over the head with it, Edie. I think you tend to keep friends longer that way."

"Well, lucky for me, Wade Armstrong is not my friend."

"He's not?" It was Selene who voiced the question around a bite of French toast, a cup of herbal tea halfway to her mouth. "I thought he gave you a ride to the bar last night? And then wasn't he the one who decked Peter Dunnegan in the face for insulting you?"

Edie pursed her lips, sent her sister a glare. "He only drove me in so he would have more time to badger me about the house. And I really don't have any idea why he decked Pete. Maybe they had other things going on between them. But the fact remains, Wade Armstrong is not now, nor has he ever been, a friend of mine.''

A tap sounded at the back door, and everyone looked up to see Wade Armstrong peering through the glass. Vidalia waved him in, so he opened the door and stepped inside. ''Hello, Mrs. Brand,'' he said, greeting her first, then nodding hello to the others. He looked Edie straight in the eyes. ''I figured you could use an extra vehicle today,'' he said. ''To help with the move.''

Selene sent Edie an ''I-told-you-so'' look, lifting her eyebrows and tipping her head to the side.

Edie rolled her eyes. ''Just what good do you think a tow truck is going to do, Wade?''

''I didn't bring the tow truck. Brought the Explorer.''

''Man, am I glad to see you,'' Caleb said, getting to his feet to greet his friend. ''I figured I'd be the only guy around for the grunt work.''

Mel rolled her eyes. ''Why is it men always assume women can't lift a heavy object or load items into a vehicle?'' she asked.

Kara nudged her with an elbow. ''Hush now. Don't you remember when all Edie's stuff arrived from L.A. in the moving truck? It took us hours to get it all unloaded and stacked away out in the barn. You want us to do it alone?''

Mel crossed her arms over her chest and leaned back in her chair. ''I'm not saying we can't *use* the help. Just that we don't *need* it.''

''How about just saying we're grateful for it, daughter?'' Vidalia asked, a stern edge to her voice. Then she nodded at Wade. ''Pull up a chair and have some breakfast, Wade. After that…'' She looked at Edie. ''Well, if you're bound and determined to move today, then we'll move you.''

Her eyes said more, though. Her eyes said that she knew

perfectly well there was more going on than Edie had told her, and that she would find out the truth, one way or another.

Edie believed it, too.

Wade took off his shoes without being told and made his way to the only empty chair in sight, and everyone at the table scooted one way or the other to make room for him. Edie felt a toe connect with her shin hard enough to make her jump, so she got up and got him a plate and silverware. Even poured him a cup of coffee.

He smiled at her, but it didn't reach his eyes. He was still good and pissed over the house. She didn't know what the hell he wanted, what good he thought his hanging around here would do him, but he was up to something. There was no doubt about that. Maybe it was still guilt niggling at him for that perverted gag gift of his. But somehow she thought there was more to it than that.

You wouldn't know anything was bothering him at all, to watch him eat, though. He dug into Vidalia's hearty breakfast like a condemned man eating his last meal, pausing between bites to praise the skills of the cook.

The kiss-up, Edie thought. Trying to get in good with her mother, just to keep her on his side. Hell, if Vidalia knew about the handcuffs, she would box his ears until they bled.

When everyone finished eating, Vidalia pushed her chair away from the table, and that seemed to be the signal for everyone else to do the same. "Maya, you and Kara stay in here with the babies and take care of the cleanup chores. The rest of you, let's get on out to the barn. Um, except for you, Edie. You'll probably want to head up to your room and get your things there packed up."

Edie shook her head. "I did it last night."

Wade glanced at her sideways. "You didn't get home until after midnight," he observed.

"Now how would you know what time I got home?"

"Well, that's about the time the bar usually closes." He sent an innocent look at Vidalia. "Isn't it?"

"Yes, it is, most nights. Edie, are you telling me you were up all night?"

"I just... I was excited about the new house, is all. I couldn't sleep."

Great. Now all of them were looking at her oddly. Caleb sent Wade a worried, questioning glance. Wade shook his head very slightly from side to side, as if to say "just drop it." Vidalia probed with her eyes, but she said nothing.

Edie knew she would get the third degree from her mother the moment they were alone together, though. She wasn't looking forward to it.

The woman had more stuff than a department store, he thought as he loaded the Explorer for the second time that day. They had already taken one trip over to the new house, with his vehicle full of junk and Mel's full pickup right behind it. And none of it practical! Hardly any furniture, at least nothing usable like a couch or tables and chairs or a bed. Just foolish stuff. Paintings and ceramics and plant stands and lamps. A hammock, for heaven's sake, and a chair shaped like a giant bowl that would be impossible to get into or out of. Accent pieces, she called them. And boxes and boxes and more boxes. She had enough clothing to supply the population of a small country. The shoes alone would fill a closet.

It would take a year to get her unpacked.

Still, he worked steadily, loading the boxes, driving to the house, unloading them again. On the first trip over, Edie, Vidalia and Selene had stayed behind at the new place. By the time he, Caleb and Mel got the trucks re-loaded and returned, several of the boxes were empty, stacked near the doors.

Wade blinked at the number of them.

"Amazing what the Brand women can get done when they put their minds to it, isn't it?" Caleb asked, slapping him on the back. Then he reached past Wade to open the back of the Explorer, grabbed a box and carried it into the house.

By lunchtime, everything had been moved in and the large open living room of the new place looked as if a bomb had gone off inside it. Vidalia had insisted they take the bed from Edie's room so she would have a proper place to sleep until she got one of her own.

With a nod of satisfaction, the matriarch brushed her palms against each other. "I say we break for lunch."

"I say you break permanently," Edie said. She was sitting on the floor, her back against a tall box, knees drawn to her chest. "It's done. I'm moved. I can handle the rest."

"It'll take you a week to get all this stuff unpacked and put away," Vidalia argued.

"Yeah, but I'll enjoy it. I'll take my time, and when I get done, everything will be just the way I want it."

Her mother lifted her brows but finally nodded. "All right. If that's the way you want to do this."

"It is." Edie drew a breath, then used it to blow a strand of hair off her nose. When she did that it gave Wade a funny little hitch in his own breathing, but he ignored that. "Thank you all for your help. I really appreciate it. But you all have stuff to do, and I don't want to hold you up any longer."

"Are you trying to get rid of us, Edie?" Selene asked.

Edie shook her head in denial. "Of course not. I'm just tired out."

"Let's go," Vidalia instructed. "Let your sister have some time alone in her new place."

"I ought to do a house blessing on it," Selene muttered. "You can never tell what kind of energy might be hanging around."

"It can wait." Vidalia herded her daughters toward the door, and Caleb with them.

Wade stood where he was, near the massive windows that looked down over the falls. It was the view he'd fallen in love with and planned to make his own. Edie hadn't told him to get the hell out with the others, and he figured until she did, he would just stay where he was.

She sat still, not facing him, while they all trooped out and climbed into vehicles. She said nothing as the engines revved up and the convoy pulled out. He was beginning to wonder if she even realized he was still there.

"It's okay," she said finally. "You don't have to feel guilty anymore."

His brows bent in the middle, and he walked toward where she sat. "Me feel guilty? You're the one who stole my house, remember?"

"You've worked your tail off today, Wade, and honestly, you've been a lot of help. Let's call it even, okay?"

He hunkered down in front of her, the better to try to figure out what was going on in her twisted little head. She seemed to think she was making perfect sense. "We aren't anywhere close to even."

"Sure we are. It was just a joke. You were pissed off, and I probably deserved it. You've more than made up for it, though. I'm not mad at you."

"For *what*?"

She smiled halfheartedly. "Stop playing the innocent already. I know." Shaking her head, she glanced away distractedly. "I wish the phones were hooked up. I'd order us something for lunch."

He tugged a cell phone from his shirt pocket. "Pizza?" he asked.

"That thing won't work around here."

"What, the phone? Oh, it's pretty useless in town and the surrounding areas. But it works great up here. You've got the elevation." As he spoke, he punched numbers. "What do you like, pepperoni?"

"Mushrooms," she said. "And peppers and onions and ham and extra cheese."

He lifted his eyebrows but rattled off the order, added a six-pack of soda and one of beer to the total, and told the person on the other end where to bring it. When he dropped the phone back into his pocket, he said, "If that arrives and you try to get away with nibbling a sliver-sized slice and calling it quits..."

"I'm going to eat at least two slices," she said, and she said it as if it were a threat. "Just because I can."

It made him smile. He thought it meant she didn't plan to go back to modeling, and that made him glad for some inane reason. It was stupid of him. He should be offering to drive her to the airport instead of hoping she would stay. That way he could get his house back.

He sat down, looked at the mess around them, then at her again. "Now that the food thing is settled, you have to tell me just what it is you think I did."

She frowned. "After lunch. While we're waiting, you can help me carry some of these bigger boxes upstairs, okay?"

He sighed his impatience but did what she wanted, sensing it was important for some reason. He moved boxes. They didn't unpack stuff, just shuffled the mess around, sorting it into its appropriate parts of the house.

The pizza arrived, and he paid Max, the delivery guy, told him to keep the change. They lugged the food and beverages into the kitchen, where they sat on the counter with the box between them. He flipped it open, took a piece out. It was good, as it always was. But for some reason, watching Edie eat became the highlight of the meal for Wade. They didn't speak, just ate. He drank a beer, she drank a soda, and they ate some more. He couldn't remember enjoying a meal this much.

Finally they finished. A few slices remained in the box. "Gee, you don't even have a fridge for the leftovers."

She shrugged. "You can take it home, if you want. It'll just spoil here."

He nodded. "So?"

"So...?"

"So what is it you think I did that made me feel guilty enough to put in a full day's work moving your stuff into a house that should have been mine?"

She sighed, rolled her eyes. "The gift," she said, and when he still looked at her blankly she went on. "The handcuffs? I'll admit it gave me a jolt, but then I realized how angry you must have been over the house thing—not that you didn't have every right to be. Hell, I deserved it."

He blinked at her, waiting for her to slow down, but she kept on talking about it being funny in retrospect, about not being mad at him, until he cut in. "Edie, stop."

She broke off in midsentence and looked up at him with eyes very round and very vulnerable somehow. As if his words had the power to hurt her in some way. He almost rethought them, but hell, he didn't want her thinking that of him. "Edie, I didn't send you those handcuffs. I already told you that. You know damn well it wasn't me."

She blew out a little breath of laughter and shook her head. "Of course you did. That's why you've been slaving away helping me all day. You felt badly because they shook me up so much. I mean, you had no way of knowing they would, after all. It wasn't your fault—''

"You really want me to tell you it was me, don't you?" he asked.

She met his eyes, held them, and, finally, she nodded.

"It wasn't. But I think you know who it was. And I think whoever he is, he's the reason you seemed so shaken up after you got them. And I also think he's the reason you changed your mind about the house, and maybe the reason you were in such a hurry to move, as well."

She shook her head from side to side as if denying every word he said.

"I helped out today because I was curious. I want to know what's going on with you. Who's got you so damn jumpy?"

Bracing her hands on the counter, she slid off it, landing on her feet on the floor. "No one."

"Who is he, Edie?"

"I told you, there's no one."

"No? The same no one who chased you out of L.A., out of your former career, and then out of your own mother's house?" He slid to the floor too, put his hands on her shoulders and made her face him. "I'm damned if I know why, Edie, but I'd like to help with this. I can, if you'll let me."

She shook her head. "I don't need any help."

"Did you tell your mother about that present? Hmm?"

"Look, why the hell do you care? Huh? Answer me that and I'll tell you everything you could want to know. Just answer me. Why are you even here?"

He licked his lips, seeing the anger in her eyes where there had been none before and wondering what the hell he had done to put it there. "I...I don't know, because I'm a decent guy."

"Bull."

He lifted his brows in stark surprise. "Well, then, why do you think I'm here?"

"Same reason every other guy has ever come around me. Including the one who sent the gift. To try to get into my pants."

He flinched as if she'd hit him, wondering if she were close to the truth. Was that his motivation? He knew he was a pig, but he kind of thought there was more to this.

"I'll tell you something, Wade Armstrong. I'm more than a pretty face and a decent body. A lot more. And I want no part of any man who doesn't know that, much less one who doesn't want to know. One who doesn't even care. I'm through with that, do you understand? I'm done."

He lifted his hands from her shoulders, held them up, palms facing her. "I got it. You're done."

"Would you be falling over yourself to help me out if I were fat? Hmm? If I were ugly? Bald? Flat chested? Would you?"

He backed away from her, feeling as if he were under attack. "Look, I don't know. Maybe, okay? I got the feeling you were in trouble when I saw the way you reacted to that package last night. That was what I was reacting to, and yeah, I'd like to think I'd react the same way to a less attractive woman if she were in trouble, but it wasn't a less attractive woman. It was you, the most drop-dead gorgeous creature I've ever seen in my life. So how the hell am I supposed to know how I would have reacted to it being someone else?"

She stopped ranting. Her face softened a little, and her hands relaxed from their former fisted position. Sighing, she turned her gaze inward, looked at the floor. "I was really hoping it was you who sent the handcuffs," she said as if she hated like hell to admit it.

"Yeah?" he asked. He smiled a little at her. "Well, if you want, I can go get you some right now, and we could try them out."

She smacked him in the belly, and he faked a loud grunt and doubled over.

"You are such a pig."

"Thank you," he said, straightening.

"Take your leftovers and go home, will you? I've got unpacking to do."

He sighed. He didn't like it. He still hadn't gotten a straight answer out of her, but he didn't see that she was giving him a choice in the matter. So he took the leftover pizza and the beer, and he left.

But he didn't go home.

Edie was alone. Completely, utterly, alone in the big, strange, cluttered house. She wandered around for a while, unpacking boxes and amusing herself by deciding that the large, towering study off the living room was going to be her studio, and that the walk-in closet off the back of it would make a perfect dark room. But none of those things distracted her from the fact that she was all alone out here in the middle of nowhere. And her phone wasn't even hooked up yet.

"You're pathetic," she told herself. "It isn't even dark outside yet." The power was turned on. At least she would have lights. A little shiver went through her at the thought of having to spend the night without them. The big windows would be black as pitch. She would feel completely vulnerable. God, she needed to get some curtains!

With a sigh, she unloaded the last of her clothing into

the smaller closet and the little dresser her mother had insisted she take with her. Then she got to her feet and brushed off her hands. "Might as well go into town. Get the word out that I'm here. No sense waiting."

She barely gave herself a cursory glance in the mirror before heading outside to her car and driving down the winding mountain road toward Big Falls proper. She figured she was about halfway down that deserted, winding mountain road when the front tire blew, sending her careening out of control. She gripped the wheel hard, forcing it into submission, and after a few terrifying seconds she managed to get the car stopped. Crosswise in the road, yes, but stopped. She sat there for a moment, stunned that a peaceful drive could turn into a roller coaster ride in a heartbeat. Then she blew her hair out of her eyes and inched the limping vehicle around until it was perpendicular to the road again and as far onto the shoulder as possible.

A truck pulled to a stop behind her. She glimpsed it in her mirror, and for just an instant she stiffened at the prospect of dealing with some stranger on this stretch of road, alone. But then she recognized the man jogging toward her car and relaxed. Wade.

He yanked open her door and leaned in. "You all right?"

"Yeah."

"You sure?"

She nodded.

He nodded back. "Sure you are. You can let go of the steering wheel now."

She looked at her hands on the wheel and realized she was gripping it so hard it hurt. Her knuckles were white, her fingers red. It actually took a minute to make her grip on the wheel loosen. Then she turned toward the door and started to get out, only to have the seat belt pull against her, holding her in.

"Hold on a sec," Wade said, leaning over her. He was too close, his face in her face, his big arm and part of his chest brushing her chest as he reached across her body to unfasten her seat belt. As he drew back, his hand moved to the switch. He turned the ignition off but left the key in. Then he straightened, and she could breathe again without inhaling his scent, which wasn't bad, just irritating.

She got more irritated yet when he took her hand to tug her gently out of the car as if she were some frightened child who needed guidance in something so simple.

"That was some piece of driving," he said.

Frowning, she looked at him in disbelief even as she put her feet on the gravel and stood upright. "What?"

"You kept the car in control. It's not easy when you have a blowout. Especially a front tire. Nice job."

She blinked, still not sure he was paying her a sincere compliment. "It didn't *feel* under control."

"It was. Otherwise you'd have ended up down there, instead of safely parked on the roadside." As he spoke, he nodded, and she turned to look at whatever the hell he was talking about.

On the far side of the road, the ground fell away sharply. She lifted her head a little to see the long, long distance to the wooded land below. Then her gaze slid to the road itself and froze on the tire tracks that marked the place where her car had come to a stop. So close to the drop. Only a couple of feet.

Her knees dissolved.

Wade's arms encircled her waist. "Whoa, hold on now. I've got you." And then, without even so much as asking permission, he turned her body and scooped her right up off her feet like some knight scooping up a damsel.

"What the hell are you doing?" she demanded.

"Putting you in my truck where you can sit down before you fall down."

"I don't want to be in your truck. I prefer my car."

"Your car has a flat."

"It also has a spare."

"And I suppose you're gonna change the tire yourself?"

"What, you think I'm incapable of changing a tire? Don't forget who raised me, Wade Armstrong."

He grinned down at her for some reason. But by then he was already standing beside his tow truck, and he'd somehow managed to open the door. He hefted her up onto the seat. "Just please sit here and let me take a look at the damage, hmm? I do this for a living, you know."

She pursed her lips and crossed her arms over her chest but didn't argue. He closed the door on her and strode back to her car. She watched him bending down to look at the front tire. He made a face and shook his head. God, she hoped someone else would come along. Anyone else. Being around him so much bothered her. He was still every bit as dangerous as he had always been. He was also as shallow as ever. And just as sexy, too. Maybe more so. And he knew it.

She glanced behind her, back up the road, hoping to see one of her sisters coming along, but no such luck. The big boom on the back of the pickup blocked most of her view, anyway.

The driver's door opened, and she jumped, startled, because she hadn't seen him coming back to the truck. He climbed in, turned the key, and the thing fired up loudly. "You have a bent rim on that front tire, and the axle needs checking, just in case. You can't drive it off this mountain like that without risking another accident."

"Then what do you suggest I do, carry it off?"

He rolled his eyes. "Honey, you have noticed you're sitting in a tow truck, right? I mean, this isn't totally lost on you, is it?"

She huffed. "So you're gonna tow my car to your garage, where you can hold it hostage to inept mechanics and inflated prices?"

"I have top-notch mechanics and perfectly competitive prices." He cleared his throat. "Not to mention the only garage in town." He put the truck into gear and drove it around to the front of her car. Then he moved the levers that controlled the equipment in the back, and she heard a mechanical hum as the boom lowered. He got out again and went around behind. She refused to watch for fear he would think she was even remotely interested in what he might be doing back there. But when he got back in, she did look, and her car was affixed, nose up in the air, to the back of his truck.

"Looks like they're mating," she muttered.

He swung his head toward her so fast she thought his neck should have snapped. *"What?"*

"The car, it's…hell, never mind."

He glanced in the rearview. "Oh. I get it." Then he looked her way again, a frown on his face. "Just never heard anyone put it like that before. Guess you just have a dirty mind."

She gaped at him, but he was ignoring her now, putting the truck into gear and into motion.

"Buckle up," he told her.

She did so, even though it burned her buns obeying orders from him. They were just rolling into town when it occurred to her to wonder and, finally, to ask, "Just what were you doing out on my road, anyway?"

Chapter 6

It was after hours. No one was around in the garage, and that was good. He didn't particularly want Edie Brand in there, either. Not now. Not…yet. He hadn't had a chance to redecorate the place yet.

"Well?" she asked.

She'd been talking. He'd been preoccupied planning just what he was going to say when she walked in. If he couldn't keep her out.

"I'm sorry. What?"

"What were you doing on my road?" she repeated.

He lifted his brows and faked surprise. "You bought the *road*, too? My God, woman, you do have money to burn."

She looked utterly pained. He was good at pissing her off, he thought, enjoying it.

"I didn't buy the road. You know full well I didn't buy the freaking road. I mean, my road, as in, the road on which I live. What were doing out there?"

"Driving?"

She closed her eyes, sighed.

"Hey, just let me know if I'm supposed to file some kind of formal request when I want to use the Falls Road, Edie. I'll be glad to comply if you tell me the regulations up front."

"You're infuriating, you know that?"

He smiled. "I had a call. Errol Johnson's car died out that way, and he thought he needed a tow. Turns out he only needed a jump start. Okay?"

She looked as if she doubted him, which was pretty damned perceptive of her, since there had been no call. He'd wanted to drive by her place to check up on her, but he would never admit that. He'd taken the tow truck instead of the Explorer because it would give him a plausible excuse if he were spotted. Which was a good thing to have, he decided.

He pulled up to the front door of the garage, cut the engine, got out and started around to the rear.

"What are you doing?" she asked.

He looked up fast, realizing she'd scrambled out, too, and followed him. "I'm going to lower the car and unhook it. Why?"

"Aren't you going to take it inside?"

"Not tonight, no."

"Well...why not?" She looked at the large garage doors, then at him.

"'Cause I've already locked up for the night. I'll put it inside first thing in the morning, don't worry."

She was worried. She pursed her lips, hugged herself and lowered her head.

"What? You worried someone's gonna mess with your car out here overnight?"

Her head came up. "Frankly...yeah, I am."

He frowned harder at her. "Why?"

She shrugged, looking away. "Let's just say it wouldn't be the first time and leave it at that, okay?"

Narrowing his eyes, he tried to search her face, but she didn't let him look long. It occurred to him that someone had really messed with her head to make her so paranoid. But it also occurred to him that she might have reasons to be cautious. "Fine," he said. "Fine, we'll put her inside for the night." He went to the main entrance, and she followed on his heels. He took out his keys and unlocked the door, opened it just a little and reached inside to flip a button.

The big overhead door groaned and began to rise slowly.

He licked his lips, looking around for a diversion, and finally said, "Look, your sisters are over at the Corral." He pointed down the street toward the bar, where a light was on in one of the windows.

"It's probably Mom. She spends way too much time at work. That place is like her baby."

"Why don't you go on over and say hello while I put the car in? It won't take a minute, and then I'll come pick you up and give you a ride home."

She looked at him oddly for a long moment, then finally she shrugged and turned toward the road. "Whatever."

He sighed his relief as she walked away from him. God, what a close call. She kept walking. Wade got into the truck and pulled it into the garage with the car still attached to the back, then shut it down. Getting out, he went back to the switches on the wall, flicking one to start the huge door on its way back down again and another to turn on the lights. He took just a moment to look around him.

Every wall sported pictures of Edie Brand in various states of undress, with pouty lips and bedroom eyes and wild hair. In spite of himself, he licked his lips. Damn, she was hot, if nothing else. She might be a hyper, snooty, arrogant pain in the backside, but she was hot. No doubt about that.

"Oh. My. God."

He whirled fast at the sound of her voice. She was standing just inside the doorway he had reached through to hit the button. Damn, he'd forgotten to lock it! He felt like the kid who'd been caught with his hand in someone else's cookie jar. But he resented feeling that way. He really resented it.

"What the hell is all this?"

Wade schooled his expression and his voice not to betray just how embarrassed he was right then. "All what?" he asked in a tone of complete innocence. Then he looked around the room. "Oh, you mean the pictures?"

She tilted her head and looked at him as if he were stupid. "No, I meant the wrenches. Yes, the pictures. What the hell are you doing with all these pictures of me, Wade?"

He shrugged. "The customers like them. So do the guys who work for me. And hell, I'm a red-blooded male myself. Have you ever seen a garage *without* a few nudie shots on the walls?"

She closed her eyes slowly. "They are not 'nudie shots', as you so charmingly put it, Armstrong, they're lingerie ads. And yes, I have seen garages without them, though that's beside the point. They're all of me. Why is every one of them of me?"

"You're local. I always try to support local businesses, and it stood to reason I should do the same for our own local pinup girl."

She blinked. "You are a pervert." She said it as if it were some revelation she had just uncovered.

He turned it right back on her. "*I'm* a pervert? Hey, honey, you're the one who posed for them."

"They're underwear ads!" she shot back. "They're not meant to be used to fuel the libidos of sex-crazed grease monkeys!"

"No? What, not even this one here, where you're bent over fixing your shoe, with your ass toward the camera? What was the purpose of that shot, Edie, to show the full benefits of thong panties?"

She turned her back on him so fast he knew she was furious. And maybe embarrassed, too. Good. He walked right up behind her. "The ads are meant to tease and tantalize and titillate. Admit it."

She stiffened her spine, not facing him. "Sex sells, Wade."

"Damn right it does. And frankly, I saw nothing wrong with taking full advantage of your teasing, tempting photos as fantasy fodder when you were clear on the other side of the country."

"Fantasy fodder?"

"Hell yes. I'm human, you know."

When she turned to face him, her jaw was clenched, teeth grated, cheeks pink. "I'm not on the other side of the country anymore. And I have to live in this town."

"And I've been meaning to take the pictures down ever since you got back."

She studied his face as if trying to see through his lies. "You...you're going to take them down?"

"Yeah. Yeah, if they bother you so much, they'll be down by morning."

She pressed her lips tight together. "I appreciate it."

"You're welcome," he said.

She started to say something else. But he kept speaking. "But I refuse to take down the ones in my bedroom."

Her face went white, and she gaped at him.

"Hey, they're some of the best visual aids I've come across."

Her hand flashed toward his face, but he caught her wrist. "Will you chill? I'm teasing you. God, can't you take a joke?"

She couldn't; it was pretty clear by the high color that flooded her face, replacing the pallor that had been there before. That didn't bother him, though. What bothered him, way down deep where it shouldn't, was the moisture that sprang into her eyes.

She jerked her wrist free, turned and ran away from him. He sighed, called himself about a zillion nasty names, and then stepped outside to watch over her until she'd safely reached the bar and gone inside. Just like he'd been watching over her up there in her hilltop home.

The man was a Neanderthal. A jerk. A pig.

And if she had half a brain, she would sic the law on him. After all, she had a stalker who'd been hounding her constantly the last six months she'd been in L.A. And Wade Armstrong not only had photos of her wallpapering his garage, but he'd been very close by when the latest kinky little gift had been delivered to her.

"Well now, what are you doing here?" Vidalia asked when Edie stomped into the bar.

"Fuming, mostly. Did you know that horrible man—"

"You mean Wade Armstrong?"

"Yes, Wade Armstrong! Did you know he had magazine shots of me all over his garage?"

Her mother blinked, lifting her head from the books she'd been poring over. "What, still?"

"You mean you knew?"

"Everyone in town knew." She smiled to herself and shook her head slowly. "Mel threatened to break his face, of course, but only until I explained it to her. The man thinks he's got everyone fooled, you know. All that attitude.''

Edie held up both hands in complete bewilderment. ''What are you talking about?''

''Oh, Edie, come on now, don't tell me you haven't figured it out yet. That boy's been pining for you since high school.''

She could have been hit by a falling house and felt less shock. ''That's…ridiculous.''

''He was gonna ask you to his senior prom, you know. The boy called me up and asked my permission. Can you believe that? Of course, by the time he worked up his nerve, you were already going with…Brad or Chad or one of those pretty boys.''

''Matt,'' she corrected. ''Matt McConnell.''

''Whatever. Wade made me promise never to tell, but…well, things have their time.''

Edie sat down hard. Fortunately there was a chair behind her. ''He…he *liked* me? I didn't think he even *knew* me.''

''He didn't think you knew him. Now he has all those photos. Tells folks it's to remind him he's risen above the people who brushed him off back then. The ones who saw him as unworthy of their time or notice. You seem to have become the poster girl for everyone who ever slighted him, Edie.''

''But I never slighted him.''

''Not the way he sees it.''

Edie sighed, lowering her head, remembering the way Wade used to walk around school. He always had this ''don't get too close'' attitude, always exuded a sense of danger, and that was what kept people away. She'd been scared to death of him in high school. All the girls had.

It occurred to her then that high school wounds ran

deep. Deeper than adults liked to acknowledge. Some kids never outgrew them. Which made sense when you put it into perspective. Some kids, tragically, didn't even *survive* them. She'd had no idea her behavior had caused Wade any pain. At the time, however, she'd been pretty wrapped up in her own little world, her own little dramas.

"Mom, did Wade leave town before I came back home?"

"Not that I know of, hon. In fact, that shop's open every single weekday, holidays included."

He would have had to be in and out of town a lot to have been responsible for all the harassment her stalker had doled out. Enough so that it would have been noticed. She could double-check, try to verify his exact whereabouts on the day the man had actually attacked her...but hell, deep down, she knew it wasn't him.

Her mother's hand covered hers. "You know, of course, the real reason he kept all the pictures isn't resentment at all. It's because he never got over you."

Edie blinked fast, looking up at her mother. "I think you're way off base on that one, Mom."

Her mother shrugged. "Guess you'll figure it out, one way or another." She slid the book into the desk drawer, closed it and twisted a key in the lock. "Come on, hon. I'll give you a ride home."

"All right."

Edie didn't like the new house, she decided. She didn't like it at all. Especially not that first night, with no phone hooked up yet, and no car in the driveway. She locked the place up tight but didn't sleep. She tried. She paced. She unpacked some more. She set her minuscule portable television up on cardboard boxes and got a fuzzy picture from a local station, via the rabbit-ear antenna. She was going

to need a satellite dish out here, she mused. No cable ran
this far out of town.

It was dark outside. Darker than hell, and with those
huge windows, she felt as exposed as a shooting-gallery
duck. Damn. She hated being afraid—especially when
there was no reason for it. The gift hadn't come from her
stalker. Probably. It could have been anyone in town. Just
because Wade Armstrong denied it, that didn't mean he
hadn't done it. And what about Pete Dunnegan? She'd
given him a hard time at the bar. Granted, that was after
she had received the gift, but he seemed to have fixated
on her before he ever arrived that night. And there were
others. There had to be lots of others. Righteous, zealot-
types who found her work offensive and vulgar and
wanted to put the fear of God into her. Oversexed types
who wanted to use her to fuel their fantasies.

She stopped there, closed her eyes. She had set a neatly
folded stack of towels and washcloths on a shelf in the
bathroom attached to her bedroom, and now she just stood
there staring at them, her hands sinking into the plush fabric. She really shouldn't be surprised at having picked up
a sicko in L.A., should she? Hell, she probably had several
of them who could be potentially dangerous. Maybe her
agent had been right when he'd said she should have expected it.

Sighing, she picked up a pretty bath towel in a deep
forest-green shade, and a hand towel and washcloth of soft
mint green, and moved to the hardwood rack on the wall
to hang them just so. She needed this place to feel like a
home, not like an empty shell full of boxes. Putting her
bathroom together helped.

She wandered back downstairs, into the living room,
located her bathroom supplies and refused to cast a shivery
glance toward the large black windows as she carried the

box back upstairs with her. She unwrapped a new bar of soap and located a soap dish, setting both on the sink. She dug for her toothbrush and hung it in the rack. It looked lonely there. Bit by bit she unpacked her shampoos and conditioners and makeup and facial-care creams and masks, and placed them all around the bathroom. Hairbrushes, combs, hair dryer, curling iron, straightening iron, crimping iron, hot curlers, hot oil treatments. She unpacked bath beads and salts and loofahs. She found her favorite plush green rug for in front of the tub, and a big white cotton robe, which she hung on the hook on the inside of the bathroom door. She put her matching slippers on the floor beside it. Then she looked around the bathroom.

The walls were bare. They needed something.

Thinking of that made her think of the walls at Wade Armstrong's garage and his choice of how to decorate them. It had been mortifying to walk in there and see all those photos of her. She'd felt as exposed as if he'd walked in on her changing and caught her half dressed.

Why, though? She never felt that way with anyone else. She had seen her calendar on walls before. She usually experienced a mixture of pride and discomfort at being on display that way—pride because someone had liked her work enough to plunk down seventeen bucks for it. Discomfort at the thought of why they liked looking at her that much. Since the stalking had begun, the discomfort level had grown far larger than the pride. That really should have been her first clue that her time as a model was over.

Walking in and seeing her photos all over Wade Armstrong's garage had felt different, though. Different from anything in her experience. She'd been embarrassed. And more. Angry. He wasn't like those other men who had bought her calendar. He *knew* her. That was it, she realized slowly. He knew her in person, face-to-face. They had been in high school together. He *knew* her. To her mind, that ought to mean he didn't need the photos. Because he knew her, he should also know that they were not her. That they were little more than airbrushed, retouched, high-gloss personas she put on to do a job. That the real her was so much better, so much more.

At least, she had always hoped she was more. He didn't see that, though. He saw only the body, the face, the hair, the poses and the lighting.

Maybe he thought that was all she was. And maybe the reason that upset her so much was because she was afraid he might be right.

No. He wasn't. He was dead wrong.

Licking her lips, she sighed and turned to the tub to run a bath. The bathroom was looking more homey. She didn't even want to look at the bedroom yet. She was glad the bed was at least put together. Wade and Caleb had done that earlier in the day, under Vidalia's supervision. Pouring a generous amount of bath salts into the water, inhaling the sweet, soothing scents of lavender and chamomile, Edie stirred the water with her hand. It ran deeper and deeper, filling the room with warmth and steam and diffusing that soothing scent.

She rose from the edge of the tub, slid her clothes off and left them lying on the floor. She didn't have a hamper yet and made a mental note to get one. For now, her jeans on the floor just made the place seem more lived in. Finally she stepped into the still-running water and leaned back. The heat felt good, seeping into her bones, soothing her. It had been a long day. But, in a way, a good one. It could easily, she thought, have been the first day of the rest of her life. A new beginning for her.

If only that damn gift hadn't arrived.

What if it *had* been her stalker?

She closed her eyes tight, shook her head. She refused to believe it. It wasn't. It was that simple. It wasn't him. Someone in town was screwing with her head, and she would find out who. She banished the thought from her mind and relaxed into the water. The scents helped. Selene had made the bath salts for her, telling her they were a special blend designed to ease away stress and worries, to relax a person's mind, body and spirit. She believed her youngest sister was onto something, the way her muscles seemed to elongate and loosen as she rested in the water.

She let it happen, gave herself over to it, closed her eyes.

It occurred to her, for some inexplicable reason, to wonder what Wade Armstrong might be doing right now. And as she sank slowly into sleep, her mind asked the question again and again.

An image slowly took shape in her mind. An image of Wade Armstrong, lying alone in his bed, completely naked and completely erect as he looked at a magazine with her face on the cover. She saw it all very clearly. The way his eyes burned over her body on the page. The way he licked his lips. And then the way his hand slid down over his belly.

An irritating bleating sound drew her attention away from where it was utterly, mindlessly riveted. It came again and again. She popped her eyes open and sat upright in the tub, blinking in shock. She had fallen asleep, she realized slowly, and dreamed...

The sound came again. Damn, not a part of the dream. Startled, she rose from the water, dripping, reached for her robe and pulled it on, then opened the bathroom door, wondering what the hell was ringing like that.

The sound was coming from her purse, which was in the bedroom, on the mattress. She made wet footprints on

the hardwood as she hurried to it, dug around inside and
found a cell phone that didn't belong to her.

Oh God, had someone been in here? Her stalker, was it
him calling her now?

She pressed the green button on the keypad, brought the
phone to her ear. "Hello?"

"What's wrong?" a voice asked.

The voice was Wade's, and it made that dream image
flash before her eyes again. She blinked it away, but not
before a little voice in her head wondered if he looked as
good undressed in real life as he had in her dream.
"Wade?" she asked.

"Yeah, it's me. What's the matter, Edie?"

"What makes you think anything's the matter?"

"You sounded funny when you answered. Scared or
something."

She rolled her eyes. "Probably because I couldn't figure
out who had come into my house to leave me a cell phone
while I was in the bathtub!"

"You...you were in the tub?"

"Yes. Is this your phone, Wade?"

"Yeah. I dropped it in your purse earlier and just now
realized I hadn't told you. So I figured I ought to call to
let you know it was there, in case you needed it tonight.
I know the regular line out there isn't hooked up yet, and
I, uh...uh..." His voice trailed off. He cleared his throat.
"So, are you *still* in the tub?"

"No, Wade, I am not still in the tub. I got out of the
tub to answer the phone. I'm in the bedroom."

"Oh." Again a long stretch of silence. "So, um, what
are you wearing?"

She closed her eyes, completely ignoring the little tingle
that zipped through her when his voice lowered the way
it had just then. She said, "The biggest, ugliest, rattiest

flannel bathrobe you can imagine, with a collar that comes to my chin, and thirty buttons, all done up tight.''

He sighed. "You couldn't lie, even a little bit?''

"No. Not even a little bit.''

"Okay, we'll work with what we have, then.''

"What?''

"Close your eyes, Edie.'' His voice had dropped again to that deep, whispery sound that brushed her nerve endings like sandpaper on velvet. "I'm unbuttoning the first button. With my teeth...''

"Stop it, Wade.''

"Oh, come on, I was just teasing.'' His voice was normal again. Hers wasn't, and she was sorely afraid he could tell. "Listen, I wasn't just calling so you'd know the phone was there. I also wanted to apologize. For the pictures in the garage. I never intended for you to walk in there and see them. I mean it.''

"You're apologizing?'' She blinked at the phone in shock. "What are you up to, Wade?''

"Nothing. I took them down. They're gone, okay?''

She nodded slowly, thinking about what her mother had told her. "Let me ask you something. And give me an honest answer, will you?''

"Sure. Shoot.''

"Why did you really have those pictures up there?''

He was silent for a long moment. Then he said, "Keeps the customers' minds off the long wait and the size of the bill.''

"So would a TV,'' she said.

"Good idea. I'll get one.''

She sighed, rolling her eyes.

"Look, I have to go. I just wanted to ease your mind about the pictures and let you know you had a phone.''

"And make sure I was okay,'' she added.

"And ask what you were wearing," he returned. "If you need anything, or, you know, if you decide you want to have phone sex, feel free to call me back. Okay?"

"Right. Whatever."

"You have the number?"

"Oh, I've got your number all right, Armstrong."

"It's number one on the speed dial," he said.

"You have yourself on speed dial?"

"I programmed it in before I gave you the phone."

She blinked, shocked. The man was looking out for her. He was acting more like a guardian angel than a big bad dangerous sex maniac. "That was…that was nice of you. Thanks."

"You wanna thank me, just take the phone with you and slide back into that bathtub."

"Goodbye, Wade."

"Can't blame a guy for trying."

She clicked the cut-off button and tried to hold on to her anger and indignation. He was crude, ill mannered and had a one-track mind.

And that was all bull, wasn't it? A big act. Maybe he'd always been acting. Because if he was as sleazy as he pretended to be, he wouldn't have thought to leave his cell phone with her, just in case. It never would have occurred to him that she would be afraid up here all alone her first night.

Then again, it wouldn't have occurred to him if she had been an ordinary-looking woman. Would it? She blinked and felt her anger waning. She was too grateful to be as angry as his remarks and his attitude should have made her. She tucked the cell phone under her pillow, rolled onto her side and pulled a blanket up over her shoulders.

Chapter 7

Something was wrong!

She came awake suddenly, her eyes flashing open and her heart leaping against her rib cage, though she had no idea why. Something had startled her awake.

It took a moment of blinking in the darkness to realize she wasn't in her bedroom at her mother's farmhouse anymore. She was in *her* house, her *new* house. Automatically, she reached for the lamp on the bedside stand, only to be reminded it wasn't there. The bedroom wasn't in order. The bedside stand was still sitting downstairs in the living room amid the boxes, and the lamp was on the floor, four feet away. She would have to get out of bed to reach it.

Then again, maybe that wasn't the best idea. If a light came on and there was someone here, it would be pretty clear where she was, wouldn't it?

She listened, sitting perfectly still and straining her ears. What the hell had shocked her out of a sound sleep like that?

There were sounds, of course. The wind up on a hilltop like this seemed to blow all the time, and with so much forest around, there was a singing in the air. The pitch changed, lower to higher, depending on how hard the wind blew. Branches moved at its touch, brushing each other and parting again like dancers in the trees. She heard that whisper now. And far beyond it, the distant, steady hoot of an owl came to her ears. But that was all. Nothing else. No other sounds. She looked around the room, straining her eyes.

The closet door was partway open.

Her heart slammed and her skin prickled. Had it been open before? Hadn't it been closed when she crawled into bed?

To hell with this. She had the cell phone in her hand, pressed the power button that made the light come on so she could see the panel and hit speed dial and 1 before she even got herself untangled from the covers and landed on the floor. The bed was between her and the closet door now. Her eyes were fixed on that darkened closet even as she crept toward the lamp. Her heart was pounding now, hammering so hard she thought it should be audible. There was someone in the house. She could feel it. The phone on the other end rang, and rang again.

Her hand shaking, she reached for the lamp, then froze when Wade's voice came into her ear with a sleepy, "Yeah?"

She licked her lips. If she spoke, and there was someone in her closet... She sprang to her feet and lunged for the bedroom door. Even as she sprinted through it, she said, "There's someone in the house!"

"Edie? Hold on. Just lock yourself in one of the rooms and hold on. I'll be there in five minutes."

"Hurry," she said, but the phone had already gone

dead. She was standing at the top of the stairs in the dark house. She could see part of the wide-open area below, lit only by the thin beam of a crescent moon and a few stars shining through the huge, bare windows. She could see the shapes of all her boxes, the few steps down to the foyer, the closed front door that she wished she could just run through right now. But she couldn't. Anyone could be down there.

She knew she had heard something, something that woke her. And she still felt the presence. Her bedroom door stood open at the far end of the hall. The second bedroom was behind her, pitch dark, with no lamp in it and no bulb in the ceiling fixture. To her left was a linen closet. But there would be no lock on the inside of a closet door.

Which way to go, dammit?

A sound, a distinct sound, like a single footstep, galvanized her. It had come from her bedroom. She shot into the darkened guest room as if fired from a cannon, closed the door, locked it. And then she stood there, trying to listen to outside sounds over the pounding of blood in her temples and her own ragged breathing. She forced it slower. Wade would have pulled his clothes on by now. He was probably out the door, in his vehicle. She followed his actions in her mind. He was starting it up, driving out of his driveway. She wasn't sure where he lived. Somewhere in town, though. And it wasn't a big town. Even if he lived all the way at the far end, he could make it to the Falls road in a minute or two. Especially this late at night. No traffic.

She swallowed, tried to count in her mind. One, one thousand, two, one thousand… And even as she did it, she was straining, listening. Straining too hard, because now every breeze that caressed the siding sounded like a human moving. No more footfalls came, only a soft brushing, that might have been the trees outside or someone's trouser legs moving as he crept through her hall.

She thought of the gun Mike had given her. She had tucked it into the back of a dresser drawer and hadn't even thought to grab it. And she couldn't go back for it now.

She backed into the farthest corner of the room, sank onto the floor and drew her knees up to her chest. God, she was so afraid.

As he drove—not the tow truck, but his Explorer, which was a hell of a lot faster—he thought of a thousand things. He should have called a cop before he left. He should have called Caleb. But he hadn't, and he didn't have his cell phone with him, so he couldn't. And he damned well wasn't going to stop the car to call anyone now.

She had sounded terrified. God, he had barely recognized her voice.

He drove wildly, recklessly, up the steep, winding road, taking curves so fast that if he met another vehicle on the way, one of them would end up in the brush, and it wasn't going to be him. He didn't have a weapon. He didn't think he would need one, the way his adrenaline was pumping.

He skidded to a dusty stop in her driveway only minutes after she had called—the faithful Explorer hadn't slowed to less than eighty until he hit the brakes. He jumped out, yanking a tire iron out of the back and striding toward the house, which was pitch dark. Damn, if she hadn't even turned on a light...

He headed for the front door. It was wide open, and he lifted the tire iron and strode through, reaching for the light switch just inside the door, flicking it on. Light flooded the foyer. He glanced around him, saw no one, and went

on to the wide-open living area, turning its light on, as
well. No one seemed to be there, either.

"Edie?" he called. "It's Wade. I'm here. You're okay
now. Where are you?"

He heard movement, footsteps, soft and tentative, from
above, and he headed for the stairs. "Edie?" He paused
at the top.

A bedroom door opened slowly, and she looked out at
him. She wore a white cotton robe, which she clutched
around her middle. Her hair was as tangled as Medusa's,
he thought—as if she had gone to sleep with it wet. And
her eyes were bigger than he had ever seen them. She
didn't look like his favorite pinup girl. She looked like a
frightened child.

"Are you okay?"

She didn't answer that. "He was in my bedroom. In the
closet, I think."

His hand gripped the tire iron more tightly, and something hot and ugly spread through his veins. If he found
some son of a bitch hiding in Edie Brand's bedroom closet,
he didn't plan to let him leave here under his own power.
They would have to carry the bastard out. Possibly in more
than one container.

He started toward the bedroom.

Edie lunged out of the room and gripped his arm. She
didn't say "Don't leave me" but he heard it all the same.
Her hands gripped his upper arm hard. He put his hand on
her hip, nudging her behind him, but she still kept hold of
his arm as he started forward. He spotted the switch for
the hall light, snapped it on. Then he led her toward her
bedroom. As he started through the door, he reached for
the light switch.

"It doesn't work," she whispered, her voice near his
ear. Warm breath did odd things to a man when it kissed

his ear and his neck like that, even during times of great duress, he thought idly. "There's a lamp." She pointed.

Nodding, he walked to the lamp, with her still at his back; then he looked at the closet door. When he took his first step toward it, Edie released her grip on his arm, and he felt her heat fade. Glancing behind him, he saw that she had backed away, all the way to the opposite wall, and her gaze was fixed unblinkingly on the closet door.

His throat a little dry, he flicked on the lamp, lifted his tire iron and kept moving. He reached the door, yanked it open and stared inside at a dim, empty space. It wasn't a large closet, nor did it have its own light source, but he could see it clearly. Three bare walls, a clothes pole across the space at eye level, an empty shelf above it, and an empty floor below it.

He stepped aside, so she could see into the closet, too.

She shook her head slowly. "He was there."

"How do you know?"

She met Wade's eyes. "The closet door was open when I left this room and called you. It was open, Wade. It was open."

"And what about the front door?" he asked her.

She frowned at him, shaking her head. "The front door...I didn't go near it. It was closed and locked for the night."

"It was open when I got here," he said.

"Oh God..."

He saw the panic in her face as she swung her gaze left and right, fought to catch her breath as it came more rapidly than before. So he went to her, crossed the room, dropping the tire iron on the bed as he passed, and put his arms around Edie Brand. She didn't fight him. She hugged him instead. Hard. And he could feel her trembling down deep. "Whoever it was, he left. He probably heard you make that call and skinned out the front door. I'm gonna search the place top to bottom, just to be sure, and I want you to lock yourself in this room until I come back for you. Okay?''

She nodded, her head moving up and down against the front of his shoulder. ''The b-bathroom first,'' she whispered.

He nodded and turned her around, set her down on the bed; then he went in to check the bathroom. She had left clothes on the floor in there, he noticed, and the water was still in the tub.

Assured the room was empty, he went back to her. ''You still have the cell phone?''

She nodded.

''Great. Use it if you need to. I'll be back in ten.''

''Make it five.''

He sent her a teasing smile. ''Can't live without me that long, huh? Okay, five, then. And when I get back, Edie, we are going to have a talk.''

She blinked. ''A talk?''

''Yeah. I think maybe it's about time you told me what's been going on with you,'' he said. He leaned past her, gripped his trusty tire iron. ''Lock the door behind me.''

She nodded as he opened it and stepped through. ''Be careful, Wade.''

He pulled the door closed, waiting to hear her turn the lock, and then he moved down the hall.

By the time Wade tapped on her bedroom door several minutes later and said, ''It's okay, Edie, it's me,'' she had calmed down enough for the embarrassment to set in. Maybe, she thought, he wouldn't think too much about it. Maybe he wouldn't ask the questions she was dreading.

But he did. First, though, he took her arm and led her

out of her room and down the stairs. "The house is clear. There's no one around. If anyone was here before, he's gone now."

She nodded, but she was still nervous as he took her into the kitchen. He dragged a couple of stools in from the living room. "You want me to get you anything?" he asked. "Cocoa, coffee?"

"There's nothing here. I...haven't even shopped for groceries yet."

Sighing, he sat on a stool—which did not match the one on which she sat, she noticed—and sat across from her. "So?" he asked.

"So...I guess I was just nervous. Probably imagined the whole thing."

"Uh-huh. Okay, we'll get to that. First things first. You called me."

She nodded. "Yes. And you came running. That was really good of you, Wade."

"Yeah, but that's beside the point."

"The point being?" she asked.

"That you called *me*. Not the cops. Not your brother-in-law, or your mom, or you sister Mel, who could probably handle any intruder smaller than roughly, oh, say, Godzilla. You didn't call any of them. You called me. And I think I know why."

She lifted her head and looked into his eyes, not sure what he was getting at. "Because you told me to?"

"Sorry?"

"You left me your cell phone. You called me on it and told me to call you if I needed anything. Remember? You said you had put yourself on speed dial. That was just about the last thing I heard before I fell asleep. So when I woke, it was the first thing I thought of. Speed dial."

"I see."

"It would have taken lots longer to call my mom or sister or Caleb. Even nine-one-one would have taken longer than just dialing one."

"So you ran all those options through your mind, and you decided it would be quicker to call me." It wasn't a question.

She nodded.

"Or maybe you still aren't ready for your family to know what's going on with you."

She lowered her eyes. Oh. That was what he was getting at. Not that maybe she felt drawn to him or anything ridiculous like that. "Well, yeah. There is that," she admitted, trying to keep the relief out of her voice.

"Well, then, you need to tell me."

She swallowed hard, lifting her head, meeting his eyes.

"And don't bother telling me there's nothing going on, either, Edie. You aren't the kind of woman to panic over nothing. You heard something tonight, and you have reason to be afraid. And that gift had something to do with that reason."

"You're right. I do have reason. And there is more going on."

"Well then…?"

"It's my business, Wade. I'm not trying to be rude, and I really am grateful to you for helping me like this, but…it's my problem. I'll deal with it."

He shook his head firmly. "Not anymore you won't. You're gonna tell me. All of it. Starting right now. Or else I'm going to make a phone call to my buddy Caleb and tell him exactly what happened here tonight."

She blinked at him. "You're blackmailing me?"

"Blackmailing you?" He seemed shocked. "If I don't tell him you think there's someone after you, and you end up hurt— Look, he's my best friend. You're his family. I can't do that, Edie. You need to come clean with me.''

She grated her teeth in anger. "I'll tell Caleb myself."

"Yeah, well, I'd believe that if you had called Caleb over here in the middle of the night to protect you from a phantom in the closet. But you didn't. You called me. So what is it, Edie? Old boyfriend who can't let go? Hmm? Abusive relationship? Bad breakup? What?''

She studied his face for a long moment and, finally, she gave, sighing deeply, knowing by the stubborn set of his jaw that he wasn't going to let up until she told him. "Obsessed fan," she said at last.

"Obsessed fan?"

She nodded.

"As in…"

"As in stalker," she said.

He sat back in his seat as if pushed there. His breath came out of him in a whoosh. "I didn't expect that."

"Neither did I. My agent said I should have, though. Considering what I did for a living."

"Sounds like a real understanding asshole," he said. "As if you asked for this kind of bull."

She blinked at him, surprised, maybe, that he hadn't agreed readily with her former agent's pronouncement.

"When did it start?"

She sighed. "Last summer. At first it was just fan mail. Persistent, annoying, but not too scary. When I didn't answer it, it started getting weird."

"Weird, how?"

She looked at him, watched his face. "He starting telling me about his sexual fantasies."

"About you," he finished.

She nodded. "Yeah. And they got more and more descriptive, more and more detailed, and more and more...violent.''

"He wanted to hurt you?''

"Look, I don't want to—''

"Just tell me. What was it? Kinky? S and M type stuff?''

She nodded again, unable to look him in the eye. ''He said he would teach me my place, that he would break me, make me completely submissive to him.'' She licked her lips. ''And then the gifts started arriving.''

"Like the handcuffs,'' he asked.

She nodded. ''Yeah. Like the handcuffs. With little notes telling me what he wanted me to wear, giving me daily orders as if he really expected me to do what he told me.''

"What kind of orders?''

She shrugged. ''Stand by the back window and take off your blouse. Don't wear bras anymore. Sleep naked from now on. You name it.'' She shook her head. ''It was creepy, because I knew he was watching me, to see if I would obey. And he seemed to get angrier and angrier when I didn't.''

He swore softly. ''You went to the police?''

"They told me until he did something illegal, their hands were tied. Advised me to keep all the letters and gifts, along with a file on when they were received, the type of packing, mode of delivery and anything else I could think of. They also advised me to hire a bodyguard.''

Wade was listening, leaning forward, watching her face, literally hanging on her words, she thought. ''And did you?''

"Yes. Mike was good, too. Just not quite good enough.''

His eyes flared wider. ''This guy got to you?''

She nodded. "He got into the car with me after a party one night. Mike had gone back inside to get something I'd left behind. The valet had his back to the car. The next thing I knew, there was a blade to my throat, a hand over my mouth and hot breath in my ear telling me to stay perfectly still or die."

Wade got slowly to his feet. His face seemed to darken to the shade of blood. "Did he rape you?"

She shook her head slowly, left, then right. "No. He...his hands were all over me. Then I said the wrong thing, and he lost it. He started...choking me. Strangling me." She closed her eyes. "I thought it was over. But Mike came out, and he ran for it. But I knew he would come for me. To punish me for disobeying him."

Wade's face had betrayed a wealth of anger until, finally, he walked across the kitchen, putting his back to her. She wasn't sure why. "And that's why you decided to come home?"

"Yes. That happened just before Christmas. My contract was about to expire. I told no one other than Mike that I was leaving. I didn't want to spend another night in L.A. He made sure I didn't have to. He packed my things and hired a mover to ship them after I left, and he was very careful, everything in his name, nothing in mine. He leaked that I was in drug rehab to one reporter, and that I was having a facelift to another. No one, *no one*, knew where I was."

"Except Mike."

She looked up. Wade had turned briefly. "I'd trust him with my life."

"You did."

She licked her lips. "Yeah, I did." But she shook her head. "Still, I know he's not the stalker—because I saw them both together that day in the car. Mike came out, came running, and the other guy dove out the back and ran the other way."

Wade nodded as if in agreement. "And he'd have no reason to help this guy find you."

"None."

"Okay, we go with that for now. Though I'd still like to talk to this Mike."

"Wade, I told you about my problem. I didn't hand it over to you. You don't need to talk to anybody."

He sighed, then twisted his wrist and glanced at his watch. "There's still time enough left to catch a few hours sleep, you know."

She hugged her arms and shivered.

"Hey." He moved close to her chair, and, to her surprise, he put his hands on the outsides of her arms and rubbed up and down. "It's okay. I'll be right here."

"You don't have to stay."

"Don't even put up a token argument, Edie. I'm staying." He let his lips curve into a slight smile. "You know you want me to."

Reluctantly, she nodded. "As much as I hate to admit it, I really do."

His smile took full form. "Good. I'll take the sofa. Unless you want me closer?"

"The sofa will do."

"Yeah, it'll do," he said. "For tonight, anyway."

She let him pull her to her feet, and she laughed a little. "You say that as if you're planning to be here longer."

"Only till we catch this guy," he said.

She stopped in her tracks, blinking up at him. "But…but…"

"You can help me move my stuff in tomorrow." He leaned down, pressed a kiss to her forehead. "Don't thank me."

"Thank you? Look, Wade, it was great of you to come rushing over here and all, but there is no way in *hell* you're moving in."

He stood back just a little, facing her squarely. "Look, I hate to fight with you when you've had such a rough night, but you really don't have any choice in the matter. And really, when you think about it, it's the perfect solution. My place is sold. Thanks to you, so is the one I was planning to buy to replace it. By next weekend, I'll be bunking in the garage."

"Look, that's not my fault."

"It's *completely* your fault."

"That doesn't mean I'm obligated to provide you with a home."

"Far easier on me to just bunk here than to come running at all hours of the night. Hell, woman, you've seen the hazards on that road. I took it at eighty, risking my neck to get here as fast as humanly possible."

"And I'm grateful, but—"

"Besides, someone's after you. I'm not comfortable leaving you all alone up here until we make sure that maniac is behind bars."

"It's probably not even him," she argued.

"Great. If we find out it's not him, the deal's off. But until then, I'm staying."

"No," she said. "You're not."

He drew a deep breath, blew it out again. "Let's just wrap this thing up once and for all. Here are your choices." He held up fingers. "One, you let me tell Caleb and your family what's going on so they can help keep you safe." She was already shaking her head no when he unbent another finger. "Two, you report it to the sheriff and let him keep you safe, which will result in your family finding out anyway. Three, you call your old bodyguard and get him to come out here and protect you."

"He can't. His partner is sick. He can't leave now."

Wade ticked off another finger. "Four, you hire a new bodyguard."

"Right. There are so many of them in Big Falls, Oklahoma."

"Exactly. So what remains is choice number five. You settle for me."

She crossed her arms over her chest. "Where do you get off telling me what to do?"

"What, you have other options that I don't know about?"

"Yes, as a matter of fact, I do. Six, I get myself a great big dog. And take some self-defense classes and... and...and..."

"Catch the guy yourself?" he asked. He tilted his head to one side, studying her face.

"Well, why not?"

"Because you'd get yourself killed, that's why not. Look, if you want to learn self-defense moves, I think that's a great idea. I'll teach you. And if you want a big dog, well, hell, I *have* a big dog."

She lowered her head, sighing.

"So?"

Lifting her gaze, she met his eyes. "I'm not what you think I am, Wade Armstrong."

His frown was swift and deep. "And what do I think you are?"

"An airhead. An empty-headed ditz with a pretty face and a decent figure. And probably something of a slut to boot."

"Hold on, now." He held up both hands.

"I'm not."

He shook his head slowly. "No. You're certainly not. If you were, I'd have had you in the sack by now. Hell, woman, you've been home almost six months."

She turned away. "I don't like men who only see me for my looks and my body. And you're one of them."

"You think so?"

"I know so. The photos in the garage said it all."

"The ones in the bedroom say more."

"Pig."

He smiled. "That's my girl. Got her spirit back. Come on, I'll take you to bed." He took her hand.

She yanked it away, gaping at him.

"I meant, I'll walk you up to your room. Sheesh, get your mind out of the gutter, will you?"

"You're infuriating."

"I know." He walked beside her up the stairs to her bedroom, checked the closet and bathroom one more time, and then stepped to the door to leave. "I know something else, too," he said, one hand on the doorknob.

"What's that?"

"Your name was on the honor roll every marking period in high school. You didn't hang out with the brainy kids— did your best not to let it show—but you were one of them all the same. I *never* thought you were an airhead. Except when it came to your opinion of me." He opened the door, stepped through it. "Good night, Edie."

Then he closed it behind him.

Chapter 8

Despite the fact that she went to bed wondering just what he thought her opinion of him had been, Edie sank into sleep almost instantly, and she slept like a baby. When she woke to the sun streaming in through the uncurtained bedroom window, she wondered why that was. After the scare she'd had, she should have been jerking awake every hour or so. But she hadn't. Not once.

The idea whispered through her mind that maybe it was having Wade in the house that made her feel so safe. But she dismissed the thought as utterly ridiculous.

She wondered if he was awake yet. Was he up? Had he looked in on her while she was sleeping? For some reason, the idea of him standing over her bed in the dark, looking at her while she slept, sent a tingle up her spine. A forbidden one. Just like the ones she used to get in high school when the other girls talked about how dangerous he was. How experienced. How...*talented.*

She closed her eyes and told herself to knock it off. She

was a grown woman now, and she knew perfectly well
what kind of man he was. The kind who would date a
model because of her looks, only to dump her for someone
younger and prettier the minute she let her hair go gray or
put on a few pounds. The kind who couldn't see any
deeper than the surface. And just because he was still sexy
as hell didn't change that.

A soft tap came on her bedroom door, followed by his
voice. "You still in bed?"

"No, I'm up."

"Damn." The knob turned and the door opened. She
sat in her bed where she had just said she wasn't. "You
are such a liar," he said.

"Did you hear me invite you in?"

"No. Invite me louder next time."

She rolled her eyes. "I didn't invite you at all."

"Good thing I'm not a vampire, then." He grinned at
her, coming farther inside. "You know, you lied last night,
too. On the phone, when I asked you what you were wearing?"

She shrugged.

"That is not exactly an ugly flannel bathrobe," he said,
nodding at the white cotton robe she still wore. His eyes
burned her as they slid lower.

She looked down at herself and realized the robe was
gaping open, exposing bare skin from her neck to her na-
vel. The tie had loosened during the night. She grabbed it,
yanked it together. "Don't look too close, Wade. You'll
ruin your own illusions."

He smiled. "What do you mean?"

"Do you think I really look like those pictures all you
perverts drool over?"

"I do not drool on them," he said. He tipped his head

and looked up and to the left. "I *did* try licking one once, but the ink tasted terrible."

His words, though teasing, made a hot pool of lava form in her center. Damn him.

"Hey, I was kidding you. Come on, I'm not an idiot. I know those things are airbrushed and retouched. But if you're worried that seeing that little birthmark just below your belly button or the V-shaped scar on your collarbone is going to shatter my illusions, forget it. Real women aren't perfect, Edie. Makes 'em more interesting."

She blinked at him in shock. He'd only had a momentary glimpse of her body, but he seemed to have seen every visible detail in that glimpse.

"So are you gonna get up, or are you waiting for me to slide in there with you? I gotta tell you, I think I would enjoy exploring your body for other imperfections."

"I'm getting up. And you really should stop with the sexual innuendo."

He didn't reply, just stood there as she slid out of the bed and started for the bathroom. He said, "Hey." She paused, turning back around to face him. "If it really bugs you, I'll cut it out. I'm just playing with you, Edie. I'm nothing like that maniac who's—"

"I know that." She saw in his eyes that he really was bothered by the idea she might think that. Pursing her lips, she drew a breath and decided to give an inch here. The man had come to her rescue last night, after all. "I'll tell you something I haven't told another soul, Wade. I called my agent a month ago. I was still up in the air about what I wanted to do about my career." She lowered her head, shook it slowly, embarrassed to admit what she was about to. "It took me three days to get him on the phone. Three days of leaving messages he didn't return. And when I finally did make contact, he told me the renewal offer from

Vanessa's Whisper had been withdrawn. They found a hot young model to take my place. Then he told me my contract with his agency was being canceled, too.''

Wade lowered his head swiftly. "If I might offer an opinion here—they're out of their freaking minds."

She smiled. "I'm not a kid anymore, Wade. Hell, I've been modeling for over a decade. My age is starting to show. I cost them more, I'm willing to do less for it. My taking off without a word of warning and then dragging my feet on a decision about renewing with them was the last straw. I wasn't a hot enough commodity to be worth the trouble."

"Out of their freaking minds, and blind to boot," he put in.

She lowered her head. "It made me realize it was time for me to figure out if there really is more to me than my good looks. And even though I detest the fact that you don't seem to know or care if there is—"

"Hey, I never said—"

She held up a hand, and he went quiet. "Despite that, I have to admit, your lewd comments and constant flirting are the only things keeping my ego from being completely demolished right now."

He blinked. Then, slowly, a smile spread across his face. "Glad to be of service."

She shook her head at him. He looked more mischievous than she had ever seen him look, and a little bit too pleased with himself. "I'm gonna take a shower," she said.

"Great. You do that. I'll go get the whipped cream and be right in."

She rolled her eyes, went into the bathroom and closed the door.

The problem was, she really thought he was kidding.
The woman had no clue that he would quite possibly be

willing to drink her bathwater. Hell, up until very recently, he had been pretty much convinced that his attraction to her was purely physical, purely sexual, purely prurient.

He wasn't so sure anymore. Not since she had told him about this stalker of hers. His reaction had been powerful, and way over the top. He had actually caught himself thinking of Edie Brand as *his* obsession. How dare some other man fixate on her? Fantasize about her? She was *his* personal fantasy, and he didn't give a rat's backside how many glossy pages her body had graced.

The bastard was toast, whoever he was. His days were numbered. The thought of the guy putting his hands on her, holding a blade to her throat—well, hell, her story had shaken him more deeply than anything ever had. He hadn't known he was capable of the kind of feelings her words had stirred up in him.

So maybe there was a little bit more to his attraction to her than her body and the way it filled out a negligee. And maybe there always had been. Hell, there was the painting he kept hidden in his closet that no one—*no one*—had ever set eyes on besides himself and the artist who'd done it for him. He told himself at the time that it hadn't meant a thing. That it had been a whim.

Maybe he did care about more than the way she looked.

But he would be damned before he would admit that to her. She was still the same girl who'd held herself above him in high school, still the same girl who'd acted as if he was so far beneath her, he didn't even exist. He strongly suspected the second she got a clue he might have feelings for her that were more than sexual, she would throw him out like yesterday's fish.

So he would just keep that to himself. No sense making himself a target.

He heard the shower running, and his mouth went dry and his eyes slammed closed, his mind conjuring a picture of her standing naked under the spray. He pictured the water jetting powerfully from the spigot, hitting her breasts, making her nipples pebble. He would give a limb to go in there and lick them dry.

He was going to have that woman. Even if she had to believe it was a one-night stand with nothing more involved, he was going to have her. Oh, yes, he was. Or die with a hard on.

He walked closer to the bathroom door, leaned close to it and listened. And after a while, he said, "Hey, Edie?"

Her movements stopped. But the water kept running. "You can't come in, Wade. The door's locked."

"You could unlock it."

She was silent for so long he knew she was thinking about it. Then he heard her moving again, returning her attention to her shower without even replying to his suggestion. But she'd heard him. And he wondered just how close she had come to turning the lock before she had chickened out.

He pulled his Explorer to a stop in the gravel road in front of the Brand family farmhouse. She looked at him, shaking her head. "I still don't think this is necessary. It's daylight now. No one would try anything in broad daylight."

He looked at her steadily, serious for once. "Up there, in the middle of nowhere, it might as well be night all the time. I have stuff to do at my place, not to mention the garage, and I wouldn't be able to do it if I knew you were up there alone all day, Edie. Just humor me, okay?"

She shook her head, narrowing her eyes on him. "You aren't at all who you pretend to be."

"No?"

"No," she said. "You're almost...heroic."

"Hell, woman, I'm just trying to keep you alive long enough to get you into bed. After that, you can do what you want."

He always had to ruin it, didn't he? She sighed and, turning, opened the passenger door and got out. Before she closed it again, he said, "Don't go back there alone, okay?"

She looked at his face for a long moment. "Okay."

"I'll call you later. Keep the phone on you."

She nodded. "See you later." Closing the door, she hurried across the lawn to her family's house, opened the back door and stepped right on inside. The crew came in from the living room when they heard her. Edie looked from their curious expressions to the still-warm breakfast on the table and knew they'd been watching her through the front windows.

"So, why are you riding with Wade Armstrong this morning?" Kara asked with a lilt in her voice as she slid into her chair. Mel took the seat beside her and lifted her brows innocently as she watched Edie and awaited her answer. Selene lingered in the doorway but seemed pensive. Vidalia, of course, marched straight to the cupboard for another plate, filled it and set it on the table, instructing Edie to dig in.

Edie sighed, lowering her head and turning away from them all on the pretense of getting herself a cup of coffee. "My car had a blowout last night. No big deal, but I skidded on it for a little ways, and it damaged the rim. Wade had to tow it to his shop last night."

"Last night?" Vidalia asked. She blinked three times and stared at Edie. "And he's still with you this morning."

"I didn't say 'still.' Stop jumping to conclusions, Mom."

She lifted her brows higher, noting, no doubt, that Edie didn't deny it.

"Actually, though, he did make a proposition that I think I'm going to take him up on."

"I didn't *think* it would take Wade very long to get around to propositioning you," Mel said, elbowing Kara beside her and laughing.

"It's not like that at all," Edie lied. She carried her coffee to the table and sat down. "The thing is, he sold his house. He can't get out of the deal, and because of me buying the place he planned to buy himself, he has nowhere to go."

They said nothing. The four of them simply stared at her. Even Selene snapped out of whatever had been distracting her and came closer to listen.

"And, while I've been there, I've found several things that need some work in the house. Loose floorboard, some tricky wiring in the basement, the gutters. Stuff like that." She shrugged. "And it *is* a huge place for one person."

Four sets of eyebrows rose.

"He's going to rent the spare bedroom from me for a couple of weeks. Just until he finds a place of his own. And while he's there, he's offered to help out with the odd jobs."

"Well, I'll be dipped in—" Mel broke off at a sharp glance from her mother.

Vidalia looked at Edie again. "Do you have any idea how that's going to look to folks around here?"

Edie blinked. "Mom, I've spent the last ten years posing for an underwear catalogue. Are you really worried about my reputation?"

"Don't you sass me," her mother snapped. The woman might be dead wrong, but she would never admit it.

"I think it's kind of sweet," Kara said. "He's always had a crush on you, Edie. Why, if you could see his garage—"

"Kara!" Vidalia warned.

Edie shook her head. "No need, Mom. I saw the garage last night. And I made him take all those pictures down. He even apologized."

Vidalia's eyes widened. Mel said, "Someone call Hell, will you? Ask if it's frozen over."

"Melusine Brand, you watch your mouth." Vidalia sighed in exasperation. "And as for you, Edain—you are keeping secrets. Now, you're a grown-up woman, and it's your right to keep your private things private, but you ought to know by now that you cannot fool your mother. I know when something's wrong, and I know something's wrong right now."

"Mom…"

She snapped up a stop-sign hand. "Don't you talk to me anymore until you're ready to tell me the truth." Vidalia got up from the table and strode out of the room.

Edie got up to go after her, but Selene came forward, stopping her. "Let her have her fit. It'll make her feel better. You just drink your coffee and relax."

Sighing, looking through the doorway in the direction her mother had gone, she finally obeyed. "Just so you all know, there's nothing going on between Wade Armstrong and me."

Not yet, at least, her mind added, startling her so much she almost gasped aloud.

Selene was looking at her in that way she had. "Something is wrong, though. Mom's right about that, isn't she?"

Edie sighed and reached out to take her sister's hand.

"I'm fine. I promise." She looked at the other two, who were staring at Selene in alarm, and realized she needed to change the subject. "I need a crew of volunteers today to help me get my house in order. It's a royal mess. Who wants to help?"

Selene nodded hard, and Mel and Kara, too. Kara said, "Caleb said to tell you to just call him if you need any grunt work done. He has a light schedule at the office today."

"Great. That's great." She sipped her coffee faster, eager to get busy on her house, and knowing full well she would be safe with a crowd of sisters around her.

Hours later, they collapsed on various pillows and cushions in what would be the living room, when it had actual furniture. The place was finally taking shape. The telephone company had sent a man out to turn on the service. And Edain had figured out where her studio would be—in the area that had been designated a den or study. Like the living room, it had towering windows, but unlike it, it was closed off from the rest of the house. There was a door off the foyer that led right into it, too. She liked the idea of having some boundaries between business and home.

Even more, she liked the idea that she was beginning to look forward to getting this project under way.

Selene was perched in the room's only chair—a bowl-shaped rattan frame with a huge circular cushion of brown velvet. She sat at the chair's edge, because to lean back was to fall into the piece. It was a chair for snuggling into with a soft blanket and a good book. And Selene wasn't in a snuggling mood. She was tense, her face drawn.

"Well, sis," Mel said, "everything's put away, and the boxes are stacked in the garage. Until your sexy new housemate brings his own load of junk over, there's not a lot more to be done.''

"He was going to bring a load tonight," Edie replied, not even bothering to argue over the "sexy" comment. He was. It was an indisputable fact.

"You ought to help him, Edie," Kara suggested. "Heck, he worked his tail off helping us move your stuff."

"He's probably still at the shop," Edie said.

Mel shook her head. "Nah, it closes at five. It's almost six already. And you know, it is kind of sad to think of him over there in that cracker-box house of his, packing all by himself. I mean, after all the help he was to us," she added.

"I'm all for it if it will get us out of here," Selene said softly.

They all looked at her. Kara seemed about to ask, so Edie interrupted. Mostly because she was afraid to have them all hear whatever Selene's answer would be. She was too perceptive. "So you want to drive over to Wade's place? Is that what you're saying?" she asked her sisters. "I'd have thought you'd be all in by now."

"Shoot," Mel said. "That wasn't anything. You'd think L.A. had made you soft to hear you talk now."

She shrugged. "Doesn't Mom need your help at the bar? What did she say when you called home earlier, Kara?"

"Maya and Caleb are helping her tonight," Kara explained with a smile. "Caleb's dad is playing grandpa/baby-sitter and loving every second of it."

"Let's get going, then." Selene got to her feet, pacing toward the door. "We should take both vehicles," she added, looking Edie right in the eye. "You can ride with me in the car."

"Sure." She knew she was in for it. Selene had that look in her eyes.

"Mel and I will follow along in the pickup, then. Selene, you know where Wade lives, right?"

"Yeah, Kara. I know. Come on, Edie. And be sure to lock up behind us."

They all trooped out and piled into the vehicles. The moment Selene had fastened her seat belt and started the engine of the compact car she drove, she turned and met Edie's eyes. "So who's been in that house?"

Edie didn't meet her eyes. "Lots of people. Me, Wade, the whole family, the real estate woman, anyone and everyone she's shown the house to, the previous owners, the phone company guy...."

"And that's all? You're sure?"

Edie nodded, pasting a false smile on her face. "Why, sis? You picking up strange vibrations? Think I have a ghost or something?"

Selene put the car into motion, shaking her head. "I don't know. There's something... It feels just like what I felt in our house the other night. As if someone had been there. Someone...messy."

"Messy?" She studied her sister's face. "I promise, Selene, the mess in that house was all mine."

"That's not what I mean. Emotionally messy. It's like someone walked through the place just dripping every feeling all over the place. Like tracking mud through the house."

"Emotional mud." Edie tilted her head. "Interesting concept."

"Don't humor me, Edie. And don't act like nothing's going on. We all know you're keeping something from us."

That brought Edie's head around. "Now you sound just like Mom. So do you want to tell me what you mean by that?"

"Just what I said. It doesn't take an empath to see that something is going on with you. Mom thinks we should leave you alone, let you work through it. No one else thinks it's anything all that serious. But I think..."

She stopped there, biting her lip, focusing on the road.

"You think what, Selene?"

Selene licked her lips. "I think you're in danger, Edie. I don't want to scare you, but I doubt I will, since I think you already know it." She turned to look Edie in the eye again.

Edie held her gaze for a moment. Then she finally had to let her own fall.

"That's why Wade's moving in, isn't it?"

Rolling her eyes, sighing, Edie said, "Look, this is nothing for you to worry about. I don't want the family involved, Selene, so whatever you think you know, you need to keep quiet about it."

Selene pursed her lips, and her hands gripped the wheel a little too tightly. "I'm glad Wade's there. He's good, you know. Everyone thinks he's so mean, so tough, so scary. But he is so far from those things it's almost laughable."

Edie lowered her head. "You know him that well?"

"No."

"Then how can you be so sure about his character?"

Selene smiled softly. "I saw him pull over one rainy night to rescue a puppy from a runoff ditch. The poor thing would've drowned. He didn't know anyone saw, of course. He tucked the little dog inside his coat just as I pulled up behind his truck to see if he needed help or anything." She shook her head slowly. "You should have seen him. He waved me off and got in his truck as if nothing was happening. He had no idea I'd seen the whole thing."

Edie licked her lips. "He...has a puppy?"

"Well, not exactly a puppy anymore. I mean, it was two years ago."

"He did mention a dog."

"More like a small horse, but whatever." They drove through town and turned onto Oak Street just past Wade's garage on Main. "It's right over here."

He was sitting in the kitchen nursing a cup of hot, strong coffee, with a half-filled box of dishes in front of him. He'd been having second thoughts about hauling them to Edie's place. She probably had plenty of dishes of her own. She probably had plenty of everything of her own, if the number of boxes he'd helped haul over there for her was any indication. Maybe he should just put the bulk of his stuff in storage.

A heavy head bumped his shoulder as he tried to take a sip of coffee, sending hot spatters over his hand, and he looked down into the huge brown eyes and long, speckled face of his best girl. "What do you think? Huh, Sally?"

"Raou-roo-ra." She answered him in that Great Dane speak of hers. It sounded most of the time as if she were speaking in complete, if garbled, sentences. She spoke several more lines, and he grinned and rubbed her head. "What? Timmy's in the well?" he asked.

"Ree-raw!" She loped toward the front door, her tail swinging around like a wrecking ball, and nearly took out his coffee cup. He lifted it out of the way just in time. Then he got to his feet to follow her.

Two vehicles pulled up. One behind his in the driveway and the other alongside the road, since the driveway was full up. He recognized them both. And the women inside them. The Brand babes had come to pay him a visit. And his favorite one of the bunch was with them.

He scratched Sally's head, and she danced excitedly.

Her head was high enough so she could see clearly out the glass upper portion of his front door without even craning her neck. "Guess she just couldn't stand to be away from me a minute longer," he told the dog.

She looked up at him, and if she'd had eyebrows, they would have been arched.

"Now, you stay," he told her firmly. She nodded, he thought, and sat obediently beside him. He opened the door. "What's this, the welcoming committee?"

Selene looked troubled and pensive, but she smiled a fake smile. She was a pretty thing, with her silvery-blond hair and angelic face. Mel and Kara got out of the pickup. Mel, with her deceptively pixielike frame and short dark hair, looked harmless. Many a man had found out otherwise, though. And Kara was so tall and lean she could have been a model like her sister, though she didn't seem as graceful.

His eyes brushed over all of them but fixed on Edain and, once there, seemed stuck. He couldn't look away.

She looked tired, a little tense, and she was looking at him a little differently, he thought. As if seeing something she hadn't before. She hadn't bothered with makeup today, he noted. Ponytail, jeans. Her gaze shifted down slightly to the dog at his side, and she suddenly smiled in a mushy way.

"Awwwww." She crouched a little.

Sally took her cue, springing forward like a linebacker at the snap. He tried to shout a warning, but there wasn't time. Sally hit, and Edie went right down on her backside. Wade tensed, lunging forward. But Edie's arms were around the dog's neck by then, and Sally was nuzzling her face and talking to her. As he watched, slightly amazed, Edie took the dog's face between her hands and looked her right in the eyes. "You sure do have a lot to say, don't you, girl? What's your name, huh?"

"Uh, she's Sally. And she's a little bit on the clumsy side."

"It's 'cause she's so tall," Kara said, speaking from experience.

"It's because she's young and hasn't learned how to manage her long, elegant limbs just yet. That's all," Edie corrected. He saw the look she sent her gangly sister and knew there had been a message there for her.

"So what are you all doing here?" he asked.

Edie got to her feet, brushed her hands over the seat of her pants, an action that had him riveted, and said, "We've come to help you move."

"Yep. We owe you one," Kara said with a smile.

"More than one," Selene added, but she didn't elaborate, even when he sent her a questioning glance.

He was more than surprised. But not being one to deny a gorgeous woman entry to his home—much less four of them—he held the door wide and waved them in. "Help yourself to coffee, if you need fortification before we get under way," he said. "To tell you the truth, I'm glad you're here. I was just debating how much I actually need to move in and how much I should just store."

"Move it all in," Selene said.

Edie sent her a look.

She shrugged innocently. "What? It's a huge place, and while you have truckloads of stuff, your actual supply of practical household equipment is sadly lacking. I have no idea how you got along in L.A." She glanced at Wade. "She doesn't even have a coffeepot."

"I was rarely home in L.A. And when I was, I drank instant."

Wade made a face. "Oh, woman, you are a sad case.

Fill your cups, ladies. That coffeepot is going to be the first thing I pack, so get to work emptying it.''

Mel laughingly obliged, filling a cup she found in the cupboard, passing it to Kara, then reaching for another. Then she peered around the corner into his living room. "Oh, boy. Oh, man, that is sweet."

Wade followed her gaze to his big-screen TV, his pride and joy, and nodded. "Yeah. You can't watch Monday Night Football on anything else after having one of these babies." He saw Edie grimace and hastily added, "Uh, and you can't beat it for, uh, sappy, emotional chick-flicks, either."

"Chick-flicks?" Edie asked, brows raised.

"I have a satellite dish," he attempted, and when that didn't seem to get her excited, he added, "It carries that women's network thing."

"Oh, well, in that case..." She shook her head and looked down at Sally, who was, Wade noticed, still sticking tight to her side. That was odd. His dog usually stuck to him like glue. Sighing, he slugged back his coffee, rinsed his cup and stuck it into the box of dishes on the table. "Let's get this show on the road, then, shall we?"

They each tipped up their cups and followed his lead, although, he noted, they didn't just set them in the box. Selene looked around until she found a newspaper, then yanked it to pieces, wrapping his cups in the pages. He thought it was overkill. They were cups, not the Hope diamond. It wasn't that far to Edie's house, and if a few broke on the way, it would be no great loss.

Whatever.

"Let's load the big stuff," Mel said, starting toward his TV. "We want to take extra-special care with this baby."

He got a little quiver in the pit of his stomach. If someone had told him six months ago that come May he would be moving in with the woman he had spent the last ten years fantasizing about, he would have told them they were nuts.

But it was happening. He was moving in with Edie Brand. The girl who'd always been too good for him—in her eyes, at least. Hell, maybe if he could fix this little problem for her, she would realize he was up to her standards after all.

He gave himself a shake. Yeah, right, but who was to say he even *wanted* her to? he asked himself. She would probably fall into his arms in abject gratitude once he put her stalker away. And then, he thought, *he* would reject *her*. Oh, it would be sweet to give her a taste of her own medicine after all this time.

Right, a little voice in his head whispered in a cynical tone. *Sure you will.*

Wade and Mel were carrying the big-screen TV out to the truck, and Kara and Selene were packing dishes from his cupboards. So Edie took the opportunity to do what she had been dying to do since they had pulled up out front.

It was his fault. She refused to feel guilty for snooping. He was the one who kept taunting her about the pictures of her plastered all over his bedroom. She had to see for herself.

She slipped through the hallway, opening the first door she came to, only to see a room filled with exercise equipment. It was as good as a gym, with weights and a bench, a Nautilus machine, a treadmill, and a punching bag hanging from the ceiling. Wow. Where the hell were they going to put all this stuff? She thought of the room above the attached garage, the one she had no clue what to do with.

It was big, roomy, wide open and airy. It would make a great exercise room.

Stepping back, she pulled the door closed. Sally nudged her hand until she petted the dog's head, then accompanied her to the door across the hall. Edie opened the door.

Wade Armstrong's bedroom was small, neat, not too imaginative. A bed, a dresser, a trunk, a closet, a mirror. There was a chair with a pair of jeans slung over the back of it, a hamper in the corner with clothes draping over its sides as if tossed there from across the room. And next to the bed, a small nightstand. She skimmed the walls for magazine pages with Scotch tape at the corners and saw none. He *had* been lying. He didn't have any pictures of her in his bedroom. She turned to go, then stopped and turned back again, her eye caught by something on the dressing table.

Slowly, she moved closer, eyes narrowing on the five by seven color photo in the little gold frame. It sat between the alarm clock and the telephone. It was of her, and it had been taken more than ten years ago, at the senior prom. She'd been sixteen. She had gone with Matt McConnell, and he had tried to feel her up every time he got close enough.

A little sigh whispered out of her as she stared at the photo, wondering where he'd managed to find a copy. She and Matt had had shots taken by the photographer who had been there, and this looked like one of them, only Matt wasn't in it. It looked as if it had been professionally altered. Moving closer, she lifted the frame and squinted at the photo, and realized that was exactly what had been done.

She closed her eyes, recalling her mother's words at the saloon last night. *He wanted to ask you to the prom, you*

*know. He called me, asked permission. He made me prom-
ise never to tell....*

She heard the front door and blinked away the inexplicable moisture that had gathered in her eyes. Quickly replacing the photo, she hurried out of his bedroom into the
hall, pulled the door closed behind her and started down
the hall.

He caught her before she had taken two steps. "What
are you doing back here?" he asked, sounding for all the
world as if it were an unimportant question.

"Checking out your weight room," she replied, hoping
he couldn't see in her eyes the discovery she had just
made.

"Oh. Hey, don't think I plan to clutter up your place
with all that."

"Are you kidding me? I may have given up modeling
for a living, Wade, but some habits are harder to break.
I've been driving clear to the Tucker Lake YMCA three
times a week."

"Yeah?" He looked surprised.

"Yeah. I was thinking that room above the garage
would be perfect. What do you think about that?"

He nodded. "Sounds great. But, uh, you know, it's up
to you. It's your house." He shrugged, trying to hide the
pleasure that she saw anyway. "Besides, I won't be there
all that long."

Those words pricked her just a little, made her flinch.
She wondered about that. It was an odd reaction. "Well,
we might as well enjoy all your cool possessions while
you are there."

"I have a water bed," he said, regaining his composure.

"It didn't—" She bit her lip, cut herself off. She'd almost blurted that it hadn't looked like a water bed. But
she didn't want him to know she'd been snooping in his

bedroom. "Very funny, Wade." She tipped her head to one side. "Do you really have a water bed? That's such a cliché."

He shrugged. "No. I have a normal bed. But, hey, if you had taken the bait, I would have had one by morning."

She was supposed to be offended, she knew. But deep down, she was thinking this guy liked her. He had always liked her and never let her know it. But now she knew his secret. And maybe it wasn't just a sexual thing or he wouldn't keep that prom picture in his room. He would have half-naked pictures of her all over the place instead, wouldn't he?

Was it possible, she wondered, that Wade Armstrong really was still nursing a crush on her? And why did the idea make her feel almost giddy?

Chapter 9

He was amazed at how quickly the packing and moving operation went with the help of the beautiful Brand sisters. Two pickup loads took care of the large items, and the smaller stuff fit into Selene's tiny trunk and back seat, and his own SUV. Sally sat on the passenger seat beside him on the last trip up the winding mountain road. Oh, he had a few more things to do. Odds and ends to retrieve. One final polish to slap on the place before Tommy and Sue moved in. But for the most part, his cracker-box house was empty.

Sally looked at him and mumbled in her row-roo-rah manner as if asking a question.

"I know, it's kind of scary. But it's a nice place. Lots of room. I don't get the feeling Edie's gonna be all squeamish about a few dog hairs on the furniture. And if we play our cards right, I might get lucky."

She barked. A short, sharp woof that sounded vaguely scolding.

"Oh, yeah, this from the woman I caught trying to hump the neighbor's poodle that summer before the operation."

She lowered her head. Sometimes he got the distinct impression she understood every word.

"Sorry, girl. I know I promised I'd never bring that up." He petted her head, and she leaned over to lick his ear, a sure sign he was forgiven. "Look, we'll only be at Edie's place until we get rid of the idiot who's harassing her. By then, I'll have found us a perfect place all our own. With a big yard where you can run till your heart's content. Okay?"

They pulled into the driveway, and he stopped the vehicle. Mel was backing the pickup into position near the front door, and he parked out of the way. He got out, and Sally didn't even wait for him to come around and open her door. She just lunged across the seat and out his. She hit the ground and loped to the smaller car, just as Edie and Selene were getting out of it. It was a comical sight, his giant dog standing beside that tiny car.

Edie smiled at her. "Here we are, girl. What do you think?"

The dog looked toward the house, then back at Edie again. Then she loped away at a full gallop, stretching her legs and really letting loose.

Edie glanced at Wade, her eyes alarmed. He held up a hand. "Not to worry. She'll be back. She tends to run in loops. The bigger the better."

He kept his eye on things until Sally had lapped the house and returned to the driveway to sit beside Edie again as if nothing unusual had happened.

"Too many woods around here," Kara said. She was lowering the pickup's tailgate and climbing aboard. "You should put up a fence to keep her from going too far."

"Just so long as it's a big one. A dog like that needs room to run," Selene put in.

"Hey, let's get a key over here, huh?" Mel called. "We can have doggie discussions later."

Edie stopped petting the dog and dug her keys out of her pocket, tossing them to her sister. Mel caught them, turned and unlocked the door.

They carried in furniture piece by piece. His bed frame and headboard went up the stairs into the room where he had found Edie hiding the night before. Every time he thought about someone having been in this house with her, he got angry all over again. There was one part of his brain telling him it might not even have been real. That she might have imagined the entire thing. But most of him believed her. She hadn't imagined that open front door, and it would be pretty tough, he thought, to forget to close it. Lock it, maybe, but not to close it.

It was eleven-thirty.

The living area of the big house was once again cluttered with furniture and boxes. The sisters were in the kitchen, drinking soda, ready to call it a night. His refrigerator stood now where there had been none before. He picked up the box of items taken from his bedroom, the box he did not want Edie to see, along with the large flat one that *no one* could see, and carried them upstairs. He took the big flat box into the bedroom and slid it under his bed. Then he carried the smaller one, the one that contained the old issues of the catalogue he just couldn't bear to part with, down the hall, to the smaller set of steps that led up to the attic. She probably hadn't even been up there yet. Not as nervous as she had been. Glancing behind him briefly, he saw no one. So he climbed the attic steps.

At the top he found a light switch, flicked it on. The attic was as dingy and dusty and full of cobwebs as an attic should be. It was also empty, except for one cardboard box that wasn't dust covered. It hadn't been up there long enough to be.

Wade set his own box down and, frowning, moved toward the other one. Could it be that Edie, too, had a box of belongings she didn't want anyone else to see? He licked his lips, wondering just how many commandments he was breaking as he reached out, tugged the lid open.

He realized what the box held at the first glance. The item on top was a black vinyl hood, its only opening a round one at the mouth. That opening could be sealed, though, with the large red ball dangling from a strap hanging to one side. A buckle on the other side would fasten it in place.

This, he realized, must be the box that held the "gifts" Edie had received from her stalker.

Swallowing bile, he moved the mask aside and looked beneath it. Countless leather straps and buckles filled the box. He didn't take them out one by one to determine their uses. Some were restraints; some were articles of clothing. There was an assortment of paddles and whips in the box, along with sex toys of various sizes and shapes. The handcuffs were there. At the bottom he saw a stack of envelopes and knew the letters the man had written would be inside them.

"Where did Wade go?" Edie asked, glancing into the living area and toward the stairs.

"I think he went upstairs," Mel said, sipping her Mountain Dew. "Probably getting his bed set up so he can get some sleep tonight."

Kara sent Edie an innocent look. "You sure do keep a close eye on him, sis."

"She doesn't like him too far away," Mel put in. "Not that I can blame her."

The three of them laughed softly, though Selene's smile was tainted by the worry in her eyes. "I'm glad he's here," she said. "I don't like the idea of you up here all alone."

"I managed in big, bad Los Angeles all alone, Selene. I think I can handle Big Falls."

Selene didn't look convinced. "Well, still, I didn't sleep at all last night. I kept getting this awful feeling you were in trouble. And I can tell you right now, if I didn't know Wade was going to be here with you tonight, I wouldn't leave at all."

Edie smiled and lowered her head to see Sally, lying at her feet, almost *on* her feet. "Not just Wade, either, but his faithful companion here."

"A pair of heroes, aren't they?" Kara asked, looking down. "Just like Batman and Robin."

"Robin Hood and Little John," Mel said.

"Scylla and Charybdis," Selene put in.

They all sent her a look, and she shrugged innocently.

"We'd better go. It's late, and Mom's going to want a full report." Mel rolled her eyes and stood up as if girding her loins. "I'll be sure and tell her there are separate bedrooms. And I'll make it a point to mention how hard Wade was working to get his bed put together in time to sleep on it."

"You think it'll help?" Edie asked.

"Not really."

Edie got to her feet to walk her sisters to the front door. Sally was on her feet, too, and keeping pace. She walked so close to Edie's side she brushed against her thigh with every step. They stood at the door, watching Selene's car and Mel's pickup pull away, and then Sally looked up at

Edie and spoke what sounded like a complete sentence, probably a question, only in her own language.

"You need to go outside before we turn in, girl?"

At the word "outside" the dog sprang out the door. Edie ran after her, worried she might take off into the woods in spite of Wade's confidence that she wouldn't.

The dog loped around to the rear of the house, and Edie ran to keep up. Out back Sally ran the length of the lawn and back, then ran it again, before she finally stopped running laps and started sniffing around in the underbrush. She chose a bush and squatted underneath it. Edie shook her head and politely averted her eyes.

Something moved in the trees off to Edie's left. She went stiff, her head swinging around sharply. But she saw nothing.

It was dark, the only light coming from the crescent moon, bigger than last night, but not by much. Stars dotted the cloudless sky. Glittering.

A deep growling sound made her blood run cold, until she realized it was coming from right beside her. Sally had returned to Edie's side and, apparently, knew something was wrong. She was looking right at the spot where Edie thought she'd seen something.

Swallowing hard, Edie reached down and closed her hand on the dog's collar. "Come on, Sally. Let's just go back inside. Come on, girl."

She tried backing a few steps away, but the dog didn't cooperate. She pulled harder. "By God, you're strong. Come on, girl, please? Let's just go. It's probably a porcupine or...or a skunk or something."

The dog seemed to ease her stance a little. Edie pulled her toward the house. Then the thing in the brush moved once more, and Sally jumped forward so hard and so fast that Edie went down to her knees. She tried to hold on, but the dog yanked her collar, and some of Edie's skin, free and loped into the woods.

"Sally!" Edie cried. "Wade, get out here! Hurry up!"

The letters started out kinky. Then demanding. Then angry. And then they got brutal. Apparently when Edie hadn't done what her admirer told her to do—things like wear a certain item he'd sent to her at some public appearance or other—as a sign of her submission to his control, he had reacted with anger. His demands grew more preposterous with each letter. He would tell her to do things like take off her top and walk to a certain window in her house at a specific time of day, so he could look at her. And then the threats began. She hadn't obeyed. She'd worn a bra when he'd forbidden it. She hadn't put on the slave collar he bought for her to show her subservience to him. He was going to punish her now. To "break her," as he put it. The final letter, the most recent one, was the most frightening of all.

So close tonight, my pet. So close to you, and yet the bodyguard you hired to keep me from you interrupted. I wouldn't want to have to hurt him. The way I'm going to hurt you. The longer you elude me, the worse it will be when I finally get my hands on you, princess. I must mark you. I must disfigure you in a way that will remind you always of the consequences of rebelling against me. Perhaps a finger. Just one. The small one, I think. I'll put it on a chain and wear it around my neck, so you know who owns you. Be sure to keep your nails done for me, my pretty. And wear a ring, a special ring, on your little finger. The right hand, yes? You are right-handed. Yes. When I come to you, when I find you, I will bring my sharpest blade. And I'll slice off your little finger. And then you'll know. Then you'll know.

Evade me once more, my sweet, and I'll be forced to add to your punishment.

Wade felt his stomach turning, his blood boiling as he returned the letter to its envelope and the envelope to the box.

He heard Edie's voice then. Not everything she said, just two words—"Wade!" and "Hurry."

Wade Armstrong exploded out the back door of the house, shot across the lawn, snapped his powerful arms around her waist and pulled her off her feet. When he set her down again, a split second later, a large tree was at her back, and Wade turned, putting his back in front of her. He stood there with his arms slightly bent and held out at his sides, his feet wide apart, knees bent, his head turning slowly as he scanned the forest around them. "Where is he? Where is the son of a—" He broke off sharply, glancing over his shoulder at her. "Are you all right? Are you hurt?" His gaze slid down her body and skidded to a halt at her hand, where his eyes widened. Whirling, he gripped her wrist, lifting her hand, and that was when she saw the blood. "Oh sweet God, he didn't—"

"It's nothing." She turned her hand over, showing him where the skin had been scraped and how the creases of her fingers bled just slightly.

His gaze rose, locked onto hers. My God, the emotions racking him right now were enough to knock her flat. He was white. He was shaking. He looked like he was going to be sick. And she knew what he thought.

"Wade, it was just Sally. I called you because she took

off into the woods. I tried to hold her collar, and when she pulled free she took a little skin with her. That's all."

His lips parted, but only air came out. He closed his eyes slowly, opened them again, and looked marginally better. One hand rose to press itself to the tree trunk just beyond her head, and he leaned into it, letting his head fall forward. "You scared the life out of me. So there was no one out here?"

"There was…something out here." She was looking at the top of his head, until he brought it up slowly, his eyes questioning. "Something moved in the woods, over this way. I thought I was imagining it, until Sally started growling and snarling. I tried to pull her back, just get her into the house, but she pulled free and went charging off after it."

He wasn't so relaxed anymore. His spine straightened, and he looked around again, eyes wary and alert. "Which way?"

She pointed.

He aimed in that direction, put two fingers to his lips and cut loose with an ear-splitting whistle. "Sally! Come!" he shouted. Then he whistled again.

"Well, that ought to do it," Edie muttered. "Any crazed killer in the vicinity will know right where we are."

"No crazed killer could outrun that dog for more than a few yards. If it were a human she was chasing, we'd be able to hear the both of them from here. Him screaming and her chewing." He sent her a sidelong glance, a little smile. "Which would be a picnic compared to what I'd do to him."

The imagery made her feel better. His protectiveness made her feel…something else. "I didn't think Sally had a mean bone in her body," she said, deciding to address the dog's reactions instead of Wade's. "Until I heard her growling, at least."

"She's as friendly as a pup," he said. "But she's incredibly protective, too. And she's taken to you."

"That's good to know." Edie swallowed, wondering if Wade had "taken to her," as well. Was that why he'd come out here with fire in his eyes, looking like some battle-crazed berserker?

He wasn't looking at her now. He was looking into the woods, calling his dog.

Eventually she came loping through the underbrush, but she stopped every now and then to lower her nose to the ground and brush at it with her forepaws. Frowning, Wade hurried toward her and dropped down onto his haunches. Edie followed when she heard him cussing under his breath.

Porcupine quills were sticking out of Sally's snout. "Oh, no!" Edie said. "Oh, poor girl. Poor baby." She stroked the dog's head and spoke softly.

"We'll need a vet. Poor damn dog," Wade muttered. He sounded heartsick. It touched her that he cared so much for the animal.

"In the morning. We can take care of the worst of it tonight," Edie said. "Come on, let's get her into the house."

They urged the dog inside. But something made Edie keep looking back over her shoulder. She didn't think it had been a porcupine lingering in the bushes out back. She'd felt something before she'd ever heard the bushes moving. A presence. Eyes on her.

Hell.

They coaxed Sally up the stairs and into Edie's bedroom, mainly because her bathroom supplies would be nearby. The poor dog whined and spoke in long rambling sentences about how badly her nose hurt, while Edie located an old, soft blanket and made her a bed on the floor. Then she looked up at Wade. "A pair of pliers. Just small ones."

He looked her in the eye, shook his head. "No. No way am I letting you rip those things out of my dog with a pair of pliers."

"Easy, Wade. Come on, I've done this a dozen times. When we were kids we had this coon dog who just wouldn't leave the porkies alone. He came home every other week all summer with a snout full of quills. I know what I'm doing here."

"It's going to hurt her."

"Not as much as you think. And we'll never get a vet to see her tonight. It's past eleven. You don't want her to have to suffer all night with those things in her snout, do you?"

He was sitting on the floor now, legs crossed, Sally's head resting on his lap. "You sure you know what you're doing?"

She nodded. "Just stay there. She's comfortable. Tell me where the pliers are and I'll get them."

He opened his mouth, then closed it again and gently slid himself out from under the dog. She whined in protest, but he soothed her. "They're out in the garage. I don't want you out there alone. I'll get them."

She nodded and watched him go. While he was gone, she gathered everything else she would need. A bowl of warm water and a soft cloth, some triple antibiotic ointment, a pair of scissors.

When he returned, he sat beside the dog, noticing the way her head was now resting on a pillow, sending Edie a look but not commenting.

"Now, she's not going to like it, but it won't hurt as much as she'll think it will. You'll have to hold her head."

Sighing, he put a hand on either side of the Great Dane's big head. She looked from him to Edie with trusting brown eyes.

"The thing with quills," Edie said, gently putting her fingers at the base of one to keep it from pulling as she worked. "Is that they're hollow, like straws. That makes a kind of vacuum." Holding the quill at its base, she lifted the scissors and snipped off the end. Sally flinched at the sound. "They come out much easier if you break the vacuum by snipping off the ends." She moved to the next quill, and the next. The dog flinched each time, but didn't fight or seem to be hurting any more than she had been already. When the quills were snipped, eight of them in all, it was time for the hard part. "Now this is gonna hurt a bit more, but I'll be quick. Hold her firmly, Wade."

He held the dog. Edie exchanged the scissors for the pliers and quickly plucked each quill from Sally's snout. She kept her fingers on the skin to keep from pulling unnecessarily. Sally whimpered at each tug but didn't cry out at all. When it was done, Edie took the soft, warm cloth from the basin of water and gently cleansed the dog's wounded snout. Tiny beads of blood welled from most of the punctures. She warmed the cloth once more and this time just let it rest over the sore, tender areas. "There, now, doesn't that feel better? Hmm?"

Sally sighed, her eyes falling closed as the warm, wet cloth soothed her pain away.

Edie looked up at Wade, and he quickly averted his eyes. But not in time. She saw how wet they were. The man was moved nearly to tears by seeing his dog suffer. She could barely believe it.

He reached past her for the ointment and lifted the wash-

cloth long enough to daub some of it gently over each
wound. Then he wrapped gauze around Sally's snout.
"Just until the ointment has time to soak in a bit, girl,"
he promised. "I won't leave you muzzled all night. Can
you stand it for an hour, do you think?"

She opened her eyes to look at him as he spoke, sighed
loudly and lay back down again.

"She's feeling loads better already," Edie said.

"You're right, she is."

Edie dropped the cloth into the basin, picked up the
scissors and ointment and gauze, and got to her feet with
her arms loaded.

Wade got to his feet, as well, took several items from
her, and led the way into the bathroom. At the sink, he
dumped the water, cleaned the basin, hung the washcloth
over the edge of the hamper and then scrubbed his hands
with soap. Then he stood there looking at Edie as she set
the medicine and scissors back in the medicine cabinet.

"What?" she asked.

"Your turn," he said.

She frowned, but even as she did, he reached for her
hands, drawing them into the flowing water. He took the
soap and then, holding her hands between his own, rubbed
them into a lather. He washed each finger, ran his fingers
between them, dragged them across her palms leaving
soapy trails. And he paid close attention to the area where
Sally's collar had skinned her up a bit.

Slowly he moved her hands beneath the faucets, letting
the water rinse the suds away. Then he located the ointment she'd only just put away and applied it to the crease
of each of her four fingers.

"I'm sorry Sally hurt you like that. She's usually very
gentle."

"It wasn't her fault," Edie said. She tried not to let her

breath hitch the way it wanted to when his fingers danced over the insides of hers. "Something in the woods frightened her."

"When I saw your hand, the blood, I thought..." He shook his head, not looking her in the eyes. But his fingers caressed her smallest one in a way that told her he knew—he knew about her stalker's threats. He knew specifics.

"You went through my things, didn't you? You read the notes."

He met her eyes. "I was just stashing a box of my stuff in the attic," he said. "I didn't go looking for your cache of evidence against this pervert."

She pulled her hand from his. "But when you found it, you felt free to go through it. Read the letters..."

"I'm here to protect you from this idiot, aren't I? Don't you think I can do that better if I know all the facts?" He took the gauze from the cabinet and pulled her hand firmly back into his. She didn't fight him. She let him wrap the four fingers in a few layers, then tape them off. It would keep the ointment from rubbing off overnight.

"I think you should have asked me first."

He finished taping the gauze, and, to her surprise, he nodded. "Yeah, you're right. I probably should have. Look, Edie, this guy is dangerous."

"You think I don't know that?"

He lowered his head. "I think we should let the police know what's going on here. Let your family know."

"No." She shook her head firmly. "No, I don't want my sisters or my mother becoming this guy's targets. And I know they will, if they know. They'll be all over this thing, trying to protect me. It's bad enough you've muscled your way into this mess. He might very well attack you next, just for getting in his way."

"Yeah," he said slowly, walking away from the mirror and nodding. "Yeah, that would be perfect."

She frowned hard at him. "No, it wouldn't be perfect! Are you insane? I don't want your blood on my conscience."

He turned again, shaking off whatever insane thoughts he'd been thinking. Instead he said, "You were great with Sally. Thanks for that."

"She's a great dog." She sighed, closing the medicine cabinet and walking back into the bedroom. She stared down at the now sleeping dog for several minutes. "You've had her since she was a pup?"

He nodded. "Yeah. We, uh, bumped into each other on the road one day, and the mutt followed me home. I couldn't get rid of her."

Not the story her sister had told her, she mused, but this version didn't rule the other one out, either. "You never had her ears or tail cropped?"

"Don't even get me started on that topic," he said, and he said it quickly.

She smiled. "What? A subject we agree on? You've got to be kidding."

He searched her eyes a little. "I think men have gotten pretty full of themselves when they think they can improve on nature and go about hacking up little puppies to prove it."

"Amen to that."

He lifted his brows. "You agree with me?"

"Yeah. I do."

"Huh. Well, gee, lemme push this theory a little. 'Cause it's not just dogs I don't like seeing surgically altered, you know. It applies to people, too."

She smiled at him. "Is this your roundabout way of asking if I've had work done, Wade?"

"You haven't," he said. "I saw the original, remember? I'd know."

"Photographic memory?"

"Where you're concerned, yeah."

She blinked, not quite sure how to respond to that. Instead, she turned away so he wouldn't see the color rushing into her face. "It's late," she said. "I...we should get some sleep."

She saw him nod in her peripheral vision. "Leave your door open, Edie, so I can hear you if you call out. I'll do the same. And we'll let Sally stay where she is, if you don't mind. I have a feeling she wouldn't let that gauze stop her from taking a bite outta crime if your maniac should show up."

She nodded, daring to face him again now that they were on a safer subject. "When she wakes again, I'll take the gauze off."

"You won't have to," he said. "Good night, Edie."

"Night."

He hesitated there by the door, looking at her. His eyes fixed on her lips, and she knew what he was thinking, and she thought he knew that she knew. Maybe he wanted her to know. She licked them involuntarily and saw his eyes react. Then they met hers. Full of messages, thoughts, images, sensations. She wondered if her mouth fascinated him as much as his fascinated her.

Sighing, he left the room and walked down the hall.

She heard him for a few minutes. Wandering through the house, checking the place, making sure the doors were locked, shutting off the lights.

She felt good with him there. She felt safe.

Chapter 10

Wade didn't sleep at all. Because up until tonight, he'd had no idea just how serious Edie Brand's trouble was. Not until he had read those letters, seen the box of gifts. She had glossed over it when she'd told him what had scared her back to Big Falls. An obsessed fan—the idea had seemed nightmarish, especially when she had described the man's physical attack in her car that night. But seeing the letters, reading their chilling words, made it more real. More immediate.

Things were far worse than she had made them sound. The man wasn't just obsessed, he was insane. It dripped from every word of his letters.

And he was utterly, completely, focused on Edie Brand. Having read the letters, Wade would have been surprised if the man *hadn't* followed her back here. He wouldn't give up until he'd tracked her down, no matter how difficult doing so might be.

Wade felt as if he had gotten himself in over his head.

Edie needed more help than a small-town mechanic could give her. Damn, why hadn't she confided in anyone?

But she hadn't.

She'd confided in him.

Trusted him.

Asked *him* to help her. Reluctantly, yes, but it came down to the same thing. He had been handed the chance to be Edie Brand's hero. And he damned well wasn't going to screw it up. Screwing it up would only verify all the lousy things she had ever thought about him. It would convince her she'd been right all along to hold herself above him, aloof from him, to look right through him.

No. He had to do this. He had to show her he was equal to the task and ten times the man she had ever given him credit for being. And then she—and this whole town— would have to rethink their preconceived notions about Wade Armstrong.

His successful business hadn't accomplished that. At least, not enough to satisfy him. His decades of upstanding citizenship hadn't, either. But this would. Saving the local celebrity from a madman would show them all. It was a chance he had been waiting for his entire life.

And his attraction to Edie Brand had nothing to do with it. Yeah, he liked the way she looked. He'd always liked the way she looked. But that was the extent of it. There was nothing more. Or, if there was more...damn, if there was more, he was an idiot. But if there was more, it was unrelated to this.

He spent the night unpacking. He put his bed together and put his clothes away, and thought and thought about what he should be doing to put Edie's stalker out of commission. When he opened a box to find his laptop computer, which he normally used for keeping the books during his off hours, an idea occurred to him. He quickly located the nearest telephone jack, glad to find one right in his bedroom, and plugged the computer in. Then he went online.

A search under Edie B. turned up countless hits. Thousands. Her photos had been plastered on more Web sites than anyone else's ever, according to one site he read. A few claimed to have nude shots of her, but they really only displayed Edie's head on someone else's body.

Wade knew that at a glance. He had committed her body to memory—even the parts he'd never really seen. He knew what she would look like. He knew what she would *feel* like. You couldn't fool Wade Armstrong with a fake.

Eventually he found a reference to a tabloid article and located it in the magazine's archives. Nothing about the stalker. Nothing about the gifts or the attack. It was a sensationalistic bit of hype that consisted of a cover photo of Edie with a handsome, muscular hunk on her arm at some function or other, with the caption, "Edie B.'s Mystery Date Exposed!"

He studied the guy for a long moment, hating him, wondering if he could be the stalker. But when he clicked through to the article and read it, he realized the guy might be his best lead. It gave his name as Michael McKenny, and said he was a friend and a business associate of Edie's, but that nothing romantic was going on between them.

Just like a tabloid to scream promises of illicit information in the headline and then report inside that there was nothing to report.

He clicked back to the photo, copied it onto his hard drive, made a note of the man's name and saved the file. Then he ran a search on the name Michael McKenny and found, once again, dozens of sites, though it was clear that most of them had nothing to do with this particular Michael McKenny. Too many to go through in a single night to see if any *were* relevant, though, so he logged off and took a break. Time to make a pot of coffee.

As he stepped into the hall, he heard soft sounds from Edie's room, so he tiptoed closer and peered into the darkness through the open door.

The hall light was on. It spilled through, just enough so he could see clearly. Edie was lying in the bed. Her hair spilled over her pillow artlessly. It was messy, not carefully arranged by some photographer. Her nightgown was a big dorm shirt with a teddy bear on the front. She lay on her side, having kicked her covers free, and her long legs were drawn up nearly to her chest. She was almost in the fetal position. Which meant she was scared, even in her sleep. Insecure. Lonely.

His gaze slid slowly back up her body again, over the rise of her hips, the dip of her waist, to her arms and shoulders and neck and, finally, to her face.

Her eyes were open and looking straight into his.

He felt his widen and almost jerked in surprise, but he managed to hold it together. "You made a noise in your sleep," he said. "I was just checking on you."

She blinked at him and nodded once, when he'd fully expected her to scold. "You're still wearing clothes," she said, her voice thick.

"Sorry. I'll take them off, if you want."

She smiled at him. Didn't snap or call him a pig. Just smiled a crooked, sleepy little smile. "Not what I meant."

"I know."

She rolled onto her back, patted the mattress beside her. He almost choked but managed to walk steadily into the bedroom, to sit down where she indicated. He turned sideways, toward the head of the bed, so he could see her better.

"Why haven't you been to bed yet?" she asked softly.

"You haven't asked."

She gave him a look that told him he was pushing it. He shrugged innocently but amended his answer. "Just didn't feel sleepy."

She sat up a little, propped on her elbows. "I should take the gauze off Sally now," she said.

He shook his head, then pointed and watched her eyes follow his finger. The dog lay on the floor, head pillowed on her paws. The gauze that had been wrapped around her snout was a foot away, as if she'd tossed it aside.

Edie laughed softly.

"She's pretty good at getting rid of anything that needs getting rid of," he said. Then he saw the look in Edie's eyes and knew she was thinking the same thing he was. The stalker needed getting rid of. Sally might not be able to handle that, though.

She looked away, pulling the covers up over her as if she were cold.

"You looked like you were sleeping fairly well, considering."

She shook her head. "In fits and starts. I drift off, then just jerk awake all of a sudden with my heart racing." She rolled over and looked at the clock. "Thank God it's almost morning."

"You didn't get to bed until after midnight." He heard the tone of his own voice and winced at the worried, tender sound to it.

"You didn't get to bed at all," she said.

He would not tell her that part of the reason he hadn't slept was an irrational, gnawing fear that if he fell asleep, something bad would happen to her, and he wouldn't be able to prevent it.

It was stupid. He could hear her perfectly from his room. And Sally was in here with her, besides.

He looked at her, rolled his eyes, sighed and finally turned himself around and lay down on his back, beside her. He was on top of the covers. She was underneath. His head missed the pillow, but it didn't matter.

"What do you think you're doing, Wade?"

He glanced at her. "You've got three hours before decent people get out of bed. Go to sleep, Edie."

"Wade, we can't just—I mean, this isn't a very…"

He turned his head to the side and looked at her face. "Go to sleep."

She held his gaze for a heartbeat. Then she drew a breath, lowered her head onto the pillow, and sighed it out as she let her eyes fall closed.

Once again, she'd surprised him.

That was nothing, though, compared to the shock that shot through him when she rolled onto her side, facing him, nestling just a little closer. Her hands closed around his upper arm, and her face lay so close that her cheek just barely rested against his shoulder.

He closed his eyes and bit his lip to keep from groaning out loud.

He never touched her. He still lay there, flat on his back, in exactly the same position in the morning. Despite the fact that she was snuggled up to him much more closely than she had been when he'd come in mere hours earlier. He hadn't moved. Yet he had slept.

Was still sleeping.

She lifted her head carefully, so she wouldn't wake him, and just looked at him for a long time. She let her eyes trace the contours of his face. The harsh line of his brows, the straight, arrogant nose, the sculpted cheekbones and the firm jaw. His lips were full, softening the whole look of his face. Her eyes stayed riveted on them for a long while. What was so enticing about them? That dip at the top, maybe? She thought about pressing her own lips to them. Just to see what they would feel like. What he would taste like.

But, of course, she couldn't do that.

She'd slept like a baby with him close to her. She hadn't had another bad dream, hadn't started awake again, not once, since he'd come to her. Would it be wrong of her to ask him to do this every night? Probably, considering how badly he wanted to have sex with her. It would be almost cruel to make him lie there, night after night, on his honor not to lay a finger on her.

She was surprised he had managed to do that for a few hours of one night. And…maybe even a little disappointed.

Idiot.

She slid out the other side of the bed and padded across the floor to check on Sally. Her wounds were still puffy, but not as angry looking as they had been last night. She would call the town's only vet after eight. It was only quarter of. She would just have time for a quick shower first. She grabbed some clothes to wear, stepped into the bathroom, closed the door and reached back for the lock. Then, licking her lips, she drew her hand away. She told herself she wasn't really hoping he would just walk in on her. She wasn't. Of course not. She just…didn't see the need to lock him out. Not after he'd shown such remarkable restraint last night.

Wade spent a few hours helping her put the house in order. It still wasn't perfect. Lots of bare places on the walls, lots of missing pieces, but he personally felt that once his big-screen TV was set up in the living room, the place was damn near perfection. He hadn't had time to mount the satellite dish on the roof yet, but later.

They'd had to cut the work short in the middle of the day to take Sally to the vet. And while one or the other of them could easily have taken care of the task alone, Wade was hesitant to let Edie out of his sight. Which was why he was letting the guys handle the garage on their own today.

He tried to gauge his reasons as he drove his SUV down the twisting road with Edie beside him and Sally on the back seat with her head nearly hitting the roof. He figured it was partly his new awareness of the serious threat this guy stalking Edie represented. How dangerous he was. And partly because she hadn't locked the bathroom door this morning while she had taken her shower.

She probably thought he hadn't noticed. As if every nerve ending and every sensory receiver in his body didn't quiver to full awareness every time she moved a muscle or took a breath. He had been wide awake from the moment she'd lifted her head from his shoulder this morning. He had been lying there, striving not to move as she looked at him. And he knew she was looking, because he felt her breath on his face and her eyes burning into his skin. He heard her soft sigh, too, just before she turned away. Felt it waft over his lips. It had taken every bit of self-restraint in him to lie there like the dead and not reach for her.

And the second she went into the bathroom, he was on his feet, moving closer, listening. She closed the door, yes, but she didn't turn the lock.

There could be several reasons for that, of course, but the only one he cared to ponder was the one that said she was hoping he might walk in and join her. And that was enough fantasy grist to keep his imagination working overtime for a solid month.

He smiled to himself as he thought about it.

"What?" she asked.

He jerked his head sideways, wiping the smile off his face. "Nothing. Nothing. I was daydreaming."

"About what?"

He shook his head. "No way. You get pissy when I talk about stuff like that. Besides, it wouldn't be appropriate now that we're sleeping together."

She blinked as if stunned. "We are *not* sleeping together."

"We are so."

She pursed her lips as if to keep from speaking, leaned back in her seat and faced straight ahead. Another mile later, she said, "So you were daydreaming about us sleeping together?"

"No. But since you're so hot to know, I was daydreaming about you in the shower this morning. And how you left the door unlocked for me."

Her jaw fell open. She just gaped at him, and her cheeks got so pink and her eyes so wide, he almost laughed out loud. "I wasn't sure, of course, if it was an invitation or just an oversight, though I suspect the former."

"You are such a pig."

"Whatever. If it's not an invitation, then you ought to lock the door."

"I don't have to lock the door if I don't want to. It's my house."

"That's true. It's your house. But if you leave it unlocked next time, I'll probably start to assume that it *is* an invitation, and I might walk in. I mean, if I tell you that up-front, and then you don't lock the door, you can't be mad at me if I walk in, right?"

"I most certainly *can* be mad at you if you walk in."

"No, you can't. Because I told you in advance. I mean, gee, Edie, take a look at this from my point of view. If I say, 'Don't leave your doughnuts out, or I'll eat them,' and you say you're going to leave them out anyway, and I'm not supposed to eat them, and I say, 'Look, lady, I'm a doughnut-holic. If they're out, I'm eating them,' and then you leave them out and I eat them, how the hell can you blame me?''

She turned her head slowly as he spoke and stared at him with eyes that got so wide he thought he had maybe grown a second head. And when he finished she said, ''What the *hell* are you talking about?''

He closed his eyes, gave his head a shake. ''I don't know.'' The damned woman had him so hot for her he could barely think straight, he mused. He turned the wheel, pulled into the parking lot of the veterinary clinic and snapped Sally's leash onto her collar. ''Come on, girl.''

As he got out, the dog did, too. Edie got out her own side, and Sally damn near pulled his arm out of the socket, trying to get to her. She walked close to the woman's side. He scowled at his traitorous dog. She looked back at him and wagged her tail.

''Did you see that? Did you?''

Edie asked the question even as she helped him transfer bags of groceries into the back of the SUV from a shopping cart. They had finished at the vet's office and stopped for supplies on the way back.

''Did I see what?''

''Everyone in that store was looking at us. And whispering as soon as we were out of earshot. God, it's all over town already.''

''What is? That we're sleeping together?''

''Shh!''

He grinned, took the last bag from her and placed it in the back. She was looking around to see if anyone had heard that remark. No one had.

"When is my car going to be done, anyway? At least we wouldn't be joined at the hip if I had my car."

He shrugged. "We can stop at the garage and check on it."

She got into the front. Sally was lying across the back seat, waiting patiently. Edie closed her door, reached for her seat belt and felt eyes on her. She whipped her head around, scanning the parking lot, even as Wade got in his side.

"Wade," she whispered.

He closed his door, glanced at her. "What's wrong?" For once his voice wasn't sarcastic or teasing.

"Someone's watching us."

He nodded, reached over and smoothed a hand over her hair. "Everyone's watching us, honey."

Her head turned slowly. The feel of his hand stroking her hair like that—the heat, the friction of his calloused palm, the pressure, the way his fingers threaded, tugging gently as they moved through, then danced over her nape like hot wires…made her shiver. "What…are you doing?"

"Do you think it's him?"

She nodded. "I do. I know it's foolish, but I do…."

He shrugged. "If you think he's watching, play along." And as he said it, he leaned closer, brushed his mouth across hers. Softly, barely touching. Then again.

"I don't get it," she muttered. But her hands had risen already to close on his shoulders.

"Might flush him out to see you kissing another man," he said. His lips brushed hers again. "Shake him up." And again. "He makes a mistake, we nail his ass. Understand?" He spoke with his mouth close to hers. Every breath, every movement of his lips, sent a ripple of heat right down her spine.

"I understand," she said.

"Good. Then kiss me. Like you mean it, Edie."

He did not have to ask her twice.

It didn't take any effort at all. All she had to do was stop resisting the force that tugged her mouth to his like a magnet. Once she did, their lips touched, parted briefly, then locked together with some kind of erotic suction that she liked way too much. And she forgot all about whoever might or might not be watching. She forgot about her stalker. She forgot everything except that this was Wade Armstrong, the hottest, baddest, most dangerous male creature she had ever known. And that she had wanted to kiss him for as long as she could remember.

It was every bit as exciting—and as frightening—as she had always thought it would be. His tongue was devilish, persistent, invasive, and it stroked paths of molten desire everywhere it touched her. His hands cupped the back of her head to hold her at just the right angle for his kiss. He could tip her slightly this way, or that way, or backward, to deepen his access. All at his will. She didn't care.

Her heart hammered against her ribs, and her body melted. Her hands were splayed, one in his hair, one flat against his back, and she was kissing him now, too. Sucking gently at his tongue, then petting it with hers. God, he knew how to kiss.

He moaned real deep and pushed her back against her door, his body sliding over hers as his mouth plundered.

A sharp rapping sound came from the passenger-side window.

Suddenly Edie remembered the reason for the kiss and broke it, only to crush her face against Wade's chest.

His hands were on her back, soothing. His voice was near her ear. "It's okay, it's not him."

How did he do that? Know exactly what she was thinking?

Slowly she lifted her head, saw his eyes, the look in them as he helped her get upright again, and finally she turned to look at who stood outside the SUV.

Her mother looked back at her, her face drawn and tight. Beyond Vidalia, Edie saw Mel, fighting a grin, Selene, looking all knowing, and Kara, wide eyed with surprise.

A tap on the other side of the car made them both turn to look out the window beside Wade. Maya and her husband Caleb were looking back at them, each holding a baby.

Wade cleared his throat, rolled down his window. "Hey there, Caleb. How's it going?"

"Better for me than you, pal." He looked past him at Edie. "Best roll your window down and talk to your mother, hon."

Too late. Vidalia was already opening the door. "Are you goin' to sit there and pretend I'm not even here, child?"

"Mrs. Brand," Wade cut in. "It's not what you think."

"What I *think* is that my daughter is making out with a man in public. Which wouldn't be quite so bad except that the entire town knows the man is also living with her, under her roof, out of wedlock."

"We were just—"

"I'm a grown woman, Mom," Edie said, cutting him off.

"Then try acting like one."

"Just because I don't live up to your values, it doesn't mean—"

"*My* values? I'd be happy if you'd live up to *any* values at all, girl." She shook her head. "I knew there was a reason you were in such an all-fired hurry to get a place of your own, Edain Brand, but I never thought it was just so you could move in with the first man to strike your fancy.''

''I didn't.''

''And *you!*'' Vidalia said, spearing Wade with her eyes so powerfully it made Edie wince. ''If you had one ounce of respect for my daughter, much less for me or my family, you'd marry her.''

''Mother...'' Edie said again.

''Don't you 'mother' me, young lady. It's obvious now to the whole town what your living arrangements are with this man. Which would be just fine by me if you didn't feel the need to advertise it. Just how am I supposed to hold my head up in church on Sunday? Hmm?''

She slammed the door and strode away. Wade was out his door before Edie knew what the hell had happened. He said only, ''Stay right here,'' as he left to go chasing after her mother.

Chapter 11

Edie started to get out of the car. Mel leaned against the door from the outside and shook her head.

Edie cranked down the window. "What the hell do you think you're doing? Wade is talking to Mom, in case you haven't noticed." And God only knew what he might be saying, Edie thought.

"Ah, let him take a swing at it, sis," Mel said. "Hell, he can't be any worse at it than you are."

Edie crossed her arms over her chest and leaned hard into the back of the seat. "No one could get along with that woman!"

"The rest of us don't seem to have too much trouble," Maya said. She was on the opposite side, speaking through the open driver's window.

"Speak for yourself, Maya," Selene said softly. "Mom is easy for you because you're so much like her. Your values and hers mesh perfectly. It's not so easy for the rest of us."

Maya crooked her brows. "Oh, come on, Selene, you're exaggerating."

"No, she's not," Edie said. "If Mom disapproves of something, then it's forbidden. No leeway. No chance she could possibly be wrong. She's fine with you because you got married, didn't move far away and had a pair of babies. Exactly the way she had always planned."

"That's not true. She gets along with me because I make an effort," Maya defended. "And so does Mel. Tell her, will you?"

Mel licked her lips. "Actually, I make an effort, too. But she still gripes about my Harley and feels she needs to lecture me at least three times a year on why a woman shouldn't kick a man's ass when it sorely needs kicking."

"She's only stating her opinion," Kara said. She spoke softly, meekly, for the first time on the subject. "She doesn't make you get rid of the Harley or anything."

"No. Because it's not *that* offensive. And because she's still distracted from my minor offenses by Edie's major ones. First posing in her underwear, and then living in sin with the town bad boy."

"We are not living in sin."

"Once she bends Edie and Wade to her will, she'll move on to me, I imagine," Mel went on.

"No, I think I'll probably be next," Selene said softly.

They all looked at her. She blinked the troubled look out of her eyes and forced a smile. "So you say you're not sleeping with him yet?" she asked.

"No."

"Honestly?"

"I haven't had sex with that man, Selene."

Selene shrugged. "Sorry. Don't get so touchy. It's not my fault you need your head examined."

"You got that right," Maya muttered.

Her husband sent her a shocked look. "What do you mean by that?" he asked.

"Well, hon, I love you right to pieces, but I'm not blind. The man is hot."

Caleb rolled his eyes and shot Edie a look. As if this were all her fault.

"Oh my *God.*" Kara dropped the three words like lead weights, and everyone turned to see what she was gaping at.

Halfway across the parking lot, Vidalia Brand was hugging Wade Armstrong's neck. It was a halfhearted hug, but a hug all the same. Then she let him go and backed off a little, nodded firmly and, turning, came back to the SUV. When she stopped near Edie's door, everyone was staring at her. She didn't return anyone's look except Edie's. "I'll expect you for dinner tonight." She snapped her eyes to Wade's. "Both of you."

Then, turning, she strode away. Shrugging and shaking their heads in bemusement, the others left, too, Maya and Caleb to go into the grocery store where they had been heading in the first place, the rest heading to their cars. They'd stopped them along the roadside when they'd spotted Edie and Wade making out in the grocery store parking lot. They had been on their way to the bar, Edie surmised.

Wade got in, turned the key, fastened his seat belt.

She stared at him, waiting, but he didn't say a word, until finally she couldn't stand the silence another second. "Well?" she asked.

"Well what?" All innocence, those eyes of his.

"What did you say to my mother?"

He drew a breath, sighed. "Sorry, kid. But that's between me and your mother."

"Did you tell her about him?"

"Who? Your stalker?" He shot her a sideways glance

while driving. "Come on, do you think she'd have walked away if I had? She'd have taken you home by the scruff of your neck and set a dozen bodyguards on you."

Pursing her lips, she relaxed in her seat just a little. "That still doesn't explain why she hugged you."

"Look, Edie. You're gonna have to tell her the truth sooner or later. I can't cover this up forever. And when you do, whatever I told her just now will be entirely moot. So let's not hash it over."

"No, let's hash it, Wade. What did you tell her? Why were we kissing?"

"I was kissing you to shake up your stalker. You, on the other hand, seemed to be attempting to swallow my tongue."

"Which would have been impossible if you hadn't had it halfway down my throat," she shot back.

"Well, I try to give the ladies what they want."

"And what gave you the idea I wanted that?"

"Well, there was the fact that you opened wide and said 'ahh.' And then there were these fingers digging into my skull to pull me closer."

She punched him hard in the shoulder.

"Ow!" He rubbed the spot. "Come on, Edie, I was just playing."

"What did you tell my mother?" she demanded.

He sighed, shook his head. "I told her you had a boyfriend in L.A. who gave you a hard time when you dumped him, and that you thought you caught a glimpse of him in town. I, hearing this, proceeded to kiss the living hell out of you, without your permission, in an effort to help you get rid of the guy once and for all. It was all an act. You fought me every step of the way, and that was all there was to it."

She stared at him.

"It's the truth, I swear it. I was trying to give the ex-boyfriend a clear message on the off chance he really had come to call. You thought it was an idiotic idea and were in the process of shoving me off you when they interrupted."

She lowered her head, feeling a twinge of guilt. "You took all the blame."

"Yes."

"Made it sound as if I wasn't even involved in the…the kiss."

"Exactly. Although I want us to be real clear on this. It wasn't just a kiss. And you *were* involved."

He looked at her, waiting, she knew, for her to admit it. Slowly she lifted her head, met his eyes. "I got…a little…carried away. It's been a long time since I've…you know."

He tucked a loose strand of hair behind her ear. "No, I don't know," he said, his voice softer now. "How long?"

She shook her head, refusing to answer him.

"How long, Edie?"

She shrugged. "A year…or so."

He shook his head slowly, licked his lips, seemed to be thinking very deeply about something as he maneuvered the car along the narrow road to her house. He opened his mouth once but closed it again, and she could clearly see he was debating whether to say something or keep it to himself.

"What?" she asked.

"No. You don't want to know. Trust me."

She watched his face, weighed his words, but her curiosity got the best of her. "Yes, I do. Go on, say it."

He glanced at her, lifted his brows. Finally, he sighed. "Okay, I will. But you have to hear me out without interruption. And I'm serious now, I'm not playing with you like…like I have been up to now."

"All right," she said, waiting.

He cleared his throat. "You are clearly attracted to me," he began.

"Of all the arrogant, conceited—"

"Uh-uh-uh. No interruptions, remember?" She slammed her lips together, all but biting them to keep quiet. "I wasn't finished. I'm attracted to you, too. Now, us both being adults, responsible, unattached, disease free—unless there's something I don't know?"

"You son of a—"

"Okay, okay. Just asking. Sheesh." His eyes were damn near twinkling. How he must love teasing her this way. "I was going to say there's no reason we couldn't end your little…dry spell."

She blinked at him, waiting to see if he was finished before she commented. "You're asking me to have sex with you?"

"Hell, no, I'm not asking. I'm offering."

She thought steam should be shooting out her ears.

"Look, you want to, I want to. It wouldn't mean anything. Just two adults, giving each other a little physical release." He turned to stare right into her eyes. "I'm very good, you know."

"Oh, are you?" she asked, putting all the sarcasm she could muster into the question.

"Yeah. I could make you scream."

"You're practically doing it already."

He shrugged, turned his attention back to the road. "Listen, it's up to you. I don't care one way or the other. Just know the offer's on the table, should you decide you want to take me up on it."

"Don't hold your breath, Wade."

He glanced at her and smiled. There was some kind of sexy fire in that look, in his eyes, and her blood heated in response to it.

But she would sooner die than admit it.

He carried in his share of the grocery bags, then went directly to his room when they got back to the house. Kicking the bedroom door closed behind him with one foot, he walked straight toward the small bathroom, peeling his shirt over his head as he went. By the time he'd reached the bathroom, he'd managed to heel off his shoes as well, and he crossed the threshold hopping on one foot while stripping the sock off the other. The jeans and shorts were next, and then he cranked on the taps, good and cold, and forced himself under the shower spray.

He had to bite his lip to keep from yelping out loud and giving himself away. He would be damned before he would tell her that the conversation they'd been having in the car had affected him far more than it seemed to have her.

The water cooled him down in a hurry. He stepped out of the flow, dripping on the floor as he reached for a towel, realized he hadn't unpacked any yet, and walked, shivering, back into the bedroom to paw through the few boxes still stacked in the corner. One of them contained towels. Beach towels, mostly. He liked them big and roomy, so he bought a lot of beach towels. He rubbed himself down briskly, then started to dress. All told, the entire operation hadn't taken more than ten minutes, he thought, zipping his jeans, looking for a shirt. Which was good, because he didn't want her to know about it. If she did, she might guess the reason.

No doubt about it, talking about sex with his lifetime fantasy girl was not a safe game to play.

Talking to her mother had been, he realized belatedly, even more dangerous. The things he'd said to the woman...

"*Wait, please, Mrs. Brand...Vidalia.*"

She stopped. She was halfway across the grocery store's medium-size strip of blacktop, standing in an empty slot near the yellow length of cement. An empty cart was at her elbow. "*I don't want to discuss this with you, Wade Armstrong. In my day a man showed discretion. A man cared enough about a woman to want to protect her from gossip.*"

"*It's because I care about her that I kissed her just now,*" *he blurted. Then he paused, wondering why it had come out the way it had, but decided it was good. He would run with it. He just couldn't give away Edie's secrets in the process. He'd promised he wouldn't tell.* "*Look, she thought she saw someone she knew in L.A.*"

Vidalia's scowl eased. She narrowed her eyes. "*Someone she didn't want to see?*" *she asked.*

"*Yes.*"

Her brows went up. "*Is my daughter in some kind of trouble, Wade? Because if she is, and you don't tell me...*"

"*It's nothing like that. There was a guy, a boyfriend, you know. Nothing serious, at least, not as far as Edie was concerned. But he saw it differently. I guess he didn't take the break-up very well. For a while he kept bugging her, and when she thought she glimpsed him here, well...*"

"*She was afraid he had followed her home,*" *she said slowly.* "*So you decided to send this fellow a message.*"

"*Exactly. That's all that kiss was. An act, just a ploy.*" *He shrugged.* "*One that probably wasn't even needed. I don't think it was who she thought it was in the first place.*"

"*I see.*"

He nodded, watching her face, waiting. He didn't know what she was waiting for, but he got uncomfortable as he searched his brain for more to say to her. Words eluded him, though.

She finally sighed. "So there's nothing else you want to tell me?"

He looked her in the eye. She had pretty eyes. Dark, Spanish eyes. Her parents had been Mexican, and it showed in her face. She had the kind of looks that only got better with age. "No, ma'am, I can't think of anything else. I mean, except that we aren't, er, we haven't—"

"Slept together?"

He averted his eyes, because they had slept together. Just not in the way she meant. "Of course not."

"But you love her."

He felt as if he'd been electrocuted, her words sent such a jolt through him. There was a solid whap of impact, dead center of his chest, and then tremors of aftershocks shooting outward to his fingertips, to his toes. "We're just friends," he managed, and it sounded more false than anything he'd ever said in his life. He sounded about as convincing as he had when he'd been caught smoking in the boys' room at thirteen. He ditched his butt as the principal walked up and said, "Wade Armstrong, have you been smoking?" And he said, "No, sir, I haven't," releasing the puff he'd been holding in his lungs with the words.

Vidalia Brand was speaking again. "I'm not a blind woman, Wade. And you don't have to worry about me saying anything. Your secrets are safe here."

That was irrelevant, he thought, since he didn't have any secrets other than Edie's.

"Frankly, I think she's plumb out of her mind not to return your feelings."

So did he. No, wait a minute, that wasn't right. He didn't have any feelings. He still thought she was nuts not to be all over him, but that was another matter.

"So what's holding her back, hmm? This old boyfriend? Or is she still harboring some damn fool notion about going back to L.A.?"

"Nah, she thinks she's above me, just like she always did."

He stood there for a second, looking at his feet, wondering who had just spoken for a split second before he realized it had been him. That last thought had emerged aloud, during some sort of psychotic break in time. He snapped his head up, met her eyes.

She was frowning at him. "Well now, Wade, are you sure? That just doesn't make any sense to me."

He opened his mouth, wondering how the hell to dig himself out of this hole, then realized anything he said at this point would only make it worse. "I—I really can't talk about this, Vidalia."

"Oh." She said it on a sigh, a look of stark pity coming into her eyes, and the next thing he knew she was hugging him to her. "Oh, poor Wade. I'm sorry." She let him go, looked him in the eyes and smiled. "I didn't raise any fools, you know. You be patient. Edie'll come around." She patted his cheek, gave him a wink, and turned to walk back to the SUV, where she'd delivered her dinner invitation-cum-demand.

Wade sighed, sinking onto his bed. So, he thought, let's review. Vidalia Brand was now under the impression that he, Wade Armstrong, the lone wolf of Big Falls, was pining away with unrequited love for her pinup-girl daughter. Furthermore, she had given him her blessing to pursue Edie's hand, and he wasn't quite sure but he *thought* perhaps the woman intended to *help*.

Could things be any worse?

The telephone rang. He hadn't plugged a phone into the jack in his bedroom yet, but it didn't matter. Edie got it downstairs on the kitchen extension. He got to his feet, went to the bedroom door and opened it, just out of curiosity. He'd left this number with the boys at the garage in case they needed him. He stepped to the top of the stairs and peered down. And he could see her.

She was standing with her back to him, just inside the arching doorway into the kitchen, holding the phone to her ear. He saw the way she stiffened, saw her move the phone away from her ear as she turned her head slowly to stare at it. Her face, her eyes, were stricken. She slammed the phone back into its wall cradle.

"Edie?" He ran down, taking the stairs by twos, reaching her, grabbing her shoulders.

She looked up at him, eyes wide, wet. "It…was him," she said. "It was him."

He pulled her to him, held her, surprised when she clung, pressed her face to his chest. He found himself rubbing her back with one hand, her hair with the other, muttering stupid phrases to reassure her—even knowing they were meaningless. It wasn't okay. She wasn't safe. And he wasn't at all comfortable with the black rage surging up from some deep hell pit inside him at the man who had shaken her up this badly.

The phone rang again, and she went so stiff he thought she would break in his arms. He set her gently aside, reached for it, picked it up and spoke in a voice he didn't recognize.

"News flash, dirtbag. You have a serious problem, because if you want her, you're gonna have to come through me. You understand that? Me. I'm in the way, and I'm not moving. Deal with me first, or you might as well quit right now."

There was silence on the other end of the phone. Then a voice said, "Wade?"

It was Caleb's voice. Wade closed his eyes, muttered a cuss word. "Caleb? You still there?"

"Yes. I'm coming over. Be ready to talk to me, because I'm not leaving until you do." There was a click as Caleb disconnected.

Wade licked his lips, put the phone down, turned to Edie. "I'm sorry. I...I blew it. Caleb heard all that and now he wants answers."

She was just looking at him, though. Staring at him as if she'd never seen him before in her life. She didn't look angry. And the fear that had clouded her eyes before was gone. There was something else there now. Something he'd never seen there before.

"I didn't mean to give it away."

"I know." She broke the hold of her eyes on his, looking at the floor, the walls, anywhere, it seemed, but at him. "It's all right. He's not going to want Maya and the babies dragged into this any more than I do. And if he tells her, she will be. And he can't tell the others without telling her."

He nodded. "Are you all right?"

"Uh-huh." She paced away from him now, back into the kitchen, but she gave the phone a wide berth, as if it were going to nip at her if she got too close. She'd been stacking canned goods into one of the cupboards, and she returned to that task.

"What did he say to you, Edie?"

She didn't turn, didn't look at him. "He said, 'How dare you betray me with another man? Don't you realize what you've done? You have to die now. You have to die.'" She just kept stacking cans in the cupboards. Mushrooms, vegetables, soups. "He never said that before. Always threatened to rape me, hurt me, dominate me. But never to kill me."

"He's not going to kill you. He's not going to lay a finger on you."

"Isn't he?"

"Not while I'm still drawing breath, lady."

Her movements stilled. Slowly, she turned, a can of creamed corn in one hand. "Why do you care?"

"Because I am Edie B.'s most obsessed fan. Me. The guy's way out of his league." He said it lightly, teasingly, with a little smile meant to ease the darkness from her eyes.

She said, "You're nothing like him. Nothing."

He lowered his head. "Glad you realize it."

"I do." She sighed, raising her head slowly. "You should leave, Wade. You shouldn't be anywhere near me until this maniac is caught. You're making yourself a target."

"I'm not going anywhere."

She licked her lips, holding his eyes with hers. "I've kept it to myself too long. I'm going to tell Caleb, go to the police, whatever I have to do. But I don't want you getting in the way."

"We've got no choice but to tell Caleb," he said, matter-of-factly. He picked up where she had left off, stacking groceries into cupboards. "But if we go to the police, it's liable to be all over town in no time flat. The cops are just local boys with badges pinned on them. They'll tell their wives, their drinking buddies. It'll get around."

He glanced at her. She was leaning on the counter, both arms braced straight, her head hanging between them.

"Edie?"

She lifted her head slowly but didn't look at him. "I'm tired. I'm so tired of this."

"I know."

"Selene already knows something's going on."

He thought about that. "She's sensitive."

"She's downright eerie."

He smiled, glad to hear her tone lightening up marginally. "Caleb will be here any minute. I'll put on some coffee."

"Yeah. God, I don't want to deal with this." She pressed two fingers to her temple as if it ached.

"Then don't."

Her head came up, hand frozen in place beside it.

"Go upstairs, run a hot bath, dump some of that sweet-smelling stuff in it. Soak and relax. I can talk to Caleb without you backing me up."

She closed her eyes, and he knew the suggestion was tempting her. "It's my mess," she said. "I shouldn't leave you cleaning up after me all by yourself."

"Caleb and I are friends. And it's not just your mess anymore. Hasn't been since you confided it to me."

She smiled with one side of her mouth. "You keep it up and I'm going to have to start doubting your badass image, Armstrong."

"Don't even go there, woman, or I'll be forced to prove otherwise."

She sighed, hesitated, looking longingly toward the stairs, but with wariness in her eyes. "Scared to go up there all alone?" he asked.

She met his eyes and almost nodded.

"Take Sally with you. Leave the door open so I can hear you if you call."

"I seem to recall someone telling me what would happen if I left the bathroom door unlocked again," she said, her voice lowering, along with her eyes.

"Hey, I'm not gonna ravage you with your overprotective brother-in-law in the house. What do you think I am, a caveman?''

"Uh-huh," she said, nodding emphatically. "Caveman."

"Ugh." He swatted her on the backside as she moved past him to go up the stairs. He watched her as she smacked her lips, making kisslike noises at the dog, who jumped to attention and trotted along beside her. Who the hell could blame her? The two vanished up the stairs, and he was still staring at the empty space where they'd been when Caleb came in without knocking and strode across the living room, stopping only when he stood facing Wade in the kitchen doorway.

He said, "Okay, I'm here. So tell me what the hell's going on, Wade."

Wade nodded distractedly. "I'm in trouble," he said softly. He dragged his gaze from the empty stairway and focused on his friend. "Damn, I never even saw it coming, but I am in serious trouble."

Chapter 12

Edie soaked. Sally lay on the floor beside the bathtub and snoozed. It was almost as if the dog sensed Edie's need to have someone close by. She had been shaken right to the core by that phone call.

And shaken, too, but in a far different way, by Wade's behavior. The way he had grabbed the phone and spoken in a deep voice that was so menacing it scared *her*. There had been something in his tone, some emotion so tenuously held in check that every syllable vibrated with a tightly restrained violence.

She shivered when she thought about it now, dunked her head and rose from the water again. The bath was supposed to relax her. It didn't. It refreshed her, and as she sat there she began to feel cowardly for hiding up here while Wade dealt with Caleb, confessed that they had been keeping dangerous secrets. Caleb would be furious, no doubt about that.

She glanced at Sally, who lifted her head expectantly. "I should go face the music, too, shouldn't I?"

The dog said something that sounded like "Roo-rah-roo."

"Yeah, that's about what I thought. All right, then." She got out of the tub, towelled down and put her clothes back on. It didn't take long. She didn't fuss. She hardly ever fussed anymore. Especially anytime she thought she would be around Wade. The less fuss the better, where he was concerned. She hadn't given it conscious thought before now, but she supposed it had been deliberate. A test, in a way.

It hadn't seemed to cool his attraction to her in the least. She had expected that it would. What surprised her was how much she was *enjoying* not fussing.

God, when she thought about how long a simple bath used to take her. She would exfoliate, wax and moisturize every inch of skin. She would wash and condition every bit of hair on her head. And the after-bath rituals took even longer than the bath itself. There was the scale to face—always with a deep dread in the pit of her stomach that she might see an extra pound or two on the dial. There was her hair. She would mousse it, flip it upside down to blow it dry, then spritz it stiff. After that, she would pull on a robe and sit down at the makeup stand for at least another twenty minutes of eyebrow plucking, lash curling and face painting.

For just a minute it hit her how good it was to take a bath just for the joy of it, and to get up and pull on a big soft robe, then towel-dry her hair and not worry about it. She honest to God didn't care. Wade might. But if he did, tough. He was the one who wanted to move in here and play big bad bodyguard. She'd warned him he might get his illusions shattered. And she hoped she'd been shattering them steadily. She stuck her feet into the scruffy slippers beside the bed, let the towel hang from her head like a nun's wimple and headed down the stairs, Sally at her side.

She heard only a single phrase, spoken by Wade, but it was enough to stop her dead in her tracks. He said, "I can't stay here indefinitely."

Edie backed up a step, waiting, listening.

"Sure you can," Caleb was saying.

"No, not the way things are. It's not sane. It's not healthy. She's deluding herself if she thinks I can live under the same roof with her and not touch her. And so am I."

"You'll manage." There was a clap. She imagined Caleb's hand smacking Wade's shoulder. "I'll get the P.I. here by tomorrow. He's good, and he's discreet."

"Thanks, pal."

"You're welcome."

Edie backed up some more as Caleb and Wade came out of the kitchen into the big open area that combined the dining and living rooms. Wade walked Caleb to the door as Edie stood on the stairs, hidden in shadow, trying to analyze what she had just heard. Wade wanted her, still. He wanted her so much it was difficult for him to stay here, despite the lighthearted teasing and flirting that seemed so cavalier. She wasn't sure how she felt about that. God, she hadn't been wearing makeup or doing anything more with her hair than pulling it into a ponytail. Look at her, she thought.

And yet part of her reacted with a longing that shouldn't have surprised her as much as it did. She'd always been attracted to him, drawn to him. Even in high school.

That wasn't important now. Two things were suddenly very clear to her. First and foremost was that she didn't want him to leave. She felt safe with him here, and she hadn't before. No, she wanted him to stay. So the second thing followed—she had to make it easier for him to be around her and not desire her. She glanced down at her attire, smiled slightly. Hell, she couldn't look much worse than she did right now. If he could look at her now and get turned on, he was hopeless.

Wade closed the door when Caleb left, and as he turned, Edie came the rest of the way down the stairs to hide the fact that she'd been lurking there. He caught sight of her immediately, sent her a reassuring smile. "He just left."

"I know. I was coming down to take my share of the fallout."

"Guess I'm just too fast for you, Edie." He met her halfway across the floor. "Besides, there was no fallout."

"He wasn't angry that we kept him in the dark so long?" she asked, lifting a brow in doubt.

"Well, he was at first. But he knows we were just trying to keep the family out of it. He's cool with that."

"Is he?" She doubted it.

"Providing I let him help, now that he does know." Taking her elbow, he led Edie to the sitting area of the living room, where his couch now held court before the giant TV, and set her down. She far preferred the cozy, if eclectic, grouping they'd put together facing the fireplace. A few odd chairs, including an antique rocker from her mother's attic, her own bowl-shaped super-sized rattan one, and Wade's favorite recliner. A couple of end tables, a plant stand, and it looked almost homey.

Not without a fire crackling in the hearth, though.

She sat on the sofa at his urging, and he sat opposite her. "Caleb wants to bring a P.I. friend of his down here to help us out with this."

Edie pursed her lips. "I don't think—"

"Just let me finish."

She sighed but bit her lip and held her objections off, for the moment.

"You know Caleb's background. He comes from a long line of big money and political power. This guy he wants to bring in isn't some two-bit gumshoe, Edie. He's good. And he's discreet. Wouldn't stay in business long if he wasn't, not with the kind of clients he's had."

"So you think we can trust him to keep this quiet? I don't want my sisters getting in the way of any of this, Wade. Much less Mom."

"If Caleb says we can trust him, we can trust him. He's gonna call the guy from his office, and he'll get back to us later. Let's at least see what the fellow has to say."

Rolling her eyes, she said, "It doesn't look as if we have much choice but to hear what he has to say."

"You're mad at me." He sighed. "Well, hell, be mad at me, then. If it'll keep you alive, you can be mad at me from now till hell freezes over."

He seemed almost petulant. That changed at the sound of a loud, rumbling motor outside. He surged to his feet then, instantly protective, and went to the door to peer outside. "It's a delivery truck," he said. "You ordered something?"

"Oh, it's my equipment!" She rushed up to the door beside him. Her towel had fallen from her head and was draped around her shoulders. Excitement surged in her veins. It was so good to have something positive to think about. "Let him in, Caleb."

She ran to the room off the foyer, the one that had been a den. It was a twin of the living room, except the floor-to-peak glass window was slightly smaller. "Have them bring everything in here!" As she spoke, she moved a few stray boxes out of the way. The one containing her camera and lenses, she carried into the living room, placing it on the coffee table, out of harm's way.

The deliveryman came in, carrying a large carton, and Wade came a few steps behind him with a smaller one. Then they both went back for more. On the final trip in, the man in his brown shorts and name tag shirt—Bill, it said—looked at her with a little frown in between his brows. "Aren't you...?"

Closing her eyes, she nodded. "Yeah, I am." She felt almost apologetic for her appearance. But if that part of her life was over, she would have to get over the feeling that she had to look picture perfect any time she was seen by anyone in public. Or even in private.

He smiled at her. "You look much prettier in person, Miz. B."

She blinked so rapidly that, for a minute, the man's smile appeared in strobe. "I—I—I—thank you." She heard Wade laugh softly, so low and muffled she knew it wasn't meant for her ears.

The deliveryman smiled and headed back out the door. Baffled, she turned around to see Wade in the doorway of her soon-to-be studio, arms crossed over his chest. "That guy shouldn't be driving without his glasses," she muttered, shaking her head.

"Oh, I don't know."

"What do you mean, you don't know? You're telling me you think I look good in a baggy bathrobe with uncombed hair?"

He seemed to take that as an invitation to look at her. And he did. From her head to her toes, then back again, and she swore his eyes burned every part of her they touched. "You know, it wasn't all the makeup and skimpy clothes and big hair that made you beautiful in those magazine shots, Edie. Besides, there's something...incredibly sexy about a woman without artifice. No makeup. No fancy hairstyles. You're not even wearing any jewelry, are you?''

His voice had dropped. Deepened to a soft, velvety caress that set her nerve endings tingling. She shook her head.

He was coming closer now. "You didn't dry your hair, did you?''

She shook her head, not moving. Unable to, for some reason. Her hair was still damp, half dry, maybe, and she imagined it looked like a rat's nest.

"It curls when you let it dry all by itself. Little waves that don't have any plan or pattern to them. Especially at the ends. And there's a little frizz.''

She lifted a hand to self-consciously smooth her hair.

"And then there's the robe. Honey, I hate to tell you this, but it's sexy as hell.''

"I thought…it was kind of ugly.''

"Just bulky,'' he said. He was so close now that she could feel his breath on her face. His hands came up to the wide collar of the robe, touched it. He didn't try to open it, just slid his fingers over the soft material. "Makes a guy want to slide it off. And it's patently obvious you aren't wearing anything underneath.''

"You're impossible. I thought this getup would turn you off like a lightbulb.''

"Is that why you came down here wearing it?''

She pursed her lips, refusing to answer.

"Keep trying. I could get to like this game.'' His hands had wandered upward now, to her chin, which he caught between a thumb and forefinger. "We haven't talked about what happened in the truck this morning.''

She lifted her eyes to his. Big mistake. They were too

intense right now. "You mean...the kiss?" Her tongue
darted out to moisten her lips.

His luscious mouth curved very slightly. A sort of smile.
"I liked it."

"It was an act."

He shook his head. "You liked it, too."

Yes, she had more than liked it. "No," she said. "I
wasn't—"

"You liked it, too," he repeated. He moved closer, and
still closer. "Say it, Edie. Tell the truth. Tell me." His lips
were so close to hers now that they brushed her mouth
with every word, sending shivers right up her spine.

"I liked it, too," she whispered.

"Good. 'Cause I'm gonna do it again."

"Yes."

He kissed her. At first it was just their mouths in contact,
and his hand on her chin, holding her to his mouth. But
then, as he tasted her, probed her with his hungry tongue,
she felt him shiver. His hands moved to her shoulders, slid
down her outer arms, and then locked with her hands, fingers interlacing. She felt the wall at her back. His hands
pressed hers to it. And he kept on kissing her. Licking her
mouth. His hips pressed against hers, and she felt him.
Then he slid one leg between hers, nudging her thighs
apart, the robe with them, and moved his hips against her
again. His arousal pressed right into her now. She was
exposed down there. And open. And damp. And he was
hard and insistent, encumbered only by the jeans he wore.
Rough denim. He rubbed it against her, over her.

He broke the kiss, his eyes open and blazing into hers.
She saw the question he didn't voice. She didn't know the
answer.

He released her hands and moved his to her hips, pushing the robe even wider to do so. Then he held her to him,

grinding against her as he slid his palms up her waist, over her rib cage, until his thumbs touched the undersides of her breasts.

She was shivering, shaking with need.

"How long," he whispered, "since a man has touched you here?" His thumbs moved upward, over her nipples, then down again, up and down again. She felt them tighten and ache.

"Too long." Her voice was broken and hoarse.

"It's a crying shame." He drew his thumb and forefinger together on them. Pressure, then more. Squeezing the distended buds tight, he rolled them, pulled at them, pressing a little harder, and a little harder. "Too much?" he asked softly, his mouth at her ear, hips moving against her still.

She knew his eyes were on her face. She didn't care. It felt so good. She didn't answer; instead, she arched toward his hands, every inch of her centered where his calloused fingers held her nipples captive.

He gave a sharp pinch that made her suck in her breath as a bolt of pleasure bit through her. Then he did it again, and she would have gone to her knees if he hadn't been holding her up.

Very suddenly, though, he let go. His hands shot to her sides, capturing her hands, lifting them. She was burning up, and she didn't argue. When he placed her hands under her breasts, lifting them, she didn't ask why. And when he stepped away just slightly and looked at her breasts held up that way, as if in offering, and licked his lips, her knees buckled.

"Oh, no, you don't." He slid a hand between her legs, cupping her there to hold her upright. "Keep your hands where they are," he told her. Then he wrapped his free arm around her waist and tugged her away from the wall.

In an instant he was on the couch, her body across his lap. He bent his head and latched on to one of her proffered breasts with his mouth even as he shoved her thighs wider and drove a finger inside her. She gasped for breath, but he didn't let up, and she sure as hell wasn't going to ask him to. The sensations coursing through her were so intense she could barely think or breathe. She existed for his fingers, for his mouth. He was sucking hard now, scraping her nipple with his teeth as his fingers moved in and out of her. And then his thumb found her most sensitive place and pressed, rubbed, rolled, until she was shaking all over. He kept it up, took her to the very brink of exploding; then he pinched her pulsing kernel between thumb and forefinger, and bit down on her nipple at the same time. Harder, she said, out loud or in her head, she wasn't sure, but he complied. She felt his teeth, his pinching fingers, and she exploded in pleasure so intense she thought she might die with it.

And then he folded her up in his arms, and he held her. Just held her, while the ripples and waves of mind-numbing bliss washed through her, leaving her limp and shaken and feeling utterly vulnerable. As if he knew, he held her. Pulled her robe tight around her body, let her curl around him and against him, and held her. No demands. Nothing.

And he hadn't even…

"Wade, you didn't—"

"Shh. Rest now. Be still."

She closed her eyes, the languor of afterglow completely enveloping her. He was so warm, his arms so strong around her. Her eyes were heavy. Leaden. "You make me feel…"

He was stroking her back, holding her close. He said

nothing. He didn't have to. He wouldn't let her go; she knew it without him saying it aloud.

She wasn't sure how to finish her sentence as she drifted off to sleep. He made her feel…safe? Yes. Good? Oh God, yes. But something else. He made her feel…cherished. In a way no one else had ever done.

"Oh, yeah," Wade muttered softly as she slept in his arms. "I'm in trouble." Very gently, he managed to get off the couch without disturbing her sleep. She was really out. He didn't imagine she'd been sleeping all that much lately, with all that had been going on.

He looked at her there for a minute; then he had to close his eyes to resist waking her up in some creative fashion. Gently, he pulled her robe together around her, so she wouldn't be cold. Then he walked into the den, where all her boxes waited to be opened. He ought to be at the garage, taking care of business. Or going through his house one last time to retrieve any remnants of the life that seemed to have dissolved like sugar in hot coffee. But he wasn't going to. He unpacked her boxes instead.

He lost track of the time as he got into his task wholeheartedly. He had to go out to the truck twice for tools. He had both his toolboxes in here with him now, along with a stepladder and nail apron. He was actually enjoying figuring out how to put various lighting fixtures together, guessing what other items were for, looking around the room to try to guess where Edie would want things.

He wasn't aware he'd been at it for over two hours, and was even less aware that he was being watched—at first. Then he felt her eyes on him like a touch.

He was on a stepladder, fixing a bracket to the wall with a screwdriver, when he felt her and stopped, then turned to stare down at her. "You're dressed," he said. And of course he wanted to take the stupid statement back the minute it left his lips, but it was too late.

"You were expecting me not to be?"

He licked his lips. She wasn't quite meeting his eyes when he looked at her, and he detected the heightened color in her cheeks. He wasn't sure what to say about what had happened between them. So he decided to act as if it hadn't happened at all. "These brackets here are for those screens you ordered. You know, the ones with the various background designs on them?"

She nodded, looking around the room. "The backdrops." He wasn't sure if he saw approval in her eyes or not. She kept her expression blank. Of course, there were torn boxes and brown paper strewn everywhere. Hunks of foam packing and plastic wrap littered the floor. Long-necked poles with light fixtures on them stood in every corner of the room. They were bendable beasts that looked like something out of a vintage science fiction film, especially with the collars some of them wore. Removable, interchangeable, they ranged from shiny tinfoil to actual mirrors. And there were shades, too, like hats the lights could wear. They came in silk and other materials he hadn't identified, and in all the colors you could imagine. There was a tripod, probably for her camera, along with a case of new lenses and a supply of film. Beside that box were a pair of others he hadn't even opened. Their labels read "Dark Room Equipment."

"I didn't mess with that stuff," he said as she looked at it. "I figured it was probably chemicals and such."

She nodded, still saying nothing.

He bit his lip, waiting. Had he overstepped? Did she hate where he was putting the brackets? "Hey, I can move these if you want them in some other spot. Just say the word, it's no big deal."

"They're fine. Perfect, actually. That's exactly where I was thinking of putting them."

"Oh. Okay, then." He frowned, but she didn't speak. Finally he shrugged. "Hey, now that you're awake, I can get the power tools. This hand screwdriving action is for the birds." He dropped the small screwdriver into its slot on his tool belt and came down the stepladder.

"Wade, don't you think we ought to talk about what happened between us a little while ago?"

He stopped, on the floor now, hands on the ladder, his back to her. "I don't see any need."

"Well, I do."

He pursed his lips, tried to come up with an answer that would neither embarrass nor insult her, while protecting his own secrets. "Look, you were tense, Edie."

"I was *tense?*" The emphasis she put on the word made him cringe.

He forced himself to turn, to face her. "Are you sorry it happened?"

"Yes. No." She threw her hands up. "I don't know. Why? Are you?"

"Not in this lifetime."

Her eyes shot to his, but he looked away fast. Damn. Why couldn't he censor himself around her? "Listen, we are both attracted to each other. You've been scared to death day and night for way too long, and you were on edge. I know for a fact that a good healthy orgasm is the best thing in the world for easing tension."

Her brows went up high. "Oh, you know that for a fact, do you?"

"Well, sure I do."

"Done a lot of research on the subject, I suppose?"

He shrugged. "Some. You know, in the past, doctors

used to get their female patients off as a treatment for nervous conditions.''

"Did they now? Well, my goodness, this is just getting more fascinating by the minute.'' She leaned sideways, resting her shoulder against the wall. "Do tell.''

"Well…well, it's true. I mean, women weren't expected to enjoy sex back then, so their husbands rarely took the time to try to see to it that they did. After a while the frustration would…well, hell, it was a common thing for a doctor to…'' His face was getting hotter by the minute, and he couldn't even think of how the hell he'd gotten onto the subject. Much less how to get off it.

"So, in this case, you were just…playing doctor?''

He regained his composure in a hurry. "I wasn't *playing* anything.''

She blinked, straightened away from the wall, and it was her turn to look uncomfortable, to avoid his eyes. "Then you were serious?''

He looked at her, opened his mouth, closed it again, and finally lifted his hands, palms up. "I don't even know what you're asking me here.''

Her eyes shot to his like arrows. Stabbed just as deeply. "What did it mean, Wade?''

"What do you want it to mean?'' It was a lousy answer; he knew that.

She made fists and sort of growled at him. "You're infuriating!''

"I know. Look, we both wanted it, and it happened.''

"Oh, come on. You couldn't have gotten anything out of that, it was all…one-sided.''

He was stunned at that statement, and for a second he said nothing at all. Then he drummed up his courage and moved closer to her. He reached out, his hand brushing her cheek, gently turning her face to his. "If you really believe that," he said, very softly, "then you are sorely deluded, lady. I was in heaven." He swallowed hard. Her eyes softened and pulled at his, and he almost leaned closer before thinking better of it. Finally he turned away. "Now I have to go get those power tools."

He strode out of the room without another word.

Hours later, she still could not believe the man. She wanted to know what the hell he was thinking, what he was feeling, besides lust. Maybe nothing. Maybe that was why he had nothing to say on the matter, because there was nothing else there. And she wanted to know why he hadn't taken the opportunity to have sex with her, when he'd been pretty damned open about the fact that he wanted to. He'd had the chance and hadn't done it, and what did that mean?

She was feeling so many things, she couldn't even begin to sort them out. She tingled every time she met his eyes, or touched him. Even a casual, accidental brush of his hand sent shivers up her spine. She was mortified at the thought of having let herself go so completely under his masterful touch, while he had apparently been in complete control the entire time. God, what must she have looked like? Sounded like? She couldn't believe she could act that way in front of him.

That would probably seem odd to him, if she said it out loud, she thought. But it shouldn't. Oh, sure, she'd been spread all over in various states of undress, in front of millions. But she'd always been in control. She had known exactly what emotions her face conveyed. She had been safely hidden behind her makeup and her image. And she had known that any flaws, no matter how slight, would be airbrushed away before anyone could see them.

This man had seen her soul, naked.

And maybe he didn't even realize it. Which made it even more humiliating.

"You're awfully quiet," Wade said as he walked beside her up the path to the back door of her family's farmhouse.

She could already hear the noise spilling from inside. Warm noise, happy noise. It flowed out with the comforting yellow light from the windows. "I just can't believe my mother invited you to dinner. She knew about your little wallpaper design at the garage, you know."

"Did she?"

He had the gall to seem unconcerned.

"Uh-huh. She didn't like it."

"Neither did Mel. She threatened to kick my ass once, unless I took your pictures down."

"She did?" The thought made her smile for some reason. "But you didn't comply, did you?"

"Nope."

"And yet all I had to do was ask you."

He shrugged. "They were your pictures."

The back door opened, preventing her from demanding a more satisfying answer, or from wondering too long just what she would consider satisfying. What did she want from him? Was she hoping he *did* feel something for her, or praying he didn't?

"Oh, they're here! Hi, you two!" Maya called from the doorway. She didn't have a baby in her arms, but that wasn't unusual. When her sisters and mother were around, Maya was rarely allowed to hold the twins for more than a moment at a time.

"Hi, Maya," Edie returned, trying to sound light, casual. "What's for dinner?"

"A nice ham, with the works. Mamma made gravy, I did the biscuits, and there's pie for dessert."

"Be still my heart," Wade muttered.

"Careful what you say, Wade," Maya said, grinning. "We have enough cholesterol here tonight to make your heart think you mean it literally."

He laughed, and the sound was so warm, so genuine, that it startled Edie. She glanced up at him sharply, because it occurred to her to wonder if she'd heard his laugh before. If she had, it hadn't been this one. This one was real.

"Hey, is that Sally out in the car?" Maya asked.

"Yeah. She hates to be left home alone," Wade said.

"Well, bring her on in. She's welcome here."

"I'll get her," Edie said. She saw Maya take Wade's arm, tugging him into the house. She saw her sisters send him warm smiles, and her mother's eyes looking genuinely glad to see him.

What the hell was up with all of this?

Sighing, she trudged back along the walk to the SUV, unlocked the back door and took the leash from the floor. "Come on, Sally girl. You've been invited to dinner."

"Roof!" Sally said, sounding overjoyed at the prospect.

Edie reached in and snapped the leash to her collar, took the end in her hand and led the dog out of the SUV. Despite the vehicle's size, Sally's forefeet hit the ground before her rear ones left the seat. Edie closed the door and started forward.

Then she stopped as a chill slid up her spine. Like a finger of ice on her back.

She quickly glanced down at the dog, hoping to see Sally looking utterly relaxed so she could tell herself she was imagining things.

Sally had gone still, too, though. Her ears were cocked forward, as much as unclipped Great Dane ears could be. Her eyes were alert, her stance stiff and tight. She was sniffing the air, and growling deep and low in her throat.

"It's all right, girl."

She looked around, the lawn, the road, the woods on the opposite side. He could be anywhere. Sighing, she led the dog forward, tried to shake off the feeling of impending doom. Aloud, in a voice intended to project, she said, "One of these times, I'll just let you go tear the bastard to bits. It would make my life simpler."

Sally kept looking back toward the road, growling, tugging a little.

"Or maybe I'll just buy an Uzi and start peppering the entire area. What do you think, girl? You just look toward the sick bastard and growl, and I'll point and shoot. Hmm?"

"Edie?"

It was Caleb. He'd come out the back door and was heading toward her. She met him halfway. "Hi, Caleb. What's up?"

"Everything okay out here?" As he asked the question, he looked past her, toward the woods across the road.

Whatever had been there was gone now. That sense, that prickling awareness, had vanished as soon as Caleb had come outside. Sally had stopped growling, too. "I just get jittery sometimes," she said. She did not want to see Caleb go loping off into the woods, unarmed, after a lunatic. "But there's no one around out here."

"You sure?"

She nodded.

Caleb took her arm and led her toward the house. "Wade was pretty much under siege from the second he got in, but he sent me out after you."

"Under siege?"

"He's suddenly a very popular guy with our family." He opened the door, and she stepped inside, saw everyone gathered in the living room, all cozy, chatting like old friends.

"I noticed that," Edie said softly as Caleb came in and closed the door. "Any idea why?"

"Maya won't say a thing. She doesn't need to, though. It's fairly obvious they have him picked out as the next Brand-in-law."

Her jaw dropped, and she blinked rapidly. He was right; that was exactly the way the family was acting. "Oh my God," she whispered.

"What did you expect them to think?" Caleb asked. "Short of telling them the real reason you two are living together, I don't see how you can change this. Might as well play along."

"This has to end," she muttered. "This absolutely has to end."

Chapter 13

Edie hadn't liked it when Wade had refused to leave her home alone the next morning. He had to go into town, he said. The garage needed his attention. Her car was probably done, and he also had to be sure his house was ready for its new owners, who would be moving in within a couple of days.

He wanted her to go with him. She wanted to stay home and try out her new equipment. Ever since it had arrived, she'd been getting a steady stream of ideas, and suddenly she was excited about the new direction in her life.

But, of course, Wade had been stubborn, and no, leaving Sally there to guard her would not be sufficient. Fortunately Kara had shown up in the nick of time, saving her from any further arguments. Wade wasn't fully satisfied with Kara's presence. But it seemed to ease his mind marginally. He promised to be back soon, made Edie promise to call if anything felt off. And then he left.

Kara wore jeans with tapered ankles and a sweatshirt

that read Where In The World Is Big Falls, Oklahoma? Her long, dark hair was caught up in its usual ponytail, and she looked rather troubled as she watched Wade's oversize tow truck wheel out the driveway.

"He's so protective of you," she said. "It's just about the sweetest thing I've ever seen."

"Yeah, he's a real sweetheart." Kara sent her an odd look, and Edie covered quickly, grabbed her sister's hand and tugged her toward her studio. "Come here, you've got to see this."

Kara came along, then paused and looked around the room. "Wow. You're really gonna do it, aren't you?"

"Yeah. Yeah, I think I am. I've always loved taking pictures. I mean, it was only a hobby, but I couldn't help but learn a lot about photography with all the time I spent in front of the camera. And…and you know, I think I'm pretty good."

Kara smiled at her. "Is Mom ever wrong about anything?"

Edie sighed. "No, not really. Irritating as hell, isn't it?"

"Watch your mouth, young lady," Kara said, her tone mimicking her mother's.

They both laughed. Kara's smile died first, though, and she looked pensive and nervous again.

"Okay, so you wanna tell me what's wrong, or do I have to guess?"

Her sister shook her head. "Nothing, really. I just…thought maybe you could help me figure out what's wrong with me."

Edie blinked. "What's wrong with you? Kara, there's nothing wrong with you. What are you talking about?"

Kara shook her head, then lifted her arms expressively and looked down at herself. "I'm like the ugly duckling in a family of swans. I trip over my feet. I look horrible in everything I put on. I'm too tall, too skinny and too clumsy. I'm sick of it.''

Smiling slowly, Edie took Kara's hand in hers and led her out of the studio, back into the living room and then up the stairs to her bedroom. Sally lifted her head to watch them walk past but didn't get up from her spot on the rug in front of the fireplace. In the bedroom, Edie marched Kara up to a full-length mirror and stood beside her. ''Now look in that mirror.''

Kara looked; then she grimaced.

''Kara. Come on, stand up straight. You slouch all the time. Come on.''

She straightened slowly.

''See that? You and I are just about the exact same height. I think I may be a half inch taller. That's all.''

Kara blinked. ''We are, aren't we?''

''Uh-huh. And you're not too skinny. I'll bet we weigh close to the same amount. And I've put on weight since I was modeling. So now, tell me you're too tall and too skinny when you are the height and weight of a famous ex-lingerie model.''

Kara frowned. ''I don't understand.''

''Of course you don't. That's because you see yourself as gangly and unattractive, not because you are. Look at our faces. Look at me. I'm not wearing any makeup. Look at you. Your nose. Your eyes. Your cheekbones. Anyone could tell from fifty feet away that we're sisters. Except for coloring, we're very similar.''

Lifting a tentative hand, Kara touched her own cheek, staring at her reflection intently now.

''Wanna have some fun, Kara?''

Kara looked at her uncertainly.

''Let's make you a model for a day, hmm?''

''Oh, I couldn't….''

"It'll be just like playing dress up when we were kids. And it'll give me a chance to try out my new studio. Come on, Kara, please?"

Kara sighed, and Edie knew she had won.

She gave her sister the full treatment, hair, makeup. Then, on a whim, she made herself up, as well. She dug through her closets, pulling all the high-fashion suits and dresses and accessories from the depths, and hauling all of it down to the studio. And then she posed Kara, and shot frame after frame. She shot Kara alone, Kara with Sally, and herself and Kara side by side. That was so much fun they did it again and again, changing outfits and hairstyles, adding wigs and hats, posing in silly, crazy ways, while Edie experimented with the lighting. They even put a feather boa and a wide-brimmed hat on Sally, and shot her over and over.

They had a blast, and by the time they finished, several rolls of film were used up, and they were both exhausted from laughing so hard. They picked up the studio, then collapsed on the sofa in the living room.

"Wait till you see them, Kara. You'll realize you're a full-blown beauty."

"That won't change the fact that I trip over my feet."

"So you take a ballet class or yoga or something. If you even need to. My own theory is, once you stop thinking of yourself as an unattractive klutz, you'll be as graceful as anyone."

Kara sighed, thinking hard about that. "And what about the jinx thing?"

"There is no jinx thing, Kara. It's all in your head."

"Every man who gets close to me gets seriously injured in a freak accident of some sort! That's not in my head."

Drawing a deep breath, Edie sighed. "Probably just a string of bad luck, or coincidences, then. And even if it wasn't, Selene could probably fix you up with some kind of charm or talisman that would help.''

"So she keeps saying," Kara said.

Edie sighed. She glanced at her sister. "You like that outfit?"

"It's gorgeous," Kara said. She was wearing a floral print summer dress with a flared skirt and draping V-neck collar. "It makes me feel almost…petite."

"The right clothes will make a world of difference. We should go shopping, you and I. Get you a whole new wardrobe."

"I shouldn't need one," Kara said. "You don't. You look as good in jeans and a T-shirt as you do in designer clothes."

"That's only because I feel just as good in jeans as I do in designer wear. It's because I have confidence. When you look good enough for long enough, you will, too. You just have to build up your self-esteem."

"Really?"

Edie nodded. "Yeah. And remember that it isn't what's on the outside that counts. I had all that licked years ago, and here I am, starting all over, trying to figure out who I am underneath it. And what that person wants to do with the rest of her life."

Sighing, Kara looked at her watch. The morning had rushed past, Edie realized. It was early afternoon. "You can go, if you want. Wade will be back any minute."

"You sure? He didn't seem to think you should be by yourself today."

"He's nuts. I was by myself for years in L.A. Go ahead, if you need to."

"I did tell Mel I'd help her wash the cars this afternoon."

"Not in that dress, I hope."

"No way." Kara got to her feet, started rushing for the door.

"Slow down, sis," Edie said. And when Kara glanced back at her, she went on. "You're always hurrying everywhere. No wonder you trip yourself up a lot. Walk slowly, deliberately, as if you know exactly where you're going and have all the time in the world to get there. And stand up straight."

Sighing, Kara straightened and walked slowly toward the door. She was stiff in the heels, a little wobbly, but she would get it in time. She paused by a chair where the clothes she'd arrived in were piled and picked them up. Edie would rather have burned them, but she couldn't say so. A little at a time, she thought.

She watched her sister get into her car and pull away, and smiled, thinking she now had two projects going. Her studio and her sister's new image.

Halfway down the twisting, mountain road from Edie's house, Kara saw a car off the side of the road and a man standing in the middle, waving his arms. She stopped to see if she could help.

Wade had spent two hours getting up to speed at the shop, and another three at the house, where he wound up helping Tommy move some of his larger items in, including a pretty little baby bassinet. White wicker, with a frilly hood. Tiny mattress pad inside.

Cute.

He couldn't believe, however, that his weight room was about to become a nursery.

He got home at five. Home? He told himself to knock it off already and focused on parking Edie's car. He'd decided to drive it back from the shop, since the repairs were finished. She could drive him into town the next morning and drop him off, and then he could bring his own vehicle home tomorrow night.

Home. Hell, there he went again. It was a little soon to be thinking of Edie's house that way, wasn't it? But it felt like home.

He tensed a little when he didn't see the car Kara had been driving earlier in the driveway. Maybe she'd only just left. He hoped so.

He shut the car off and walked inside. The door was locked, so that was a good sign. At least Edie was exercising a hint of caution. Not that he'd expected otherwise. She was scared half to death.

Using his key, he opened the door, stepped inside, looked around. "Edie?"

There were clothes scattered around. On the furniture, on the floor. Edie didn't answer. "Hon, where are you?"

Still no answer. He moved through the house quickly, his heart in his throat. Her studio was empty, as were the other rooms on this floor. He ran upstairs and searched it in about a minute flat. Still no sign of her. Pounding back down the stairs, he ran for the phone, halfway to dialing nine-one-one, when he heard a thump that seemed to be coming from her studio.

He set the phone down and ran in there. And finally he noticed the red scarf tied to the doorknob of the closet she had said she was going to use as a darkroom.

Sighing, he walked up to the door, tapped on it. "Edie? You in there?"

"Yeah, just a sec."

He waited patiently for his heart to return to its normal rhythm. Then she opened the door.

The closet was big, formerly a walk-in number, but the fumes were terrible, and he resolved to get some kind of ventilation system installed before another day passed. She was wearing a painter's mask that probably did very little good. She had pans full of chemicals on a shelf, and photos hanging everywhere. She'd been busy.

"You're later than I expected," she said, reaching past him to flip on a light switch.

"So you decided to scare me half to death so I'd call next time?"

She frowned at him.

"I searched the entire house, Edie. When I couldn't find you, I was afraid..."

Her frown vanished. "Oh, Wade. I'm sorry, I didn't think. I was just so excited to see how I did. Look at this, look." She pointed at a photo hanging to dry. He looked. It was his Sally, wearing a goofy hat and feather boa. And he'd be damned if she didn't look as if she were mugging for the camera.

"That's pretty undignified," he grumbled.

"It's gorgeous. She's a natural. I took a bunch of her. And Kara, too. Look."

He did, and then he looked again, squinting this time. "That's Kara?"

"Of course that's Kara. She's gorgeous. She just doesn't know it."

"She looks more like you than I realized." He smiled. "Has she seen these?"

"Not yet. I can't wait to show her."

"It's gonna change the way she sees herself, I'll bet."

Edie tilted her head, studied his face. "You think?"

"Sure."

"In what way?"

He shrugged. "Well, she doesn't seem to think of herself as particularly beautiful or sexy." Then he shook his head. "Of course, I would expect any younger sister of yours to have trouble with her self-image."

Her brows went up; her lips parted.

"Don't be offended," he said. "It's just that you're a lot to live up to. You know?"

"There's more to me than the way I look."

"You still think I don't know that?"

"Do you?"

He frowned at her. "Can we get out of here? It stinks to high heaven."

She nodded, looking back at her photos. The phone rang. "In a minute. Get that for me, will you?"

He headed out of the little darkroom, through the studio and into the living room, thinking on the way that she would need a phone in her studio. Probably a separate line. She should have space for an office, and a red light for that dark room so people would know when not to open the door. Also that ventilation he'd been thinking about. Hell, there was enough work here to keep him busy for months.

He picked up the phone. Vidalia Brand said, "Well, hello, Wade, hon. How are you?"

"Just fine, Vi, just fine. Yourself?"

"Couldn't be better, but I seem to be short a daughter. Is Kara still there?"

"Nope. She must be on her way home."

"All right, then, I suppose she'll get here shortly. You give Edie my love, all right?"

"Will do, Vi."

He could almost see her smile through the phone lines. The woman liked him. It made him feel kind of warm and mushy. She disconnected, and he headed back to the darkroom.

"It was your mother," he said. "She was looking for Kara."

Edie backed away from the photo she'd been staring at. "She isn't home yet?"

"No. Why? When did she leave here?"

"Two hours ag—oh, no."

"What? What is it?" He didn't like the way her voice had gone soft, or the way her eyes had widened and were fixed now on the photo.

"Look, look at this!"

He leaned over her and looked. It was a photo of Kara and Edie, posing in full makeup and big hair, back to back, facing the camera, arms crossed over their chests. It was a great shot. A fantastic shot. "I don't see—"

"The window behind us. Look."

He looked. A man's face peered through the window in the background of the photograph.

"He was here," she said softly. "He was here, and now Kara is missing." Her eyes shot to Wade's. "Oh God, Wade, what if—"

The doorbell chimed. He took Edie's hand, held it tight in his, drew her close to him and looked her dead in the eye. "I'm not gonna let anything happen to your sister. You hear me?"

She nodded, but he wasn't sure if it helped. The doorbell rang again, so he drew her with him through the studio to the front door. When he whipped it open, he was ready for a fight.

Caleb stood there, though, a tall stranger at his side.

"Hey, Wade. This is the P.I. I told you about," Caleb said. "Alexander Stone, Wade Armstrong."

"Thank God," Edie said. "You're just in time."

It was, Alex Stone assured her, too late for discretion. Edie agreed with the slate-eyed stranger, and fifteen minutes later the State Police were in the driveway and her entire family was in her living room. All of them demanding answers.

"I can't believe you had some lunatic after you and you didn't tell us," Vidalia said. Her eyes were wet with worry, her tone harsh. "Especially once you realized he'd followed you back here."

"I know. I'm sorry. I should have...I just..."

"Hold on now," Wade said, drawing Edie close to his side, his arm around her shoulders almost protectively. "Edie bought the house and moved into it because she thought it would draw this guy away from the rest of the family. She didn't tell you because she knew you'd want to get involved, and she was afraid you'd be at risk if you did."

"They would have been better off knowing," Edie said softly, her head hanging, eyes burning. "If Kara had known there was a risk..."

"He's not going to hurt her," Selene said. She had been sitting silently in the rocking chair until now. She looked up with her round, pale blue eyes. "It's Edie he wants. Not Kara. He has no problem with Kara."

"This is ridiculous. Why are we just sitting here?" Mel barked. She was pacing, pushing one hand over and over through her short dark hair. "We should be out there looking for her!"

Alex Stone glanced up from the front door, where he stood speaking to a uniformed cop. He nodded to the man, who left; then he came up the shallow steps from the foyer into the living room with the others. "You left someone at your house, ma'am, in case Kara shows up there or tries to call?"

Vidalia nodded. "Maya's there with the babies. Caleb went back over to join her."

"Good." He looked at Edie, who stood, restless and frightened, then at Mel, who was wearing a rut in the floor with her pacing. "Look, the State Police have set up roadblocks. This man has no reason to harm Kara."

"This man has no *reason*, period," Mel snapped. "He's a maniac."

The man nodded. "Yes, but a maniac with a goal. He wants Edie."

"He'll contact her," Selene said softly.

Everyone looked at her. The second she said it, the phone rang, and Edie was so startled she thought her heart would explode at the sound. Wade held her tighter, searched her face. "I can get it...."

"No," Edie said. "It's me. I..." Swallowing hard as the shrill sound came again, Edie went and picked it up. The police were supposed to be putting wiretaps on her phone lines, but they hadn't had time yet. They wouldn't be able to trace...

"Hello?"

"Ms. Brand? This is Lieutenant Daniels. We've found your sister's car."

She blinked, shocked at the sound of the male voice— it wasn't the one she had expected. Then she realized what he'd said and looked toward Wade. "They...found Kara's car."

Wade took the phone from her hand, spoke briefly, then hung up. "Okay, they found Kara's car hidden along the edge of one of the side roads. About halfway down. It had been driven into the brush there."

Edie couldn't speak. She couldn't form the question in her mind.

"Was there anything in the car?" Vidalia asked. "Or any*one?*"

"No, nothing."

"I'm going to head down there, take a look for myself," Alex Stone said, heading for the door.

"I'm going with you."

He glanced back at Mel. "There's nothing you can do, Miss—"

"But there's something *you* can do?" Mel shook her head. "If the police miss anything, Stone, I'm far more likely to spot it than some buttoned-up city slicker."

His face hardened a little. "I'm a trained professional, Ms. Brand. I know how to study a crime scene."

"I know the woods. I know the car. I know the road. I know my sister." She strode to the door, yanked it open. "So are you driving or am I?"

He sighed, giving up, shook his head and walked to the door. "I am."

Sighing, Edie turned and went into her studio without a word to anyone. She saw her mother send Wade a glance as she left, and she knew he was coming after her.

"Where are you going?" he asked softly, catching up, hands on her shoulders.

"I can't face them. My God, Wade, this is my fault."

"How the hell do you figure that?" His eyes searched hers, and she saw the worry in them, the caring.

"I'm the one who posed for those magazine shots. I'm the one who drove this man over the edge, made myself a target, put myself right in front of him."

"It's your fault he became obsessed with you? Well, hell, then we may as well blame every rape victim and every battered wife, while we're at it."

"It's different."

"No, it's not. No one is responsible for this guy's behavior but him. Dammit, Edie, there is no man on the planet who fell for you harder than I did, and you don't see me going around kidnapping your sisters, do you?''

She blinked, staring up at him, shocked by his words, and not fully understanding what he meant by them.

He lowered his head, turning away. "I shouldn't have said that. Not now. I'm sorry."

"Wade, I—"

"Don't. Just...where were you going?"

"To the darkroom. I thought I'd try to enhance the photo. See if I could get a better look at his face, or..."

"Good idea. You do that. I'll handle things out here."

"But...don't you think we should—" Then she shook her head. "No, you're right. We...later."

"Yell if you need me. I'll leave the studio door open." He walked in with her, checked the windows to be sure they were locked, then called Sally in, as well. "Stay," he told the dog.

She obediently lay down near the door. Edie watched him moving around the studio. She didn't want him to go. She wanted to make him explain what the hell he'd meant by that remark he'd made moments ago. But she couldn't ask. Not now, with her sister in danger. Not now, when she didn't know how he would answer her and was even less sure how she wanted him to answer.

She stood there, hand on the darkroom door. He looked at her as if about to say something. Then he seemed to think better of it and started out of the room.

She lurched forward, caught his upper arm and spun him around. He looked at her, a frown bending his brows. Edie rose up and pressed her mouth to his. He reacted with a start of surprise; then his arms curled around her waist, and he bent a little, kissed her back, held her close.

She didn't want to let go, but eventually she released

her grip on his neck. Lifting his head, he stared down at her face. "What was all that about?"

"I..." She closed her eyes, stepping away from him. "I'm just so glad you're here right now."

He lifted his brows a little but quickly hid any other response before it could show on his face. "I'm here. And I'm not going anywhere."

She swallowed hard, looking away quickly, because she knew she wasn't as good at hiding her emotions as he was.

Too late, though. "What? What is it?"

She drew a breath. "I heard you telling Caleb you couldn't stay here indefinitely."

He smiled a little self-deprecatingly. "Call me fickle. I'm here for as long as you need me to be, Edie."

"Even if it's unhealthy? Insane?"

"Even if." He leaned in, kissed her on the tip of her nose. "Now go play with your photo and see what you can do."

She nodded, turned and hurried into the darkroom. Once inside, she leaned back against the door. He touched her with the most incredible tenderness—as if he cherished her. He treated her intimately. Maybe he did feel something more than desire for her after all.

Sighing, she got to work on the photo.

A long while later, she was staring at the blown-up shot she'd isolated of the stalker's head. He wore a black ski mask. It was too blurred to make out details, but that didn't matter. What did matter was that his hand was beside his head, and in his hand was a white square that looked like a folded piece of paper. The way he held it, the way those eyes from behind his black ski mask seemed to be looking directly into the camera lens; it was almost as if he were posing. As if he *wanted* her to know he was there. Along with the paper.

She went to work again, focusing on it and it alone, blowing it up until she could barely make out the lines of blue ink on its surface. Lines that seemed to spell out the first two letters of her name.

It was a note, and it was for her. Blinking, she flipped on her light and opened the darkroom door. Sally lifted her head and looked at her expectantly. Glancing to the left, Edie saw the open studio door, the steps up and the living room beyond. Wade was out there, holding hands with her mother, speaking softly to Selene. They were drinking something, and she smelled cocoa and realized he was doing everything he could think of to comfort her mother and her sister. God, he was something.

She stepped into the studio, ducked past the open door quickly, silently, and went to the far window, where she had captured the image of her stalker. Leaning close, she looked outside. It would be dark very soon. But it was still light enough for her to see the white square of paper. He'd tucked it into the window frame. She opened the window carefully, reached out and pulled the paper free, careful to touch as little of it as possible.

Then, unfolding it with hands that shook so much she could barely control them, she read the note.

Hello, my pet. It's been a long time. You've made me very angry, you know. Letting another man be with you. Touch you. You've been a very bad girl, but I suppose you know that. Maybe you crave the punishment I am now forced to apply. Maybe you're simply foolish. Either way, you've left me with no choice, pet. I'm going to have to hurt you. Badly. I'm going to have to inflict a great deal of pain and suffering on you. I wouldn't be doing my job if I did less.

You belong to me. You have violated my trust. You will be punished. And you will submit to the suffering you have earned and you will thank me for it, or your sister will have to bear it in your place. And I won't be as careful with her. Permanent damage is irrelevant where she's concerned. She's not my property. You are.

I will be waiting for you at midnight. There's an old barn on the road that runs past the falls. I'm sure you know the one. You will be alone there. You'll wear the black teddy—you know the one I mean. I will know if anyone else is there. And if you disobey so much as a single order I give you, your sister will suffer beyond anything you can imagine.

                                                        Always,
                                            Your loving Owner

Edie blinked down at the note as tears rose up to distort her vision. She wasn't afraid, not for herself, not anymore. She was scared to death for Kara, though. Lifting her head at the sound of Wade's voice, she glanced back out toward the living room. How the hell was she going to do this? Get out of here, alone, without letting anyone know her reasons why? Wade would never let her do this alone. No more than her mother or her sisters would.

She quickly folded the paper, tucked it into her jeans pocket. Then she hurried back into the darkroom and took the photographs that had shown her the note, tore them into tiny bits and dropped them into a wastebasket. Finally she drew a breath, lifted her chin, and walked back into the foyer and up to the living room.

Wade met her at the top of the steps, his expression warm, his hands familiar as they touched her arms. "Any luck?"

"No. I didn't find anything at all."

"It was worth a try."

She nodded, looking around the room and wondering if the man was watching her even now. She felt exposed. Vulnerable.

"You're shivering," Wade said, pulling her into a gentle hug, warming her with his body. "It'll be okay. I promise it will."

She nodded against his chest. "It has to be."

Chapter 14

It was killing Wade not to be *doing* something. He wanted to join the cops at one of the roadblocks, search the vehicles that came by, hand out flyers with Kara's face on them, something. Anything.

Alexander Stone, the designer-suit-clad P.I., and Mel had returned to the house. Selene and Vidalia Brand had gone back to their own, exhausted and worried to the point of being physically sick with it. Damn, Wade wanted to help them. To make it better for them. But he felt impotent.

The four of them were huddled in the kitchen, warming themselves at their coffee mugs like refugees from a blizzard. It didn't matter that it was spring outside. What was happening was cold. Brutally so.

"I don't understand why he hasn't contacted you by now," Alex said. Wade noticed the way he was watching Edie's face as he spoke. Carefully, and closely.

"I'm afraid I don't follow," she said, but she looked away. Averted her eyes in a very un-Edie-like manner.

"Sure you do. He took your sister to get to you. That's only gonna work if he contacts you to tell you what you have to do to get her back."

"Well, he hasn't."

"Are you sure?"

Edie shot her eyes to Alex's. "Are you calling me a liar, Mr. Stone?"

"Whoa, whoa, hold on a minute here," Wade said, cutting in. "Stone, you don't have any way of knowing this, but you're looking at one tight family here. Edie would cut off a limb for any one of her sisters."

"That's what I'm afraid of."

Wade blinked. Mel, who'd been glaring at Alex, suddenly shifted her eyes to Edie. "You keeping secrets, sis?"

"How can you ask me that?" Edie said. And it occurred to Wade that it wasn't an answer.

"How can I not? You kept this whole thing to yourself until you had no other choice. It makes me wonder what else you aren't telling the family, you know?"

Edie shot to her feet, and so did Mel. They glared at each other across the table. Edie blinked first, turned away. "I'm going up to my room." She shoved her chair out of the way and stomped out of the kitchen.

"The hell you are," Mel shot back, shoving her own chair aside and lunging after her.

Wade and Alex got to their feet, too. Wade made it to the living room in time to see Mel grip Edie's upper arm and jerk her around.

"You tell me what you're keeping from me, Edie, or I swear I'll—"

Wade was there in a heartbeat. He put his hand on Mel's, removed it from Edie's arm. "Leave her alone."

"You stay out of this, Armstrong. This is a family matter.'' She shot a look at Edie. ''Kara is my sister too, dammit.''

''Yeah. But the guy who took her is *my* stalker.''

''What the hell difference does that make?''

Edie set her jaw, turned her back on Mel and strode away up the stairs.

''Damn you, Edain Brand!'' Mel shouted after her.

Wade squeezed Mel's shoulder. ''Just let her be. She's shaken up. She needs time.''

Turning slowly to face him, Mel shook her head. ''She's hiding something! Dammit, Wade, can't you see that in her face?'' Wade said nothing, so Mel looked beyond him, seeking help from the stranger. ''You wanna back me up on this, or are you just gonna stand there taking up space?''

Alex Stone cleared his throat, stepped forward. ''I would watch her very closely tonight if I were you, Wade. I don't know the girl well enough to know if she's lying, but her sister certainly ought to.''

''Right through her teeth,'' Mel said.

''Go home. I'll deal with it.''

Crossing her arms over her chest, Melusine Brand lifted her chin. ''I'm not going anywhere, Armstrong. If she decides to go off on some half-baked rescue mission all by herself, you're gonna need all the help you can get.''

''I'll watch her all night. She's not going anywhere.''

''You're underestimating her. If she has her mind set to do it, she'll find a way.''

Behind him, Alex made a sound that was a cross between a snort and a laugh. Mel's attention shot to him. ''Sorry,'' he said quickly. ''I'm not—you make her sound like some kind of superhero or something. What do you think she is, Wonder Woman?''

"She's a Brand woman," Mel said. "And that's plenty."

Stone stopped smiling, swallowed hard.

"You can have the sofa," Mel said to Alex. "Not to sleep on, just to relax while you keep the front door under watch. I'll go find a comfortable spot near the back door." Even as she said it, she yanked a blanket and a throw pillow off the sofa, and strode away.

Alex met Wade's eyes. "Man," Alex muttered, "I pity the poor slob who winds up with *that* woman someday."

Wade shook his head. "Mel? She's not at all like she seems."

"No?"

"Nope. She's worse." Then he smiled a little. "But she grows on you."

"Fortunately I won't be here that long."

Sighing, Wade changed the subject. "You really think Edie's keeping something from us?"

"The perp should have made contact by now. Is there any way he could have called her without you knowing it?"

Wade thought carefully, finally shaking his head. "No, that phone hasn't rung once that I didn't know who was on the other end."

"E-mail?"

"She doesn't have a computer. I do, but she hasn't used it."

Alex shook his head slowly. "There was no note in Kara Brand's car. I'd have expected him to leave one there, if nothing else. But nada." He shrugged. "Maybe she's telling the truth. Either way, Wade, stay close to her tonight. And stay awake, just in case."

"Will do."

Feeling as if he were facing the longest night of his life,

Wade headed up the stairs. He didn't even bother going
to his own bedroom. He went, instead, to Edie's. And her
door wasn't locked, so he opened it and stepped inside.

Edie was sitting on the floor in front of her open chest
of drawers, a pile of lacy fabric beside her. She had to dig.
She didn't own the pieces she wore in the shoots. But she
had been given many items from the catalogue over the
years. She'd bought others. Never had much call to wear
them, however.

She finally found what she was looking for. A black
teddy similar to the one she'd worn in the shoot that
seemed to be her lunatic's focus. She hoped it would be
close enough.

"You okay?"

The deep voice—Wade's voice—came from behind her.
Her back was to him. She shoved the black teddy underneath her blouse, wrapped her arms around her waist to
hide it there and turned to look up at him. "Yeah. I'm
okay."

His eyes looked doubtful. Then curious as they skimmed
over the pile of lingerie on the floor. "Dare I hope you're
getting dressed up just for me?" He said it lightly, an
attempt to tease her into a smile or a little banter.

"That's not who I am," she muttered.

"And you still think I don't know that." It wasn't a
question. He moved closer, finally sitting himself down on
the floor opposite her. "You probably haven't even worn
most of these things. Oh, you might someday, for the love
of your life, in the privacy of your bedroom. But the sex
kitten in the pages of *Vanessa's Whisper* was a role you
played. Like an actress. And maybe you were a little too
convincing for this nutcase out there to understand that it

wasn't real. But you have to remember, Edie, I knew you before.''

She met his eyes. "Yeah," she said very softly. "You did. Tell me something. Truthfully, Wade, what did you think of me back then?''

He looked a little alarmed. "What do you mean?''

She sighed, a deep, tired sigh. "I've been playing that role for so long, I started to forget what else I was. It's coming back to me now. Now that I'm home, with my family. This house, and the photography, and...and you. But I want to know—maybe I even *need* to know—how you really see me.''

He licked his lips, drew a deep breath. "In high school, I thought you were damn near perfect. Not just the way you looked. The sound of your voice. Your laugh. Your walk. But I also thought you were full of yourself. Hanging out with the popular crowd. Looking right through me. I wasn't even sure you knew I existed.''

She stared at him for a long moment, realizing that the admission hadn't been an easy one for him. "I did, you know.''

He shook his head.

"All the girls in my crowd did. You...well, you had this reputation.''

"Of being trash. The son of trash. The guy most likely to fail. A loser.''

"Is that what you think?''

He nodded.

"It's not what we thought of you.''

"No?''

She shook her head slowly. They were sitting on the floor, legs crossed, facing each other. "You were considered the hottest guy in town. But also the most dangerous.''

"By whom?" he asked her, his eyes fixed to hers.

She lowered hers. "My crowd. My friends." She paused. "Me."

His brows were arched when she peered up at him.

"It was rumored you could convince any girl to have sex with you and you only needed one date to do it. It was common knowledge that no girl could say no to you."

He smiled widely. "And you believed that?"

She shrugged. "I was raised to believe keeping my virginity intact until graduation, if not marriage, was essential if I wanted to get into heaven. And I was sure that if I spent any time with you at all, I'd be doomed to hell."

Her voice had softened. Deepened. His smile died.

"So I looked at you. God, I looked at you a lot. But only when you weren't looking back. And I avoided you in every way I could think of. And then I went home and dreamed about what it might be like if I weren't such a good girl."

When he spoke, his voice was hoarse and choked. "I thought you detested me."

"I didn't. In a way, you were my sexual fantasy long before I was yours."

"Not quite, hon. You were already mine. Way before you posed for any magazine ad." He reached out and tugged the teddy from underneath her blouse. "And you don't need this. Not for me."

"No?"

He hesitated for a long moment. Then he finally said, "Do you really want to know how I see you, Edie?"

She nodded wordlessly.

"Maybe it's time I showed you, then." He rose slowly to his feet. Reached a hand down to her. "Come with me for a second."

She took his hand and let him pull her to her feet. He

led her out of the room, into the hall, down it to his bedroom, and then inside. He took her to the bed and nodded at her to sit down. She did. He knelt in front of her and reached underneath the bed. He pulled out a large, rectangular cardboard box, only an inch or two deep. Then he stood it up on one end and peeled the front away, revealing a canvas, a painting.

It was a painting she should recognize, she thought. A classic image of a beautiful woman standing magically on the surface of a dark sea. She was nude, except for the sheer fabric draped over her thighs and billowing out behind her in the sea wind. She had seen this piece before. Everything in it was the same…except for the woman. The woman wasn't the woman in the original piece. It was her. It was Edie.

She blinked in complete shock, her gaze shooting to his. "What…how…?"

"The original was called *Evening Mood*. It's by Bouguereau. A print of it used to hang in the library in town. It always struck me. One of your layouts made me think of this painting. And something about the tilt of your head—" He gave his own head a shake. "I couldn't get the idea out of my mind. So I found an artist and hired him to do this."

She was still not saying anything. She couldn't find words.

"No one knew. No one's ever seen it but me." Then he lowered his head. "I guess it seems pretty foolish. Call it a whim. But this is how I see you. How I've always seen you. As something…more."

She was still staring at the woman in the portrait. She was beautiful, her nudity awe-inspiring and lovely. Not dirty.

Shifting his weight from one foot to the other, Wade

leaned the painting against the wall and started to put the cardboard cover on it again.

Edie reached out and caught his wrist, tugged him toward her. She slid her arms around his neck, then leaned up and kissed him.

He kissed her back, twisting his arms around her waist and holding her close. But then he stopped, lifted his head away, frowning at her. "You're crying...."

"No, I'm not." She leaned in again.

He held her off. "Yes, you are. Why, Edie?"

Sniffling, she shook her head. "I don't know. A hundred reasons. I don't know."

"Is it Kara?"

She shook her head. "Kara's going to be fine." She was sure of that now. She glanced at the clock on his nightstand. An hour and a half until midnight. It wasn't long enough. Why the hell had she waited so long?

Pulling herself gently from his arms, she walked back across his bedroom, closed the door, turned the lock.

He stared at her, and she knew he was confused by her changed attitude toward him. She wasn't sure what was behind it herself, but she knew that later tonight she might very well have to bear the hands of some other man on her. A man who saw her only as the sum total of all her airbrushed images on glossy pages. Even if she gave him what he wanted, he would hurt her, but he would let her sister go. So she would do what she had to.

But first she wanted to know the touch of a man who saw her as something more. And finally she realized without any doubt that this man did see her as something more. And maybe he always had.

She took her clothes off, piece by piece, as she walked back toward Wade. Her blouse. Her bra. She was bold, utterly unconcerned. She slid out of her jeans, her panties.

His breaths came shorter and faster as she walked up to him, tugged his shirt from his jeans and started on the buttons.

He put his hands on her shoulders. Breathed her name and let her undress him, in between kissing her face, her neck, her shoulders. When his chest was bare, he scooped her up in his arms, and then he laid her on the bed. She lay naked, on her back, and he stretched out beside her on his side, head propped on his hand, elbow to the mattress, so he could look at her. Look at every part of her.

"No fake tan," she said softly. "No double-stick tape keeping my breasts standing at attention even when I'm lying on my back. No baby oil coating my skin."

"Thank God," he whispered, leaning down, kissing her breasts, tasting them.

"You're not disappointed?"

He trailed a hand over her chest, down her belly, dragged his fingers across her thighs and brushed them over her center. Then he lingered there, touching, parting. "Know why I kept those pictures all this time, Edie Brand?" he asked her. He stroked, and she shivered. "Because the real thing was out of reach. Like staring at glass and wishing for a diamond. The glass is perfectly clear. It's the flaws in the diamond that let you know it's real." He stroked again, his breath wafting over her nipple as he spoke. "Perfection is boring."

Her breath stuttered out of her as he touched her, played her like an instrument.

"Relax, baby. Let me take care of you." His fingers slid inside her, and he bent to nurse at her breast.

Edie shook with longing but opened her eyes, pushed him away. "I want you to make love to me."

"I am."

She rolled onto her side, facing him, slid her hand down

to the front of his jeans. She rubbed his arousal through
the denim. "I want you inside me," she told him.

His eyes widened a little. As if maybe he were just the
tiniest bit afraid. Edie popped his button fly, lowered his
zipper and slipped her hand inside his jeans. When she
found him there, she closed her hand around him, teasing
and taunting.

"Why don't you want to make love to me, Wade?"

He rolled onto his back, shuddering now, and she rose
above him, shoving his jeans and shorts down, out of the
way, so her hands could continue to torment him. She
leaned low, used her mouth on his chest to add to the
sensations. His eyes were closed, his head shifting from
side to side.

"Why?" Her thumb ran over the tip of him, and when
he shivered in reaction, she did it again.

With a deep groan, he gave up. His hands snapped
around her waist, moved her until he was nudging at her
wet opening, and then he pulled her down onto him, driving deep inside her. She bit her lip to keep from crying
out at the fullness, the stretching, even as he lifted her and
brought her down again, arching his hips to thrust into her
even more deeply than before. Over and over he moved
into her, and she felt the intensity move through her, center
in the very core of her and begin to build. Every move he
made, every whisper, every touch of his lips, his hands,
his skin on hers, intensified it. And she was moving, too,
over him, around him, with him. Until finally she exploded. She cried his name, quivered and shook around
him, felt his answering climax in every part of him.

As their bodies relaxed, she lay down on top of him.

He wrapped his arms around her, kissed her long and
languorously, rolled her onto her back without separating
from her and began to move inside her again.

* * *

It was, he realized, the biggest mistake he had ever made as he held her close to him in his bed, spooning against her, listening to her breathing. He had known it would be a mistake, and that was why he hadn't wanted to make love to her. Not that way, at least. What the hell did a man do when he realized his fondest dream? It could only be downhill from there on. He would never equal this, never have sex this good, or that meant this much, ever again. No other woman was ever going to measure up to Edie Brand. How could they? She had been his fantasy, his first crush, his obsession....

And hell, it wasn't as if he could keep her.

Well...then again...

She slid out of his bed at twenty-five minutes to midnight. Waiting that long had almost killed her, but he hadn't fallen asleep right away. She forced herself to wait for his even, steady breathing, and then she slid out of the bed, taking a spare blanket to wrap around her, and tiptoed to her own room. She did a quick washup in the bathroom, then put on the black teddy, adding a sweater and jeans over top of it. She slid her feet into sensible suede walking shoes and threaded a long sharp hat pin into their laces. Going into the bathroom, she turned on the shower. She locked the door from the inside, then stepped into the bedroom and closed it.

Perfect.

Her everyday jacket was downstairs, and she couldn't go down there. So she took a silky warm-up number from her bedroom closet and put it on. Lastly she dug through her dresser drawer for the handgun Mike had given her. She checked it, fumbling for a moment before she managed to release the catch and make the cylinder open. He'd shown her, but it had been a long time.

The bullets were in place. Six of them. She clapped the cylinder closed again, mentally reviewing what Mike had told her. There was no safety. You just thumbed back the hammer, took aim and pulled the trigger. She pulled everything he'd told her from the depths of memory. How to hold the gun, using both hands, one to support the other. How to look down the barrel and use the notch on the end to sight on the target. How to hold the gun down a bit as you pulled the trigger, to compensate for the recoil.

Biting her lips, scared half to death, she dropped the gun into her jacket pocket, then changed her mind. He would take her jacket off, or insist she do it. No, she needed to hide the gun better.

She rummaged around, found some masking tape, and shimmied out of her jacket, and then her sweater. She taped the gun to her side, where she could cover it with an arm, if necessary. Then she dressed again, quickly. Finally, opening her bedroom window, she climbed out.

Chapter 15

Edie shimmied her way from the second-floor bedroom window to the ground by way of an obliging maple tree, scraping her hands raw on the bark and wishing she'd thought to pull on some gloves. At the bottom, she brushed her stinging palms against each other and looked around.

It was pitch dark tonight. She had no idea what phase the moon was in, waxing or waning, although she would lay odds Selene would know. It had been a crescent last night. Maybe tonight it was gone. Or maybe it was bigger. Not that it mattered. If it was out there anywhere, it was obliterated by clouds. There was no light.

She needed a flashlight. She damn well wasn't going anywhere without a flashlight.

She glanced toward the front of the house. Wade would have a flashlight in his truck, and if not there, then maybe in the garage, where he'd put all his miscellaneous guy-paraphernalia. She headed to the truck first, opened the door, winced when the interior light came on. No buzzer, at least, thank goodness. She glanced nervously back toward the house, saw no movement inside and, sighing in relief, proceeded to ransack Wade's truck. She found a small Mini Maglite flashlight in the glove compartment. It was deep red, and heavy for its size.

Nodding, she backed butt-first out of the truck and closed the door as quietly as she could. Then, squaring her shoulders, she headed down her driveway on foot. There was a path that cut kitty corner through the woods and came out on the dirt road about 100 yards from the old barn where the maniac had told her to meet him. It occurred to her that that might be why he chose the place. It was close to her, within walking distance via a concealed route. Maybe he'd been staying there the entire time he had been in town.

She flicked on her light as soon as she stepped onto the trail. The ground was soft, no crackling dry leaves as there would be in the fall. It was still moist, and the grasses were young and silent. Her footsteps were whispers as she moved along the path, her flashlight beam arcing back and forth in front of her. Once she thought she heard answering whispers. She stopped, spun around, aimed her light like a weapon, stabbed at the darkness with it.

But she saw nothing. No one.

It must have been the wind.

Swallowing, she turned again and continued on her trek.

It took twenty minutes, by her best guess. She was worried that she was late. It had to be midnight already, she thought, when the forest around her fell away and opened onto the narrow, winding dirt road. The barn stood in the distance, a darker shadow against the coal sky.

Her sister was in there.

Stiffening her spine, lifting her chin, she flicked off her tiny flashlight. She walked a little faster. And finally she was standing there, facing the barn door. It was big and square and hinged. A cross piece made of a two-by-four held it closed. Edie lifted it slowly and pulled the door open.

The hinges groaned like the souls of the damned. She clenched her jaw, ducking backwards, expecting an attack.

Nothing. Nothing happened. No one came bursting out the door onto her. She didn't delude herself into believing he hadn't heard her or didn't know she was there. He knew. He was calling all the shots here.

Squaring her shoulders, she stepped into the darkness. "I'm here."

And then he was there, behind her and around her, and her arms were pinned to her sides. She cried out in shock and surprise, and then his breath was hot in her ear. "Ten minutes late, too," he rasped. "You must *really* want to be punished."

Edie tried to calm her breathing. Tried to halt the trembling that was rising up from the depths of her. "Where is my sister?"

"Safe. She's beautiful, you know. If you hadn't come, I just might have kept her."

Swallowing against the bile that rose in her throat, Edie said, "Where is she?"

He tightened his arms crushingly around her. "Don't be cocky, young lady. Don't forget your place." His arms held hers pinned hard to her sides, and the gun taped there pressed its shape into her inner arm hard enough to bruise. And yet it was comforting, somehow.

Now one of her captor's hands slid lower, caught her wrist, and she felt cold metal snapping tight around it. She sucked in a breath.

"Give me your other hand."

"No. Let go of me."

He let go. She was shocked and surprised, and she whirled to face him.

He stood there facing her in the darkness as she panted. She could barely see him. An outline. A dark mask. A white shirt. He lifted a hand toward his breast pocket and took something from it. It was too dark to see what. A box of some kind.

"What...what is that? What are you doing?"

"Oh, poor baby can't see? No matter. Listen."

His thumb moved on the box, and there was a scream. Kara, somewhere in the barn, crying out in pain. Horror shot through Edie, and she swung her head around, looking for her sister. But the sound died quickly, and there was only darkness.

"Kara! Kara, where are you?"

There was no answer.

"She won't reply," the man said in a rasping whisper. "She knows she'll get another jolt if she does."

"You bastard, what the hell are you doing to her?"

"Oh, it's not nearly as bad as she makes it sound. Only a few volts, really."

"You electrocuted her?"

"Don't worry, pet, your turn will come. Now let's see if we understand each other. Put your wrists together."

She hesitated. He thumbed the control again, and again Kara cried out in anguish. "No, don't! Don't. I'm doing it, all right, I'm doing it." She slammed her wrists together, and held them out to him.

He dropped the device into his pocket, put the other cuff on her, took hold of the chain in between and led her deeper into the darkness. She couldn't see. Not his face or his expression, only his outline. She felt straw under her feet and smelled mustiness. He lifted her arms over her head, draped the chain over some sort of hook. Then he stepped away, grabbing a rope and pulling.

The hook rose, pulling her up onto her tiptoes. The cuffs bit into her wrists. He tied it off there. When he came back to her, he ran something cold and sharp over her neck. "Now, let's see if you wore the black, like I told you." He started slicing away her clothes.

Wade knew when she left the bed. His heart knotted up in his chest, because he so didn't want Alex to have been right in his theory that Edie was lying to them all. Damned if he knew why. No, that was a lie, and he'd been telling himself way too many of those lately. Honesty was what he needed here. The bald, unvarnished truth. And that truth was that he wanted to believe Edie trusted him more than she trusted anyone else. He wanted to believe that she would tell him the truth, even if she kept it from every other soul in the universe.

But she hadn't told him.

And now she was up, sneaking around the house. He could hear her moving around in her bedroom, padding to the bathroom, then back out again. He could hear the shower running. He was so tuned in he could almost see her through the walls that stood between them.

Sighing, he slid out of bed, moved closer to the wall, listened.

He heard something that sounded like...

Holy God, the window?

Wade lunged to his own bedroom window in time to see her clambering around in the tree outside like some kind of monkey-girl. He could barely believe his eyes. When she landed on the ground and looked back up at the house, he pulled back just in time. When he looked again, he saw her disappear around the corner.

Hell.

He pulled on his jeans, left his room and paused at the top of the stairs. Did he really want to alert Alex and Mel to what was happening? Would Edie want that? She wouldn't, and maybe she had solid reasons for striking out on her own. She obviously knew something the rest of them didn't.

Maybe he should trust her just a little bit here.

Okay. But he had to go after her.

Swallowing hard, he turned toward her bedroom and, with a sigh, walked into it. The bathroom door was closed, the shower running. But he knew that was a ruse. He was going to have to take the same route Edie had. And fast, before she got out of sight.

"Alex!"

Alexander Stone woke to the sound of an irritated female voice and an elbow in his rib cage. Opening his eyes, he saw an agent of Satan glaring at him. Then his memory returned, and he realized it was only Mel Brand. Yeah. Okay, correct on both counts.

"Something's going on!" she hissed.

He lifted his brows and sat up straighter on the sofa, where he'd fallen sound asleep. "Define 'something.'"

"The light just came on in Wade's truck outside. I couldn't see who was in it. Then it went out again."

He came more fully alert then. What the hell would a sexually depraved stalker want with Wade Armstrong's tow truck? "Did you go upstairs to check on your sister?"

"No." She turned and started for the stairs, and he went with her, just in case. When they got to the top, she paused, staring through an open door into an empty room.

"What is it?" Alex asked.

"Well...that's Wade's room. But it's empty."

"And this surprises you?"

She shot him a look. "Shouldn't it?"

"Not if you saw the way he was looking at your sister it shouldn't." He took her arm. "Come on, let's look in her room."

"Wait a minute." Mel jerked her arm free and strode into Wade's room, flicking on the light switch. "Those are Edie's clothes on the floor!" She pointed at them as if shocked.

Alex bit his lip to keep from commenting, gripped her arm again and tugged her along into the hall to Edie's room. That door was closed, and he knocked gently. When there was no answer, he tried again.

"Oh, get out of the way," Mel said, shouldering him aside. She whipped the door open and strode right in, flicking the light switch.

The empty bed was the first surprise. The open window the second.

"Holy…"

"Edie? Wade?" Mel called. She looked at the bathroom. The door was closed and the shower was running. She didn't even hesitate before going to it, trying the door, and then shouldering it open despite the fact that it was apparently locked. "Edie!" she shouted. She rushed into the bathroom. A second later the water stopped running and she came out again. Then she looked at him. "It's empty. Where are they?"

He shrugged. "My best guess is that one or both of them had a communication from the man who took Kara today and kept it from us. They've probably gone off to try to meet his demands."

"But where?"

Alex shrugged. Then he glanced up at her. "Those

clothes on Wade's floor, they're the ones your sister was wearing today?''

She nodded.

He turned and went down the hall, back to Wade's room, snatched up the blouse from the floor and ran the fabric between his hands. It had no pockets to check. Then he picked up the jeans and turned the pockets inside out, one by one. As he shoved his hand into the final pocket, he found the folded-up piece of paper, pulled it out, held it up.

"Oh my God," Mel said. "Read it. Hurry."

He unfolded the note, read it aloud, then frowned at Mel. "You know this barn he's referring to?"

"I know it."

Her face had gone stony. He'd never seen anything quite like it. Stony. Pale and hard. She just walked past him, down the stairs into the kitchen, where she picked up the phone and dialed. He didn't know who she was talking to when she gave the location of the barn. But he clearly heard her say, "Bring my shotgun. The twelve gauge. And a box of slugs. No, not birdshot. Slugs. This son of a bitch is going down."

She hung up the phone, strode into the living room and jerked an iron fire poker from the rack near the fireplace. She hefted it in her hand, and Alex felt his stomach clench. Then she went to the door, yanked it open and finally glanced over her shoulder at him with the coldest, most dangerous eyes he'd ever seen. Those eyes didn't fit in such a pretty face. "So are you coming or what?"

Wade followed her, but keeping up wasn't easy. She had a light, and she knew the path. He had neither advantage on his side, and every time she went around a curve in the trail and her light blinked out of his line of vision, he found himself stumbling through the brush, struggling to keep on course.

By the time he got to the road on the far side of the trail, he had lost her. But he heard a scream that galvanized him. And it came from the abandoned-looking barn hulking like a shadow in the distance.

"Wade, just what the hell is going on?" a voice said, damn near making Wade jump out of his skin. Mel and Alex Stone emerged from the path through the woods just behind him.

"I don't know," he said. "She took off, and I followed. I think they're in that barn." He started forward.

Alex put a hand on his shoulder. "We should make a plan."

"Screw the plan," Mel said. She slapped her poker into her palm and strode toward the barn.

"She's right," Wade agreed. "A second ago, I heard a woman scream."

Alex nodded, his jaw firm. The two turned and caught up to Mel. They went right up to the front door, opened it slowly, cringing at the groan of the hinges, and stepped into the dark barn. In the distance, a light flickered, and Wade saw a dark form hunched over a kerosene lantern, just lowering the globe into place. As the light flared brighter, he saw Edie.

She was standing on tiptoe, wearing nothing more than a skimpy black lace teddy, her arms stretched over her head and anchored there. She looked up, as if she felt him there, saw him, and shook her head from side to side rapidly.

He stopped, holding a hand out to stop the others.

Edie said, "Listen, mister, you—"

"Master. You address me as Master, and you speak only when I tell you to." The man turned to face her.

"Master," Edie said, and damned if she didn't sound totally submissive. "Please take those electrodes off my sister now. You don't need to hurt her anymore with that little remote control you have in your shirt pocket. I'll do whatever you say."

She was telling them the situation, explaining why they couldn't just burst in. Kara would suffer for it if they did.

"I ought to give her a little jolt right now, just to teach you not to speak unless you're told to!" He strode up to Edie and smacked her hard across the face. "I can gag you. Don't make me do that."

Wade stiffened, but Alex gripped his shoulder, tugged him backward until the three of them were outside again. "We have to find Kara, get those electrodes off her."

"But he's hurting Edie," Wade argued.

"Edie's tough," Mel said. "She can handle it for a few minutes. Let's just skirt around the barn and find Kara."

Wade shook his head. "I'm staying put. I'll wait as long as I can, give you guys time to find Kara and get her safe. But if he gets too rough…"

Alex and Mel nodded their understanding and took off around the barn. Wade crept back inside, on hands and knees, crawling closer now.

Edie's eyes were on his, riveted to his. The man had bared her breasts now, though the teddy remained in place. He was walking around her, speaking slowly, and he had a short, whiplike tool in his hands, with multiple tendrils on the ends.

"So, you're ready now to receive your punishment?" He looked at her. "You may answer."

"I will be ready," she told him. "As soon as you let my sister go."

Smiling, the man reached into his pocket, and a second later, Kara screamed somewhere in the depths of the barn.

Edie's eyes welled with tears, and Wade's stomach turned. Still, he realized the sound would lead Alex and Mel straight to Kara.

"Every time you ask me to let her go, I'll hurt her a little more."

Then he lifted his whip and brought it down hard across Edie's thigh.

She never made a sound. Just held Wade's eyes.

The man whipped her again, and then again. When he lifted the lash again, Wade lurched at him. He leapt onto the man's back and knocked him face first into the musty hay on the floor. The kerosene lamp fell over and smashed, and fire swam through the hay.

Wade and the maniac rolled on the floor, amid the flames, Wade pounding the man mercilessly and taking a few solid blows himself. When he managed to glimpse Edie, she was clinging to the hook above her with both hands and pulling her legs upward, as the flames danced higher and higher beneath her.

Then the man landed a blow Wade hadn't seen coming. He saw stars, tried to get up, dropped to his knees again. Edie shouted a warning, and he ducked just as the bastard swung a board at his head. The fire was burning higher. He drove his head into the maniac's belly, and while the guy was doubled over, Wade reached out and snatched the leather hood off his head.

He looked up, and Wade recognized him. He was older, fatter than he had been in high school. But he hadn't changed that much in thirteen years.

"Matt McConnell," Wade said. And he smiled as he drove his fist into the guy's face with everything he had.

The hook above Edie was attached to a rope, and she had managed to climb it all the way up to the beam over which it was flung. Now, as she pulled herself up onto that beam, still handcuffed, she saw Wade hit the man hard, knocking him onto his back. He didn't get up again.

Then Wade turned, looking for her. She wasn't where he'd last seen her. "Edie?" he called.

"I'm up here. I'm okay!"

He looked up at her, shielding his eyes against the flames that were leaping between them. And at that moment she saw the man rising up behind Wade. He had a board in his hands, and was lifting it. "Look out!" Edie cried.

She moved her cuffed hands to her side and tore the little gun free from under the teddy. It was in her hands then, tape still dangling from it as she leveled it, thumbed the hammer back and squeezed the trigger.

The recoil knocked her off balance, and she fell from the rafter into the burning hay below, having no idea if her shot had hit its target. There was smoke, heat, she was burning, and her head was spinning from the impact, when someone bent over her.

She flinched until she heard his voice. "I've got you. It's okay, baby, I've got you." Gently, Wade scooped her up into his arms, and he carried her out of the smoke-filled barn into the night.

"Kara," she whispered. "Wade, what about Kara?"

"We got her, Edie! We got her!"

Edie turned to see Mel running toward her. Beyond Mel, Kara stood, wrapped in Alex Stone's jacket, looking bewildered and shocky.

"She's okay," Edie whispered. She tipped her head up to look into Wade's eyes. He was sooty and bleeding.

As he dropped to his knees, he said, "Everything's okay now, Edie. Everything's okay."

Then she found herself on the ground as Wade just sort of tipped over and went still.

Wade woke in his bed at Edie's house.

Women seemed to be everywhere. Vidalia Brand was clucking around like a mother hen, giving orders to the others. Mel and Selene were running in and out of his room, fetching things. Selene was arguing with her mother over which ointment to put on his cuts. Sally was pacing back and forth, looking as worried as a Great Dane could look.

And Edie was there. She sat beside his bed, a cool damp cloth in her hands as she ran it over his wounded face. "Finally awake," she said softly. "How do you feel, Wade?"

Vidalia turned to see him, sent him a wink and a nod, and then hustled her other two daughters out of the room and closed the door behind them. Sally rushed to the bed and licked his face. Edie gently moved her away, and Sally finally sighed and padded to the foot of the bed to lie down.

Wade closed his eyes, wiped his cheek dry. "I feel like I just went a few rounds with the high school football star. Oh, wait. That's because I did."

Edie lowered her head. "I can't believe it was Matt McConnell." She swallowed hard. "The police said my gunshot only nicked him. It was the fire that did him in."

"He got what he deserved. He was always a jerk." Wade lifted a hand, cupped her face. "Are you okay?"

"You're the one with the burns and cuts and bruises. I'm fine."

"And Kara?"

"She's all right. No serious damage."

"Thank God," he said, closing his eyes slowly.

Edie licked her lips. "Wade...I'm sorry I tried to go after her on my own."

"You were doing what you thought you had to," he said.

"I didn't tell you because I didn't want you to get hurt. I thought I—I thought I might have to give him what he wanted in order to save Kara. And I knew you'd get yourself killed before you would let that happen."

He studied her face for a long time. "You're right. I would have. And I'm glad you know I would have. But do you know why?"

She smiled down at him. Very slowly, she nodded. "I knew as soon as I saw that painting, Wade. You love me."

His own smile hurt his face, but he couldn't help it. "I do," he said. "And it wouldn't matter what you looked like. You know that, too, right? I didn't fall in love with the lingerie model. I fell in love with the little sophomore who always ignored me."

"Pretended to ignore you," she corrected him. "The truth is, I was probably a little bit in love with you even then."

"Yeah? And what about now?"

She lowered her eyes, licked her lips. "Now I'm just wondering if it's healthy to love someone as much as I love you."

He sat up in the bed, despite the fact that it hurt to do so, cupped her head and drew her close for a kiss. "It is when they love you back just as much." He kissed her again, tasted tears on her lips. When he drew back again, he said, "Why don't you go ask your mother how she feels about a June wedding?"

"Is that your idea of a proposal?"

"Nope. This is." He got out of the bed with effort, even as she jumped to her feet in protest. Then he dropped down on one knee in front of her, gently pushing her back into her chair. "Edain Brand, you are the love of my life. If you won't marry me, I'll be a lonely, lonely bachelor, pining away over pictures of you until the day I die—just like I have been for the last decade or so. Will you be my wife, Edie? Please?"

She slid out of the chair and sank to her knees, nodding and crying, kissing his lips through her tears. "Yes, Wade. Yes. Yes."

He pulled her close and kissed her. Sally barked and lunged at them, hitting them bodily and knocking them both sideways onto the floor. Then she danced over them, speaking volumes in her own little language.

"I think she's congratulating us," Edie said, laughing.

"No. She's asking if this means we get to keep the house after all," Wade said. He kissed her, and they managed to get to their feet. When they did, he looked toward the door and saw Vidalia standing in the doorway, sniffling, eyes wet. Her daughters surrounded her, smiling and sniffling, as well.

"June," Vidalia said. "My goodness, my daughters don't believe in long engagements, do they?"

"Thank God for that," Wade said. He looked deeply into Edie's eyes and said it again, in a whisper. "Thank God."

* * * * *

Silhouette

INTIMATE MOMENTS™
is proud to present

Romancing the Crown

*With the help of their powerful allies,
the royal family of Montebello is determined
to find their missing heir. But the search for the
beloved prince is not without danger—or passion!*

**This exciting twelve-book series begins in January and
continues throughout the year with these fabulous titles:**

Available at your favorite retail outlet.

Silhouette®
Where love comes alive™

CALL THE ONES YOU LOVE OVER THE HOLIDAYS!

Save $25 off future book purchases when you buy any four Harlequin® or Silhouette® books in October, November and December 2001,

PLUS

receive a phone card good for 15 minutes of long-distance calls to anyone you want in North America!

WHAT AN INCREDIBLE DEAL!

Just fill out this form and attach 4 proofs of purchase (cash register receipts) from October, November and December 2001 books, and Harlequin Books will send you a coupon booklet worth a total savings of $25 off future purchases of Harlequin® and Silhouette® books, AND a 15-minute phone card to call the ones you love, anywhere in North America.

Please send this form, along with your cash register receipts as proofs of purchase, to:
In the USA: Harlequin Books, P.O. Box 9057, Buffalo, NY 14269-9057
In Canada: Harlequin Books, P.O. Box 622, Fort Erie, Ontario L2A 5X3
Cash register receipts must be dated no later than December 31, 2001.
Limit of 1 coupon booklet and phone card per household.
Please allow 4-6 weeks for delivery.

**I accept your offer! Enclosed are 4 proofs of purchase.
Please send me my coupon booklet
and a 15-minute phone card:**

Name: _____

Address: _____ City: _____

State/Prov.: _____ Zip/Postal Code: _____

Account Number (if available): _____

---

097 KJB DAGL
PHQ4013

COMING NEXT MONTH